# MISSION TO AMERICA

## ALSO BY WALTER KIRN

*My Hard Bargain: Stories*

*She Needed Me*

*Thumbsucker*

*Up in the Air*

**Doubleday**
NEW YORK   LONDON   TORONTO
SYDNEY   AUCKLAND

# MISSION TO AMERICA

*A Novel*

## WALTER KIRN

PUBLISHED BY DOUBLEDAY
A division of Random House, Inc.
DOUBLEDAY and the portrayal of an anchor with a dolphin are
registered trademarks of Random House, Inc.

*Book design by Jennifer Ann Daddio*

Library of Congress Cataloging-in-Publication Data
Kirn, Walter, 1962–
Mission to America : a novel / Walter Kirn.—1st ed.
        p.   cm.
1. Missionaries—Fiction. 2. Rich people—Fiction. 3. Ski resorts—
Fiction. 4. Matriarchy—Fiction. 5. Young men—Fiction.
6. Colorado—Fiction. 7. Cults—Fiction. I. Title.
PS3561.I746M57 2005
813'.54—dc22
2005045477

ISBN 0-385-50764-X

PRINTED IN THE UNITED STATES OF AMERICA

November 2005

First Edition

1   3   5   7   9   10   8   6   4   2

*For*

**Elizabeth and her dog**

*With thanks to*

**Elwood and Nina Reid**

*With rules of health in the head and*

*the most digestible food in the stomach,*

*there would still be dyspeptics.*

—MARY BAKER EDDY, *SCIENCE AND HEALTH*
*WITH A KEY TO THE SCRIPTURES*


*My bowels boiled, and rested not . . .*

—JOB 30:27

# MISSION TO AMERICA

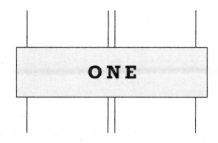

**ONE**

**Partly we did it out of pity.** We felt sorry for people who didn't know what we knew. By reading their newspapers in our village library and questioning the occasional lost hiker or adventurous dirt-road motorist, we realized as never before that life out there had become strident, disheartening, and harsh while life back here, back home in Bluff, Montana, remained harmonious and sweet. But we also had selfish reasons for what we did. Over the years we'd come to understand that there was something we needed from the outsiders, without which our charmed little world might not survive. We needed new blood. We needed wives and mothers. We needed a few brown eyes among our offspring, more dark curly hair, and less inherited color blindness. We needed to stir our lumpy hard old stock until it was soft enough to pour again. And so, for the first time since we came together one hundred and forty-seven years earlier, and in violation of our traditions of silence, modesty, and isolation, we gathered a party to go down out of the hills and mount, at long last, a mission to America.

The strange disturbed place needed help, and so did we.

Our wisdom for their vigor. We hoped to trade.

We were the Aboriginal Fulfilled Apostles and I am Mason Plato LaVerle. I won't start by recounting all of our history; it will trickle out. We approved, that's the main thing. We approved abundantly. We approved of the Prince of Flocks, whom others call Christ, and of our God of Gods, the All-in-One, but we also approved of a host of other divinities, majestic and humble, familiar and obscure, from tricky Old Coyote, the Hopi spirit, to dainty Lady Vegetalis, a garden sylph of cloudy origins. We approved of diverse ideas and teachings as well, embracing the Golden Rule, the Ten Commandments, the Hindu law of Karma, and our very own Perpetuity of Essence, which was easy to state but hard to comprehend. In the words of the Seeress, our aging leader, who spoke every week for three hours from her sunporch, propped in a wheelchair between two folded sheepskins and waving a quartz-tipped cedar cane for emphasis, Death does not end us, Birth does not begin us, and Life does not corrupt us. We stream on forever through the Etheric Flux, indestructible channels of vitality.

The doctrines we were best known for among outsiders—particularly in our first two decades, when the newspaper writers from the great cities still found our movement exotic and picturesque—related to health and bodily well-being. Edenic Nutritional Science, as we called it, was a system of eating and elimination that the inscrutable All-in-One took from earth in the days of Zoroaster and finally restored in 1889 when the disembodied Discourser spoke to the Crow tribe's Little Red Elk, who corresponded with us through coded letters smuggled from his people's place of banishment near southern Montana's Bighorn River. Food, for Apostles, was more than physical sustenance; it was emotion materialized, hardened spirit, and its ingestion, absorption, and expulsion mirrored the deepest patterns of the universe. ENS is a subject for later on, though. First I should describe the situation that we found ourselves in two years ago.

We'd gone without publicity for so long that outsiders had forgotten we existed. Then, the spring that I turned twenty-four, a handsome young AFA rancher named Ennis Lauer came from behind in the final round of *Grit!*, a nationally televised endurance contest, to beat out a Kansas federal prison guard for the top prize of half a million dollars. Quiet cunning bested boastful brawn as Lauer, in the program's closing challenge, lashed together a raft of willow branches to float six hundred pounds of cinder blocks to the finish line thirty miles away. The prison guard, who'd built a crude board sled with a harness that tied around his chest, still hadn't arrived when Lauer received the trophy and uttered his memorable five-word victory speech: "It wasn't me, but gravity."

Our leaders weren't pleased when Lauer joined the contest, but all was forgiven when he took the cup, becoming our movement's first celebrity since Francis Blair Howell, the presidential candidate who won one percent of the vote in 1960 by backing a total tax exemption for women. Lauer's fame was a thrill, for our men and boys especially, who'd grown up dominated by the Seeress and her white-haired quartet of female counselors. Now we had a hero who wore trousers. With his prize money, he erected a hillside mansion, the largest private structure in all of Bluff. It cantilevered out over downtown and cast a vast afternoon shadow over Venus Street that some people grumped and grouched about at first, until the Seeress taught them to regard it as a fortuitous giant public sundial.

Lauer had a manner and a bearing that enchanted photographers—a dreamy potency, detached yet fierce, forged by hard field work but also by meditation—and this led to a steady round of articles in newspapers from Portland to New Orleans. The Strongman Mystic of the Rockies, a hybrid of Atlas and Nostradamus. He bolstered his fame by publishing a calendar showing him in a corral among his stock with rolled-up sleeves, a half-unbuttoned work shirt, and mineral-oil perspiration on his chest (a stratagem that the Seeress reproached him for in a lengthy sermon on Illusion). The calendar sold three hundred thousand copies, helped by a story on a national news show, and Lauer, still smarting from his public scolding, devoted the funds to a spiritual effort he named the Apple.

The Initiative commenced in early June on the spacious third floor of Lauer's mansion, which he'd built in part as a community conference room to supplement the decrepit Celestial Hall. Through its tall picture windows I could see my town. It didn't resemble ordinary towns because it had almost no commercial district. Bluff's center had burned in 1965 when a fire surged down through a canyon to our west and overwhelmed our volunteer fire department, which refused all assistance from neighboring departments as well as the hated U.S. Forest Service, whom we'd been fighting in court for seven years for rights to the outflow of a thermal spring that heated the greenhouses where we grew our herbs. Not much was lost, though, just a hardware store, a welding garage, and a ladies clothing shop. Bluff operated then, to some degree, on a modified barter system called the Virtue Code, which assigned economic values to good deeds as well as to more conventional products and services. Cash was also honored for most transactions, but the co-op warehouse that stocked our food and sundries ran exclusively on Virtue Coupons. They were larger than dollars, lavender not green, and the picture inside the central oval seal was of a mourning dove sunning on a branch. Every couple of years a tax agent from Helena would storm through Bluff with armed guards and a black car and confiscate a portion of our currency, but it took only days for our printers to replace it, refining its design each time they did and adding more lines of texture to the dove's feathers.

Attendance at the Initiative's first seminar was by invitation only. My father, a Mineral County deputy sheriff who only arrested people when he felt threatened by them, and my mother, who assisted the Seeress with various clerical and domestic chores, cautioned me when I was summoned that Lauer's views had yet to be sanctioned by the leadership and therefore couldn't be discussed in public. Still, they said it was crucial that I go.

"Mr. Lauer will make you privy to certain hard truths that perhaps you'd prefer not to know," my mother said, "but which wise AFAs must no longer turn away from." Unlike my father, my mother took pleasure in speech and stressed the seams and spaces between words. "Whatever he may require you to do, though, be confident you have our blessing. If we lose you, we lose you. 'What should be, is.' "

"Lose me how?" I asked.

My father seemed pained and got up and left the kitchen, not always the strongest of men when feelings threatened. The gun he carried for work had never looked right on him. It would have looked more appropriate on my mother.

"Lose you to their fine phantasms," she said.

The conference room held five men besides myself, none of them over thirty and all unmarried. Lauer, who'd gotten his hands on a projector during one of the paid outside appearances where he performed feats of strength for business audiences and touted his notion of Etheric Stamina, conducted a forty-minute presentation on our movement's prospects in the next decades. He explained that unless we introduced new bloodlines into our active breeding pool, Bluff faced a so-called biological sunset that would enfeeble us in the near future and was, in fact, already causing harm. A hush settled over the room. We coughed and fidgeted. We knew all too vividly what Lauer meant. There were children in town who didn't seem quite right, who still couldn't read at nine and ten years old and who sat out the sports and games we'd played at their age because of sore joints and other vague complaints. The young man sitting next to me, Elias Stark, had a little nephew of twelve, I'd heard, who'd spent several months at a costly Seattle clinic learning to synchronize, for the first time, the movements of his left hand and his right eye.

"I'm going to speak sharply and plainly," Lauer said. "Someday our descendants will all be idiots. And there won't be enough of them, in any case. Our young ladies just aren't producing like they used to, and they were never prolific to begin with. In a way that's a tribute to their development. It means they enjoy the freedom to say 'no.' But there are limits, and soon we'll reach those limits."

Lauer left it there. We broke for lunch. We grazed on a buffet of local staples: thin-sliced antelope sausage on sprouted black rye, smoked rainbow trout preserved in cider vinegar, squash relish, chopped barley salad, and clover tea. No salt on anything, but quantities of pepper, cold-stone ground to protect its volatile oils. Pepper aroused the intestines, it sped their labors. Disease begins in the gut, the duodenum, and death is a matter of sluggish peristalsis—that's the great key to Edenic Nutritional Science. Our bowels should work ceaselessly, not just at intervals.

Lauer took me aside after the meal and led me into an office off the conference room decorated with framed photographs that showed him shaking hands with famous men, including Montana's Democratic senator and a champion Negro golfer with dyed red hair. Lauer was a new and intimidating type for me, clothed and turned out in a way I'd never encountered. His shoes were a cross between tennis shoes and dress shoes, fastened by Velcro straps instead of laces; his watch had a small inner dial that showed the moon phase; and he wore cologne in a town where scents were frowned upon because of their effect on certain glands involved in the metabolism of starch. It wasn't a light scent, either—all musk and smoke. It set off a drip of thick mucus behind my tonsils.

"I've been authorized by a select committee," he said, "to recruit volunteers for an historic undertaking meant to address the concerns we've just discussed. I asked around some. Your name kept coming up. I hear you speak well."

"Thank you."

"Is it true?"

"I guess."

"Not very promising: 'I guess.' Impress me, Mason. Turn a fancy phrase."

"Just out of the blue, that's hard to do," I said.

"I know it is. It's impossible. I'm teasing. Get used to being teased by me."

I nodded.

"I'm playful because I'm passionate," he said.

Lauer knew mind tricks, I learned that afternoon, and once he finished describing the mission itself, which he did without much color or expression—nine months on the road, three teams of two men each, and weekly reports to be filed with his office—he switched to the subject of Neuro-Dynamic Salesmanship, which was the topic he really seemed to care about. He told me he'd learned it from a Phoenix businessman who'd earned almost eight million dollars in one year selling therapeutic car-seat covers impregnated with ionized powdered copper. He was already using its principles on me, he said.

"Right now," he revealed, "you're in a waking trance. You'll notice that your breathing matches mine and I'm guiding your eye movements in specific patterns. I've made a request that you haven't yet agreed to, but the truth is, right now, you're powerless to resist me. Do you see how your feet are pointing?"

I looked down. My feet didn't seem to be pointing anywhere special.

"That particular posture is always a 'yes.' Don't worry, you'll learn to spot it for yourself someday. But say the word anyway."

" 'Yes'?"

"Good man," said Lauer. "You need to know that I'm funding this effort privately, which gives me a personal stake in the results. Money is going to be tight, no way around it, but if you budget wisely, and you sacrifice, you ought to do well. If you don't, we might be finished here. We're down to less than nine hundred active members. And that's the Church's figure. I think it's half that."

I'd never counted us. I had no idea.

"I suspect it's not much more than four. Which I find tragic."

After allowing this figure to sink in some, Lauer reached through the space between us and touched my knee. "Our big worry, of course, is that you won't come back once you've had a long sweet drink of freedom. So think about it. Think realistically. Not that what they offer out there is freedom."

"What is it that they offer?" I said.

"Death."

I asked him if he was referring to their guns.

"Their guns are the least of it," Lauer said. "Look at what they dump into their gullets. They eat death. They defecate death. It's all they know. And when they sleep, they dream of death. You'll see. You'll see how it saturates their souls. Just walk into one of their toy stores and count the death dolls."

I tried to imagine what such things looked like. "Skeleton figures?" I asked.

"They might as well be. Emaciated elongated young women with barely enough flesh to cover their skulls but with breasts the size of a nursing mother of twins. The Sphinx and the Griffin are more convincing creatures."

He allowed me to sit with these images for a moment before asking me, eye to eye, with an expression that I sensed he'd borrowed from the Phoenix millionaire, if I'd be comfortable doing whatever was necessary to meet potential mates during my mission and persuade one of them to accompany me back home. I wasn't exactly certain what he meant, but I felt I understood his general point: Would I devote my whole body to the task? And, further, was there someone here in Bluff, someone whom I was pledged to or had feelings for, who might prevent me from me going forth wholeheartedly?

"I'll need to talk to her," I said. He knew who I meant. There weren't that many of us.

"I'm sorry," said Lauer.

"It might be for the best. I've been wondering if we're poorly matched."

"Problems?"

"Little strains," I said.

"That ought to make it easier." Lauer slanted his head to indicate a photo hanging above his brass-buttoned leather sofa. "The short man in the bow tie I'm standing next to developed a flavorful ice cream that never melts and in fact contains no liquid. Gross sales last year of thirty million dollars. What's astonishing is that the fellow has no thumbs. Born without thumbs. Take a lesson there."

"Persistence?"

"Forward-leaningness. Focus. Mental drive." Lauer gazed off through the widest of his tall windows, the one with the stained-glass border of stars and suns. "Once you're out there, Mason, you won't miss her. Maybe at first, but then you'll be absorbed. The place has a pull, you'll discover. It hums. It hops. Death thinking does that to people. It peps them up. To be frank with you, Bluff could use a dose of that."

"I like it the way it is now."

"I don't," said Lauer. "We need to put some muscle on. This faith has turned into an endless ladies' tea that starts with a prayer and closes with a séance and accomplishes precisely nothing except to turn Tuesday into Wednesday and February into March. As long as the flowers bloom, they like to tell us. As long as our friend mister robin sings his songs. They're touched in the head, these women."

"They're our mothers."

"So they enjoy reminding us," said Lauer.


My first full experience of physical love, like that of most young men in Bluff, took place at an annual religious festival known as the Sanctified Midsummer Frolic. I was twenty-two that month, a trainee forester battling Asian beetles in the lodgepole pine stands north of town. My partner, chosen by our families, was one year my junior, a girl named Sarah Kimmel, studious, severe, and very thin, whose fingertips smelled of Scotch tape and Magic Marker ink as she reached for my face and neatly shut my eyes.

"You're going to like this, and it's okay to like it, but try not to like it too much," Sarah said. "You have to contain yourself."

"I know," I said.

"Not every time, but this time. Can you?"

"Yes."

"Because you've done the exercise?"

"I have."

Sarah looked worried. Accidents happened. I wondered if I should be equally concerned. I'd kissed girls, I'd held them, I'd roamed inside their clothes, and a few times I'd let them touch me under my clothes, but those were sneaky, unauthorized encounters, hampered by fear and circumscribed by conscience, while this one was authorized, open, and encouraged. I might explode. My whole body might fly apart.

My father had tried to prepare me for the Frolic by taking me out on a drive the previous week in his Chevrolet cruiser and speaking frankly for hours, even drawing a couple of sketches in his citation log as we idled at the edge of Martyr's Pond, the site of the 1880 hacking death of a runaway polygamous wife by a posse of vengeful Mormon patriarchs. There had been three other murders in Bluff's history, but none of them so momentous and galvanizing, perhaps because the victims were all men and at least two of them were drunken men. The dead woman's name was Eliza Wofford Bingham, and we honored her with a two-day September holiday that was my least favorite weekend of the year. From dawn on the first day to sundown on the second, all AFA males had to stay inside their houses while the women of Bluff paraded in the streets drinking from flasks of elderberry spirits and—in imitation of Eliza fleeing her killers through the thorny brush—casting off their clothing as they went. The holiday ended here, at Martyr's Pond, with a ceremony I'd never seen but once heard described as "rambunctious naked splashing."

After hastily going over the mental exercise meant to arrest my pleasure at the last moment, my father recalled the Frolic of thirty years ago, when he'd first enjoyed contact with my mother. He said he'd been tired that evening from staying up late kidding around with his buddies, and he regretted it. He was drowsy and inattentive during the ritual, while my mother, he said, was alert and fresh and avid. He told me that he feared he'd hurt her permanently and compromised their marriage before it started. He advised me to go to bed early beginning that night and to double my daily intake of citrus water.

"You'll be judged by the girl," he said, "and it will linger. I don't think it's right, and they're warned they shouldn't do it, but most of them—the lively ones—can't help it. What's worse is that what they're judging you against isn't another man but their idea of one."

"What idea? From where?"

"You'll never know. They don't know, either. Just rest and build your strength."

I asked him with some reluctance what I should do if Sarah didn't suit me. I didn't consider that I might not suit her.

"There's nothing to be scared of there," he said. He explained that my pairing with Sarah was not an accident but the result of continuous observation by our most intuitive church leaders. They'd been watching us since our childhoods, he said, and our compatibility was assured, although it might not be evident right away. "With your mother and me it took about six years. In your case, I'd be surprised if it takes two."

I tried to look cheered by this news but it was hard. Two years was more than seven hundred days.

"You're kinder than I was at your age," my father said. "You thrive on their approval. You nod. You listen. Love will come quickly, I know it. You're a knight."

"Sometimes I act that way. I'm not sure," I said.

"Acting that way is enough for them, I've learned." My father laughed and seemed eager for me to join him but something in what he'd said felt grim to me. It suggested I'd have to be false for women to like me, or at least for Sarah Kimmel to like me. Women in general were irrelevant now.

"And of course there's your other great virtue," my father said. "The midwife and I discussed it at your birth. But I've told you that story."

He had. It made me bashful. How the old woman had measured me with her thumb and marked its tip with a pen to show her friends. I knew he expected me to share his pride in this, and maybe I did, but it didn't feel proper to show it. Not to him, and not to any man. And what Sarah might think didn't matter; I'd thought this through. If she'd dabbled in much love play before the Frolic, she might feel appreciative and pleased, but she wouldn't be able to tell me without revealing embarrassing facts about her youth that AFA females simply never spoke about lest it should ever dawn on AFA men that the Frolic was not worth waiting for. And if Sarah hadn't dallied with other partners (which seemed to me more likely), she wouldn't know that I was any different. I'd know, however, and it might breed resentment to watch my oblivious, complacent mate take for granted what her worldly sisters might dote on and covet and treat me like a king for.

"Can we please just forget that old story?" I asked my father. I loved the man, but not right then. "It hasn't helped me any. It's upsetting. When you tell it to other people, it always comes back to me. I don't think you know that."

My father looked wounded, pierced. The story was about himself, I saw then, about the potential hidden in his seed that had emerged so grandly in his son. But was it even true? I wondered now. The physical fact it referred to was true enough (I'd peeked around at my buddies while growing up and confirmed that I had a modest advantage, especially in warm weather and in the morning), but the awestruck midwife and her thumb felt like devices invented to mask and soften an outright boast that my father dared not risk. He was a shy man. He rarely polished his badge and he wore a Windbreaker over his uniform even in broiling late July.

He gazed through the windshield at muddy Martyr's Pond. It was miserable being a man in Bluff sometimes. Perhaps it was even worse elsewhere. We hoped so, anyway.

"The Frolic," my father said. "I wouldn't have named it that."

"What would you have named it?"

"Hmm . . . I'll think."

"Not that they let us name things. Or ever will."

"Don't talk that way, Mason. It's a downhill road."

"Don't be so somber. Let's hear your name."

"'The Clench.'"

Exactly sixty minutes after sundown, Sarah had me lie on my back with my arms beside my trunk and my legs about a foot apart so that she could kneel between my ankles. She was as thin from the front as from the side, an index finger of a woman. She spread her hands and gripped my goose-bumped shins and seemed to be steadying her mind for something that she'd mastered while alone but found more daunting now that I was here. I asked her if she'd intended to leave my socks on.

"It's brisk tonight. I thought you'd want warm toes."

"It looks wrong," I said.

"No one's looking at you."

"You are."

"But you don't know at what. It's not your socks, young man."

Surprising. Enlightening. Her quip meant that she did know the difference, but it meant more than that. It meant she didn't care to hide her knowledge and even that she enjoyed it. And felt entitled to.

Like the five or six other young women at that year's ceremony, Sarah had made a small campsite along a stream at the edge of a cut alfalfa field. She'd pitched a loose tent of gray mosquito netting supported at its corners by sharpened willow sticks and spread out a freshly laundered flannel sleeping bag made fragrant with drops of purifying sage oil. On the ground, beside a kerosene lantern, her purse lay open, filled with her supplies: a tube of skin cream, a folded yellow hand towel, and a pocket edition of Mother Lucy's *Discourses* bound in white elk skin, stitched with yellow thread, and marked with a lavender ribbon near the end. I'd never managed to read that far myself, but Sarah was a student of theology, about to complete her fourth year at Coleman College, the Church academy for women. There was no such institution for men. Men in Bluff trained for jobs, for concrete tasks, but women cultivated a higher view that showed them what all our sweat and toil would come to. They spoke of this vista in parables, symbolically, and my hunch was that they withheld important elements out of fear of lowering men's morale.

"Your body needs to form a line," said Sarah. "North-south, to take advantage of magnetism." She grasped my heels and tugged my legs out straight, gently shaking them to relax my hips, and then, beginning with the little ones and working methodically inward, she cracked my toes. Afterward, I couldn't feel them. The lantern light through my closed eyelids was mottled pink, its patterns shifting with my heartbeat, and I could smell concentration on Sarah's breath—a burned odor, not unpleasant, like peanuts roasting—as she positioned herself athwart my pelvis.

"All the way flat. No tension. Dead," she said.

I'd assumed we'd pray first. Maybe later. She gave me all of her weight. She gave it smoothly. I drew a deep breath, then felt Sarah blow it out. That people could breathe for each other was strange new knowledge and I felt suddenly enlarged by it, like the moment I'd learned to stay upright on a bicycle. A needle of hay stubble pierced the sleeping bag and I arched my back to avoid it but couldn't go high enough without disturbing a balance that had developed. I let the stalk scratch me, its sharp dry tip, and then let it cut me when she drove me flat again. I must have made a sound then—Sarah stopped.

"Are you close?" she said. "How close are you?"

My father had said it would jolt me, but not wholly. First would come a sense that a jolt was likely.

"I'm pretty sure we're safe," I said.

She touched me near where we were connected, in a spot where I'd never been touched as an adult and hadn't wished to be. Now I wished to be. This new wish would endure until I died, I sensed, and might even float free from my gray corpse and drift forever in the Etheric Breeze, a permanent speck of quintessential Mason-ness that couldn't think or remember or speak its name but only wish and wish and wish.

"I'm supposed to be able to feel it. Here," said Sarah. "A little bump-bump or twitch that tells me when."

"Did you?"

"Not yet."

"Let's keep going."

"If you're confident."

"I'm confident."

"Confident or just determined?"

"The longer you jabber and pester me," I said, "the more confident I get."

Across the field, by some wonder of acoustics that summer in the mountains brings on sometimes, I could hear the voices of our chaperones—four ancient ladies drinking mint tea from thermoses and plotting their annual trade fair in Missoula. AFAs lived to ninety quite regularly, and not a touchy, arthritic, dependent ninety but an unflappable productive ninety that, among the women, led to supreme achievements in the crafts realm. They sewed and crocheted with the patience of near immortals, complicating and miniaturizing their stitches, detailing and elaborating their patterns. It was as though they were working their way down to some primary depth of tininess and fineness that, if they ever succeeded in touching it, might allow them to reweave the cosmos or, if their fingers slipped, unravel it. They didn't hold on to their handiworks, however; they sold them to strangers from a rented stall at a Missoula's weekend farmers' market. Their pieces commanded handsome prices. Those old crones loved their money, it was plain to see, though why they loved it wasn't clear. They rarely spent it, just packed it into shoe boxes or sewed it into the linings of their coats for their heirs to come across someday.

"I'm feeling the twitch," Sarah said, and she was off me, quickly enough to avoid a pregnancy but not to avoid a gluey wet mess. She wiped us both clean with the hand towel (had she planned for this?) and reminded me, after pausing to let things settle, that a clock had just started on our eventual wedding. Once I'd proven myself as a provider by amassing the money and Virtue Coupons necessary to buy a house and a share in the Bluff co-op, we would be married in this very field, on this very spot beside the creek. Until then, more intimate contact was forbidden; our memories of the Frolic would have to serve.

"We're in the Book of Love now," Sarah said.

In practice, this meant meeting for Sunday suppers at her family's house on Isis Street, a standard aluminum-sided three-bedroom cube built by community labor in the eighties from plans drawn up by the Church Domestic Architect. These blueprints changed only every thirty years or so, resulting in uniform little neighborhoods that I found cozy and reassuring but that the fussier women of our town (my grandmother called them "the Parisians") loved to gripe about. And, yes, each house style did have certain flaws, such as the tendency of my parents' roof to collect so much snow in the winter that when spring came the copious runoff would flood the basement and swell the soil near the foundation. Repairing the damage this caused was often expensive, but the fact that every squat white stucco bungalow clustered around ours was ailing in the same manner softened the blow.

At the Kimmels' house the problem was lack of air, which made me groggy and inarticulate during my weekly visits. Sarah's father, a laborer in the talc mine that was Bluff's chief source of outside income, suffered more spectacularly, coughing nonstop and rubbing his runny eyes until the lashes all fell out. Sarah blamed the dustiness and stuffiness for her dull skin, her dandruff, and her dry mouth. Only her mother seemed unaffected, perhaps because she seldom took a breath. The woman was a husky kitchen whirlwind who cleaned as she cooked and had no true feminine features aside from a great wild mass of dyed dark hair that looked like it had sprung down from a branch, claws extended, and attacked her scalp.

The meals she served had less flavor than the stale air. The Kimmels were fish people, their Maternal Foodway as determined more than a hundred years ago by Mother Lucy, our founder and first Seeress. The only fresh fish to be found in Bluff was trout, and Sarah's mother prepared it according to two main recipes in which I could taste her own mother's wrinkled hand: oven-baked trout fillets garnished with forest herbs and parboiled trout on stewed dandelion greens. This would be my diet once I married Sarah, so I tried to eat enthusiastically, even when my appetite was stifled by her wounding behavior at the table.

It usually showed itself midway through the meal, after the Prayer and the Lesson. The Lesson was Paul's job. Paul, the little brother—a prim blond twelve-year-old whom I was expected to take an interest in by helping him with his math and science homework and admiring his collection of fossil insects dug from the shale deposits south of town—read to us from the Three Foundational Works in a high fearful voice familiar from my own school days. He lived in terror of mispronunciations, just as I had at his age. The teachers punished them harshly. "Be always incorruptible in intention," he quoted from Mother Lucy's *Discourses*, "and indefatigable in execution. The Transcendent Immanence yields but slowly to the instrumentalities of will."

"How did I do?" he asked, looking at his big sister, who functioned as the household magistrate and ruled on all of life's little daily questions. Her mother was too distracted, her father too tired, and her little brother too young and fretful.

"Moderately inadequately," said Sarah.

The crisp extra syllables were a cruelty. Paul's eyes fogged over with shame. His throat turned red.

"Better than I'd have done. That was hard," I said.

"Mason?"

"What?"

"Respect," said Sarah.

"Sorry."

"Paul, don't cry," she said.

"I'm not," he sniffled.

"You were about to cry. Mason?"

"Yes?" I said.

"Eat. You're not eating."

"Because we're talking now."

"And now we're finished talking. Eat," she said.

After supper the parents released us for a stroll into the hills along a raw dirt logging road that was a favorite spot for couples like us, their affections stretched thin between memories of pleasure and forebodings of commitment. Whenever we passed them, we lowered our heads to show we weren't interested in their conversations, but faint vibrations passed between us anyway: of sympathy for one another's awkwardness and—between the future husbands, at least—of mutual condolence.

Sarah used our night walks to disclose to me her hopes and expectations for our life together. She planned to teach at the college once she graduated and put aside money for certain small luxuries that we might not be able to save for after she started having children. To me, the luxuries didn't sound small at all, though.

"I'd like a nice car. A Saab."

I made her spell it. The word's outlandish foreignness annoyed me. Most AFA families owned two vehicles, the husband's pickup truck and the wife's sedan, both of them used and minimally equipped. The talk that a car such as Sarah described might cause would isolate us from our friends and neighbors.

"Maybe. If it's a few years old," I said.

"I'd like a new one. The new ones are much cuter. I saw a nice red one in Missoula last August."

Sarah's grand notions all came from the same place. Because of her trips to the trade fair with her mother, who crafted cedar spoons and cooking tongs, she'd spent too much time, I felt, comparing herself to the vain free-spenders with poisonous diets whom the All-in-One had set around us as a reminder of how not to live and, especially, how not to eat. As the Seeress had been telling us for years, the buildup of yeast in people from bleached white flour promotes a restless, selfish temperament that atrophies the pituitary glands and plays havoc with natural peristalsis. If such defectives were Sarah's models now, then she was sick, too, I feared, and might grow sicker. Once she'd secured her abominable Saab, she'd look around for something else—a second Saab, maybe, in another color.

"No Missoula this year. It's bad for you," I said.

"You've hardly been there."

"That's immaterial."

"Clever long words don't suit men."

"They suit me fine."

"Where do you get them? I'm curious."

"The library."

"The library is for dandies," Sarah said. "If you have to use it, be quick. Don't sit and read there. It gives the wrong impression."

"So do Saabs."

When I finally told Sarah plainly that our marriage might be an undertaking beyond my means, she yielded a bit in the area of chastity. One night when she'd been describing her future kitchen, and specifically the built-in ovens that would allow her to run a home-based business using the Kimmel women's beloved recipes for marionberry bran cakes and the like, I let go of her hand and walked three steps ahead of her, turned around in the middle of the logging road, and announced from a formal, manly distance that I would need an extra two years, at least, before I'd be in a position to set a wedding date. I led her through a cold, mathematical formula relating my projected weekly wages to the estimated costs of aping the Missoula way of life.

She opened her hands and held them out to me at the level of my hips. "I'm frustrated. We don't touch enough," she whispered. The gap between our bodies became charged and my scalp prickled as before a lightning strike. The wish flared up. I gave in. I went to her. Her warm, grabby hands crawled into my back pockets and she lowered her face so her lashes tickled my neck. "You never push me to break the rules," she said. "I wonder why not. Don't you love me? I love you."

"I love you but not when you talk about the Saab."

Sarah kissed me then. In the kiss I could feel the squirming energies of unborn children impatient to leave the spirit world. Sarah wanted three children, she'd told me—two girls, one boy—but it felt as though at least twice that many souls were swarming up at me through her throat and lips. She moved a hand to my right front pocket, dug deep, and held me through the cloth. Her fingertips moved along me like a flute player's, with meticulous sequential pressure.

"Fine, then. A three-year-old model. But red," she said.

This was the night before the talk with Lauer that freed me to imagine no Saab at all.

The key was to make everything look like my fault. That was my mother's opinion. She'd thought things over. She'd even secretly contacted Sarah's mother, a second cousin, and discussed the matter. They agreed that although I was leaving Sarah to do the bidding of the Church, my departure might harm her social desirability unless it appeared that she'd rejected me first—and for some clear and fundamental reason that wouldn't scare off future suitors by confirming her growing reputation as a finicky, prickly, demanding shrew.

I had to be seen as a lost cause, irredeemably unmarriageable.

Rumors about the disqualifying trait that Lauer, the mothers, and I decided on were planted around town the following week. Within a few days they were rustling all about me whenever I stepped outside the house. When Sarah, as I knew she'd soon feel forced to, questioned me about the troubling stories, I planned to turn surly and evasive so as to head off any urge in her to empathize with me, accept my limitations, and love me despite them—or because of them.

While I waited for the breakup, I trained for my mission at Lauer's mansion. He taught me to indebt the people I met by sending them off with a trinket or a free book. He told me to think the words "I am now inside you" whenever I looked a prospect in the eye. He told me that an angled stance invites your listener to move in closer while a squared-off stance pushes him away. Then he showed me how to end a handshake. "Person One, who's you," he said, "loosens his grip slightly, cuing Person Two to loosen his grip in response, at which same instant Person One—the power figure—lets go completely." Another trick he showed me was to sit with my head a bit lower than Person Two's and then, very slowly, over several minutes, straighten back up until my head was the high head.

"Person Two feels like he shrunk," I said.

" 'Remote Infantilization.' That's the term."

"But how does it help me persuade him to join the Church?"

"In every interaction between two people, one plays the Parent, the other plays the Child. There's no third way," Lauer said. "But there's an art to this. The Parent can't just dominate the Child or the Child will resist the Parent. To earn the Child's respect and love and trust, Person Two needs to share his power now and then."

"Person One, you mean."

Lauer smiled at me. He held the smile in the way a person does when he wants you to ask him why he's smiling so that he can reveal a thought he's having that you, if you were cleverer or sharper, would have already guessed or had yourself.

"Why are you smiling?" I knew what he'd say next and that my response would be "Tell me, I don't know," and that his tone when he finally explained things would be the parental power-figure tone. I'd never felt so tired in all my life.

"Why do you *think* I'm smiling?" Lauer said.

His secret, when we got that far, was that he'd intentionally erred a moment ago by mixing up Person Two with Person One in order to give me, the Child, a chance to correct him, the Parent, and feel proud and "valued" as a result. Without asking me if I'd actually felt these feelings (which I hadn't, though I would have said I had just to end the session) Lauer declared the experiment a success.

It was a slip. The Child felt condescended to and erupted with his true thoughts. "If these tricks can really convert people," I said, "then people aren't worth converting. They're machines. And AFAs are fools."

I left the session, my seventh in two weeks, despairing about my mission and my life and unusually eager for Sarah's company. I assumed she'd heard the gossip by then and was weighing the risks of repeating it to me. Our walk the next night was uncomfortable and odd. A porcupine with reflective golden eyes waddled across the road and Sarah said, "Maybe people are nocturnal, too. Maybe we're happiest in the gloomy murk but somehow it's been bred out of us. You think? Maybe we lived in caves because we crave caves but maybe there weren't enough of them eventually so we moved into houses and tried to change."

She seemed to be pushing at something, but timidly. There was only one thing to push at by that time.

"Who can say?" I told her. "I know I do get restless when the sun sets."

"Or maybe it's just men," she said. "You think?"

"A lot of our primitive hunting took place at night."

"And in groups," Sarah said. "Men hunted in groups back then. No women. Just men and the mammoths. In the night."

But that was as far as Sarah was willing to go that evening.

I figured we had a week before our rupture. I passed it by getting to know Elias Stark, whom Lauer had chosen as my mission partner. His bristly stiff brown hair was more like beard hair than normal head hair and the chunks of gray in it didn't make him look mature, just troubled. His comma-shaped nostrils were the blackest I'd ever seen, as were the holes in his ears. His pupils, too. The impression was that the cavity of his skull was packed with some sort of infernal shadow matter—or maybe it held absolutely nothing and he operated on reflex, not higher thought. Still, Elder Elias Stark was local nobility: his mother was in line for Seeress someday and already endowed with Gifts and Powers. She resembled a female version of George Washington, already white-haired at fifty-two, with a broad unwrinkled polished forehead that looked like the perfect setting for a third eye.

One day I confided in him about Sarah, and Elder Stark described to me how he'd dispatched his own girl: swiftly, in one slashing cut, by criticizing her looks. He'd told her that her eyes were set too close and that her waist was too long for her short legs. He took a kick to the shins for this, he said, but the kick didn't hurt because it was the last kick.

"Sarah isn't concerned about appearance. That wouldn't work with her," I said.

"I think your plan is screwy. I think it's doomed."

"I'm trying to be merciful."

"By pretending you've been with men? She won't believe you."

"I'll deny it, but not convincingly," I said. "She'll believe me if she thinks I'm lying."

"You're too sloppy, too slouchy. Those boys are fresh and springy."

The next Sunday, at last, it came: the conversation. Sarah's mother, who knew what loomed, sighed and stared at her plate during the meal in a way that suggested she felt sorry for us, and not just for Sarah and me but for all of Bluff. Sustaining ourselves had become a chore and perhaps too much of one. Our faith had sequestered us in a mountain valley, drier, higher up, and farther back than anywhere human beings should have to dwell. The helpful talc mines still held tons of talc but the deposits were harder and harder to get at. Yes, we were safe from assault, debased philosophies, bewildering images, and harmful foodstuffs, but in our safety we'd thinned and paled and dwindled. Our blood was weak, like children's milky tea, and though our digestive tracts were scrubbed of residue, it seemed that we'd lost some essential vital filth, some energizing compost required for growth.

We retired to the sofa after our iced-fruit puddings. Paul sat on the rug and arranged his fossil insects according to age, assembling a time line that made me feel marginal and indistinct. I sensed that Sarah was working up to something but slipping sideways as she went. The struggle enriched her complexion. It pinked her earlobes.

"You're eating poorly," she said. "You yawn and slump."

"Because the windows don't open in your house."

"Drink some bentonite clay mixed in grape juice."

I promised I'd have a glass when I got home. Sarah took my right hand and cupped it on her bare kneecap, its surface creased and pebbled with childhood scars. Kids in Bluff grew up by falling down, by crashing and tumbling, girls and boys alike. The divisions came when we got older. The final division happened at the Frolic, when we were pushed together by our elders. We'd already been together, many of us, but in our own fumbling ways, on our own time, not in the ordained way and on their time.

"This is terribly hard for me," said Sarah. She had all the tales and tidbits. She had her case. She'd make it delicately and diplomatically, and then I'd be mean to her, protest, act insulted, and she'd feel well rid of me and want someone else.

But she took a route I hadn't anticipated. "I need a favor, Mason. An indulgence. Set me aside. I'm not good for you or anyone. Everything you've accused me of is true. I'm greedy and I'm a scold and I'm a needler. I need to repair those weaknesses. In solitude. Not in a house together with a husband."

We sat there in silence as Paul replaced his rocks in a tissue-lined shoe box whose lid was marked "Prehistory." I should have known by his presence that his big sister had decided not to say hard things to me or repeat hard things she'd heard from others. But he needed to go now, because this wasn't over yet. I pointed at him. He knew. He took his box away. We'd given him plenty to chew on as it stood.

"Is that all you wanted to say to me tonight? I think there might be more," I said.

"I wish it weren't so simple," Sarah said. "I'm wrong for you. Just please don't always hate me."

"Impossible."

"Thank you."

"This is nonsense, Sarah. It's me who's not fit for you, and you know why. You're sparing me because you think I'm weak. You think I don't know what people say about me and you don't want to be the first to tell me."

A snorty chuckle, rich with nose juice. Sarah covered her mouth with her left hand.

"Listen to me," I said. "Be serious. Sarah, I am a different kind of man. I am a man who can't . . . I mean who doesn't—"

Wiping her eyes and trying to hold in laughter. Rubbing away the juice under her nose. Finally saying, "Don't cook things up—just *say* things. You know what I wanted to spare you from, you goofhead? Wait—just let me laugh and get this over with." It took about a minute. "Done," she said. "What I wanted to spare you from, you silly knothead, was this, this whole ridiculous performance. Mason LaVerle, the tortured secret dandy!"

"Someone told you. Recently," I said. "Last week, when we talked about mammoths, you thought I was one. And it made sense to you. I use the library."

"And then I paid a visit to your proud father."

The midwife's thumb.

"Who hated the plan all along and told me this: 'I know you don't have any way to judge, but I can assure you, young lady, my only son was specifically crafted in Preexistence to deliver mighty carnal pleasure to the most tender depths of womankind.' He's a poet, your father."

"Not usually," I said.

"On the subject of his son, he is."

"I'd like to leave on a mission. May I?"

"Do."

"You shouldn't wait for me."

"I won't. We're incompatible and I want a Saab. The All-in-One made this work out perfectly. Go declare it, Mason. Tell the world. 'Our habit of wishing backward from what is to what might have been,' " she said, quoting the Seeress, " 'is the soft but persistent tapping that cracks the crystal.' "

"I need to memorize that one."

"You need to go."

We kissed goodbye on the front steps. I thought back to the Frolic, under the mosquito netting, when we'd breathed for each other. We'd managed the feat again. Maybe we can all do it, at certain times—any willing, good-hearted two of us. Maybe we're all fine matches for one another and someone should just throw us in a sack and shake it until we're jumbled up together and then pick us out in pairs and send us off. Maybe everything would come out the same. But things would have to come out somehow, surely, and when they did we'd have the choice we always have, and our only choice, really: approve or disapprove.

Once I'd obtained my release, events moved swiftly. One half of one moon cycle later, on June 10th, after an outdoor party and a feast attended by every living person I knew, all of whom lined up to wish me well and many of whom stuffed money in my pockets or verses they'd copied out or little charms they'd made, I left my home with another AFA whom I had not chosen or been chosen by to show a people quick to disapprove (or so we'd heard, and so we both believed) that constant approval had a faction, too. We'd invite them to join it. Come along, we'd say.

And if they asked us why they ought to, or asked us why we were so few and growing fewer while they were so many and ever multiplying, we'd smile at them in the way that people smile when they want others to ask them why they're smiling—as though we knew something they didn't, something obvious.

I just hoped my partner could tell them what it was.

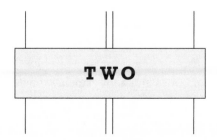

# TWO

**On our seventh night away** from Bluff we parked and locked the green Dodge camper van that we were supposed to sleep in to save money, paid for a motel room near the interstate by raiding the box of rubber-banded dollars presented to us by the lady Crafts Fair magnates, ordered by phone two tubs of cayenne chicken wings and two Dr Pepper soft drinks in barrel-size cups that advertised a movie called *The Flip Off*, and then lay on our stomachs on our queen-size beds, our neckties flipped onto the backs of our white shirts and our discount-store dress shoes kicked off on our pillows, and watched TV for the first time in our lives—seven hours of TV, without a break—until we were satisfied we'd been told the truth and had indeed come to a land of disapprovers.

"You watch," Elder Stark said, "she'll pick the federal marshall. Mustache, sidearm, badge—he has it all."

"Not the professional golfer?"

"He wears pink slacks."

"He's rich, though. He owns a boat."

"It doesn't matter. These women out here want killers. They want menace."

The show was one of those real-life dating programs that we hadn't known existed until that night but had now seen three of and couldn't turn off. The women wore blue jeans slung low around their hip bones and kept glancing down at their candy-colored toenails as they strolled along white beaches in floppy sandals, kicking up sand to display their playful natures, followed by panting nippy little dogs that they clapped at now and then to hurry up even though the dogs' tongues were hanging out. The men were suntanned brutes in pretty shirts, with dull, narrow eyes, blond hair peaked up with hair spray, and mouths that didn't quite open when they spoke or fully close again when they finished speaking. They were actual people, supposedly, not actors, but they moved and pulled faces as I imagined actors might.

"We haven't discussed the teacher," Elder Stark said.

"Not going to win. Too serious. Too stiff."

"Too much like us, you mean."

"We improved today. Especially at the end there. We relaxed."

Elder Stark crossed his ankles on the pillow and returned his attention to the program, the last in a series of twelve, apparently, and the one where the woman would select a mate. Decision making fascinated my partner. He'd grown up in a bedroom that shared a flimsy wall with his mother's spiritual counseling office, where she interpreted her patients' dreams, adjusted their diets, and heard out the regrets that AFAs are encouraged not to have but still need a kind ear for when they do. He'd learned a lot through the Sheetrock—too much, he told me—and the main thing was that we're strangers to ourselves, pointed from birth toward outcomes we resist, even though we've obscurely chosen them. He said that his years of spying had revealed to him the key to happiness and satisfaction: rush at high speed toward wherever you're headed anyway. "Momentum, Mason. It's everything," he said. "Frustration comes from fighting your own momentum."

As he sucked the wet meat from another chicken wing, I went to the bathroom and peeled a sheet of cling wrap off a water glass. At the bottom lay a curled dead spider. The motel's staff was a band of red-eyed wrecks, like stragglers from a disbanded traveling circus, and I suspected they'd placed the creature there as a tiny act of vengeance on people who weren't as yet in such bad shape. At check-in a girl with a faded neck tattoo depicting a pair of strangling male hands had blown her nose on the shoulder of her T-shirt while she was programming our plastic key cards. I offered my handkerchief and she said, "Ick." Elder Stark set a tract on her counter but she ignored it, and we didn't press her; we collected our keys and left. On a mission of just nine months we couldn't waste time on those who wouldn't have us.

"It's rough," Elder Stark had said when we reached our room, "leaving folks alone like that to suffer."

"Tomorrow we'll try harder. We're tired," I said.

"You noticed that little cross around her neck?"

"Yes."

"Those trinkets discourage me," he said.

We'd been seeing crosses everywhere. Also, roadside billboards for the Lord, T-shirts and sweatshirts for the Lord, and stickers on cars and trucks with sayings like, "Believe in Him. He still believes in you." I wasn't sure how seriously to take these things—some of them seemed to be decorations, or jokes—but my partner regarded them as evidence that we'd arrived too late. These fields had been harvested, harrowed, and replanted so many times that the soil was dead, he feared.

I rinsed out the spider and purged my sticky mouth of the cayenne and Dr Pepper tastes with three or fours swallow of neutral tepid water that made me miss the water back in Bluff, so hard and sharp, like icy liquid stone. I considered making myself vomit as I stood at the sink and faced the mirror and probed my belly with my fingertips to feel the hard, engorged outlines of my intestines. I'd mistreated them and I vowed to stop. We'd dined responsibly for the first five days, relying on almond slivers to keep from snacking and seeking out dinner spots with salad bars featuring radishes, beets, and turkey cubes, but then two nights ago, desperate for hot showers, we'd pulled into a truck stop west of Billings. I ordered the fish but the waitress wouldn't serve it, explaining that the freezer where it was kept had been contaminated by a busboy who'd urinated on the floor and walls after learning that he'd been fired. To be safe, we ordered sourdough pancakes. The corn syrup and white flour sapped our wills, and we'd been craving garbage ever since.

I opened my toilet kit and removed the products I'd picked up that morning at a Sheridan drugstore where I'd gone to buy razors and shaving cream while Elder Stark handed out pamphlets in the parking lot. The store's health-and-beauty aisle had overwhelmed me. I'd filled my basket with lotions, creams, and gels that I knew full well I couldn't afford but whose labels made claims I was powerless not to test.

"It's the golfer," my partner called in from the bedroom. "I'll be danged. She picked the golfer. Frick."

"You can use bad words. It's only me."

"Damn it, she picked the golfer. Watch with me."

"I'm getting ready to whiten my teeth," I said.

"What's wrong with your teeth? They're fine."

"You've seen the teeth here."

Even after seven days in the van, my partner and I were still learning about America. The Church's founders had called the place "Terrestria," refusing at first to vote in its elections, supply troops for its armies, or recognize its currency, and though they capitulated in 1913 in a bid to escape imprisonment, Bluff had remained a world apart. As schoolkids, as part of a secret curriculum we were forbidden to mention to nonmembers, we'd learned to refer to our incorporation as "the Arrangement" and think of it as temporary, lasting only until that fateful day when Terrestria succumbed to chaos and the Apostles were left to sift through the wreckage and usher in the New Edenic Covenant foretold by Mother Lucy. Elder Stark felt this day might come during our mission and he'd joked that the prospect excited him because it would offer us a chance to loot, starting with the luxury-auto lots. Elder Stark wasn't satisfied with the sluggish camper van that never seemed to shift out of second gear. He wanted a Range Rover with a V-8 like one we'd seen parked in Missoula our first day out.

"I'm eating your next-to-last wing," he said. "Also, I'm switching to news. We need to pay more attention to the news."

"Why is that?"

"The worse it gets, the better the chance they'll give us a fair hearing."

"That's a mean thing to wish. The news is bad already."

"It's hard to tell. We don't know what they're used to."

I pricked the plastic tube of whitener open with its pointed cap. The instruction sheet promised results that you could see in only fourteen days, but I hoped to cut this to seven by applying a thick double coating. I couldn't wait two weeks. Women who struck me as fine potential mates were already passing me by without a look. They seemed to sense it when I looked at them, though, and yesterday one had reached into her bag as if for some instrument of self-defense.

"They're broadcasting a hostage difficulty. Texas clinic. Disgruntled young male nurse. The SWAT team, whatever they call it, has bulletproof breastplates and some kind of scope or camera that sees through walls. Watch this thing with me."

"Once I'm done in here."

"Should I whiten my teeth, too?"

"That's up to you."

"Why don't I stay natural and you go whiter and whoever has more luck in meeting people, he'll be the leader. We need to choose a leader."

"You go ahead. You're older."

"You're clearer headed."

Elder Stark was being disingenuous. He knew that he'd been in command since we set out and that he had no intention of yielding power. How he'd assumed control I wasn't certain. I only knew that the first time we'd bought gasoline he'd insisted on premium, for better mileage, and that was that—the pattern was set. Next he was pointing out which passersby we should try to talk into taking the Well-being Quiz and which ones we should allow to meet their fates.

"My mom had a man she counseled who took a hostage once. He dreamed it before he did it," Elder Stark said. "He tied up his wife with twisted plastic trash bags to keep her from leaving him for another man, then locked her in a shed behind the house while his neighbors searched the woods. After a week he set her free and she refused to report him. They're still together. That tying her up with trash bags did the trick."

"This happened in Bluff? I never heard a word."

"It happened when we were little. You've heard of 'angel babies'?"

"Never."

"They're the newborns who don't come out right. The Church owns a house in Spokane where people care for them. Big heads. Short arms. Stubby fingers. Angel babies."

"Stop it."

"I heard about them through the wall."

"You make stuff up," I said. "It isn't that funny. A lot of it's danged disgusting."

"Say it: 'damned.' "

When he bantered this way, out of sight, without direction, I knew what Elder Stark was really doing. He'd unhitched his belt. One hand was in his underwear. It had happened after lights-out in the van on our second night and again the following night. I'd done it, too. An agreement took shape. We could carry on as we pleased in our own bunks as long as we spared each other the sights and sounds.

I dipped a small wand into the plastic tube, drew back my lips so they wouldn't spread saliva, and covered my incisors and bicuspids with a layer of bleachy-tasting gel. The tooth discoloration was due to diet, and particularly the "strong digestives" such as anise jelly and sweetened pine pitch that we took after heavy fatty meals. The results of this regimen, for me and others, were clear, unusually elastic skin, urine that sometimes smelled strongly of burning leaves, and tooth enamel scored by hairline etchings that I feared were the beginnings of ruinous cracks. Eating as Adam was thought to have was perilous, but at least it warded off the bloating that I was suffering from that night.

"They're saying there's no sign of life inside the clinic. It's over. The SWAT team is taking off its breastplates. I feel like we should go back to the lobby and give that poor girl with the cross another chance."

"This stuff needs to sit on my teeth for fifteen minutes."

"Shiny beautiful teeth look strange on men. That blond guy in Bozeman—the one who bought us coffee and said we could stay anytime in his spare room—his teeth were so white they were almost clear, like glass."

"I'll stop before that."

"Come watch with me. I'm lonesome."

"So sleep, then. Turn it off."

"I can't," he said. "I'm lonesome without it. I don't know how that happened."

"I do."

"How?"

"It's hard to put it into words. You forget how quiet it was before, or something. The quiet scared you, but you didn't know it. After you turn off the screen, you know it, though."

"We've never turned it off."

"It's a prediction."

Lonesomeness was a problem with Elder Stark. I'd known him before as a schoolmate and a Church friend but I'd only grown close to him during the last few training seminars, after we'd moved into Lauer's house so we could spend more time practicing being Person One. I'd learned that my new friend couldn't sleep in stretches longer than two hours due to nightmares, and sometimes, in the middle of the night, waking up on my bunk in the makeshift basement dormitory, I'd hear him sucking cough drops or crunching almonds as though trying to drown out troubling thoughts. A few times I heard him talking to himself in a croaky old man's voice. I got the tones and the rhythms but not the words. When I asked Elder Stark about this in the morning his face tightened up and he told me I'd been dreaming. A few hours later he confessed, "The Hobo paid me a visit. He keeps me company. Was he being critical or kind?" I told him the voice sounded very faintly critical and asked him what the Hobo looked like, afraid to ask him how real the Hobo was.

"He wears an old floppy hat. It shades his face. I made him up when I was five or six to look in a barn I was scared of going into for a cat I'd lost."

"The Hobo went in and you stayed outside?" I said.

"No. He made fun of me for being scared until I had something to prove. We went together. Afterward, he clapped me on the back and I felt prouder than I ever had, so I asked him to stay. He promised to pop in sometimes. My mother told me when I was twelve, once I was old enough to understand, that I didn't really invent him, either. She used to see him standing over my crib. The same floppy hat. You probably have one, too. She told me most boys in Bluff do."

"I don't have one."

"Maybe a sea pirate or a cattle rustler?"

"Why are these types all vagabonds or crooks? Do they have to be?"

"They just always are."

I let the gel dry and watched the nighttime interstate out the recessed, cell-like bathroom window. Each car and truck represented another soul out of reach of our influence, lost to its true nature. Growing up, it had always bothered me how easily we consigned non-AFAs to lives of dissatisfaction and insignificance. The universe pivoted on our heads solely, even though we'd just recently organized ourselves. The older I grew and the more I read, the more confusing it all seemed. How could a settlement tucked up in the woods at the edge of the power grid and the zip code system have a bigger lever to shift history than the millions of people who voted for the government, farmed the Great Plains, and administered the markets?

"How white are they?" Elder Stark asked me from the bedroom. His voice had brightened; he must have finished his business. With me it took forever, but he was quick.

I bared my teeth in the mirror: no improvement. Besides a nice smile, I wanted some other things. A suntan that didn't end partway up my arms and at my collar line. Hair that poked up a little, or puffed out, and didn't just lie sideways and dead flat. My mother had always told me I was handsome, and compared to the boys in Bluff I might have been, but within a few hours of leaving I discovered that they weren't much to judge by. Framed in the windshields of the cars we passed were young male heads so symmetrical and pleasing I feared that Lauer had underestimated the degradation of our physical stock. My partner showed no sign of such concerns, though, and I couldn't very well bring them up without insulting his own appearance.

"No whiter," I said.

"I'm glad I didn't bother then."

"You're supposed to be patient. It's a gradual change."

"Maybe I'll reconsider if I notice it. Right now, my brother, I think you bought a lie."

There were still a few things to do before I slept. The training course had taught us to end our days by swallowing a one-ounce dropper of filbert oil as prescribed in our six-page manual, "The Alchemy of Evangelism," which also included a recipe for mouthwash made of melon-rind juice and muckweed pulp. The nut oil was thought to condition our vocal cords and cause them to resonate at secret frequencies that listeners would find calming and appealing. The next step was to gargle with the mouthwash, which was said to ward off canker sores. Finally, we were told to shut our eyes for a five- or ten-minute Thought Retreat during which we were urged to picture a belt of pink radiation swaddling the earth and neutralizing its poisons and malignancies.

I sat on the edge of the tub and did the exercise. It had originated forty years ago in response to a pleading letter to the Seeress—the current Seeress's predecessor, who we called Swift Aunt Patricia, because we rename them when they're dead so we don't confuse them with the reigning ones—from the Peruvian Minister of Health, a secret longtime subscriber to *Luminaria*, the monthly AFA journal of ideas that our leaders hinted was widely read, in secret, by enlightened powerful outsiders. According to the minister's letter, northern Peru had recently been identified as the source of an epidemic, ROGA, rapid onset gonadal atrophy, which had sterilized hundreds of young men in the Lima slums. The bug or germ behind the outbreak was mutating too quickly for vaccines and might soon cross the border into Bolivia. Could Swift Aunt Patricia offer help or guidance?

That very day, the story went, she sent her staff home early, fed her birds, and shut herself up in the Blossom Room of Riverbright, the turreted official residence that Mother Lucy had sketched while she lay dying but failed to render the rear side of, causing its builders to leave it flat and windowless because early Apostles were strict abstainers from what *Discourses* calls the Bridegroom's Folly, defined as trying to guess another's desires in the absence of unmistakable evidence. (We grew less stringent about this as the years passed.) She prayed in the time-honored manner of her office, kneeling on an unplaned cedar plank, her feet unshod, her right palm open and up, her left palm flat across her forehead. After three sleepless days and several Etheric Contacts with Lom-Bard-Ok-Thon, the virility entity of the Pyramids, Swift Aunt Patricia discerned a trembling radiance around the globe atop her desk. The glow turned rose-colored, intensified, and hovered over South America as the Blossom Room warmed to ninety-nine degrees (or, as in my grandmother's account, was whipped by a sudden, fierce cyclonic draft that stripped its houseplants bare of leaves). Exactly four months later, under the spring moon we know as Snake Emergence, another letter came in which the minister confirmed the miracle: Peru was whole. The plague had ceased.

Such stories were hard to credit, yet I cherished them. What I couldn't imagine was telling them to strangers, even though I had little else to offer them. Ours was a church of tales, I'd come to realize, and we accorded anecdotes and gossip a higher place than formal doctrine, which we didn't really trust. It was no wonder our movement had failed to spread. Unless you grew up with us, soaking up the lore, how could you hope to understand or join us? It was all so sloppy, so disheveled, a huge loose stack of fables and fourth-hand yarns clipped to a modest sheaf of creeds with a lot of health advice tossed in.

I stripped to my shorts and T-shirt, washed my face, went back to the bedroom, and slid in under the blankets. Elder Stark's state of awareness was hard to estimate; his eyes were open, lit by the TV shine, but didn't seem to be taking anything in. We'd been asked to recite an old verse before we slept—"All-in-One of Aspects Manifold / Maker Not Admirer of Gold / One Day Red or Violet, Another Green / Ever Heard, Perpetually Seen / Mind the Turnings That We Take / And the Actions We Forsake / Help Us Never to Compare / Perfect Presence Always Everywhere"—but tonight we'd have to skip it.

"Are you awake or not really?" I asked my partner.

He rolled himself on one side to face me, the waffled print of the bedspread on his cheek. The pale areas exposed by his fresh haircut made him look boyish, vulnerable, unformed. In Bluff he'd been an ox, a horse, running loaders and graders at the talc mine and coaching boys in grappling, but Terrestria had diminished him somehow.

"That girl with the blue hands around her neck? I think we should go back to her," I said. "I'm worried she was sicker than she looked. Maybe if she completed the Well-being Quiz and she saw it right in front of her, the proof . . ."

My partner thought for a while. He watched TV. From somewhere he mustered the gumption to shut it off but he stuttered the button on the handheld button board and the wide blue eye blinked right back open, showing some kind of government reminder about how fathers who ignore their children hamper the kids' ability to read and write. Or maybe it was a movie; I couldn't tell yet. I'd heard that sometimes they made movies which seemed like news here, and also that the news showed lots of movies. It was one of the reasons the Seeress banned TV, which Swift Aunt Patricia had allowed because she'd enjoyed the humorist Milton Berle, whom she'd sent copies of *Luminaria* to in the hope that he'd discuss them on his show someday, perhaps not in words but allegorically.

Whether he had or hadn't was still debated, and there was no way to settle the debate. A lot of Apostle debates were like that. People took sides depending on their temperaments and because if they didn't take sides they couldn't debate, which passes the time in a town with no TVs.

"I should tell you this now," Elder Stark said. "I get 'prompts.' Faint little nudges. They give me information."

"Hobo nudges?"

"He told me they're not him. My nudge on that girl, from just a minute ago, said, 'Leave her be, Elias, she's contagious.' Her germ doesn't just cause a fever and a cough, it shreds the gall bladder from inside out. She's fighting it off because people here are used to it, and that keeps it weak for some reason, but you and I, if we ever caught it, we'd be crippled. Invalids."

"That's more complicated than a nudge."

"Let's pass her over, just in case."

My partner lay back down and shut his eyes, crossed his hands on his chest, and swallowed loudly. One lamp still burned. The lamp was closer to his bed, making it his duty to switch it off, but I suspected he'd left it on on purpose, spooked about going to sleep in a new place that you couldn't forget was a new place even with your eyes squeezed closed and a pillow bunched around your ears. The odors from potions they'd used to scrub the carpet. That slippery dry fabric on the quilt that felt as shiny as it looked. The shudderiness in the box springs from the trucks that also vibrated the walls, which didn't seem solidly fixed to the whole building, perhaps so they could be moved or taken out to change the shape and dimensions of the room. To me, the most bothersome newness was a thought, though. Who owned the motel, and where were they? They couldn't be here or they'd have sent the clerk back home to bed and told the maintenance people not to suffocate spiders with plastic film. The idea of a place where strangers bathed and slept having no one watching over it or taking an interest in its goings-on as long as the money it earned was counted correctly left me feeling hollow and preyed upon.

Elder Stark kept swallowing and fidgeting until he got frustrated and sat back up and patted around on his bed for the TV device. Once he'd found it, just before he used it, he said, because he knew I wasn't sleeping yet, which friends together in a little room can always sense about each other, "Now I'm thinking she's not contagious after all. I'm thinking that nudge was my greedy inner brain giving me an excuse to laze around and watch more shows and not feel low about it. If you still think she needs us, let's go find her. We'll give her the Quiz. She can tell us how her life's been. Unless she's catnapping, maybe, and needs her rest to shake her little bug. I'm of two minds still. This one's up to you."

He reached out with the device and lit the screen. A trim hairy young doctor with a face mask and splashes of dark blood on his green smock was leaning down to kiss the forehead of a beautiful woman who looked dead lying on a cart or table in nothing but her frail black underthings while a scampering puppy or white rabbit or cat (it finally turned out) was throwing the nurses behind them all into a chasing-and-stumbling mad ruckus that an audience we couldn't see was laughing and hooting about to beat the dickens.

I'd never seen such business and it took ages, close to a whole hour, probably, before my partner and I had learned enough—about the people and the corpse and the reasons the cat, which turned out to be rabid, was loose inside an important

Chicago hospital—to feel satisfied we understood it all (including why it's permissible to laugh at people crashing down and skidding sideways when right in the middle of things is a dead young lady) and could offer our full attention to the next show, which also had a part about a cat.

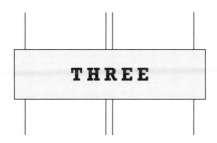

# THREE

**We'd been taught** that to sleep during daylight showed ingratitude, so we woke the next morning at the minute specified in the latitude-adjusted sunrise table printed in our little instruction pamphlet. The air in the room was a fog of nighttime body smells veined with whiffs of undigested chicken. I had crust in the corners of my eyes and mouth and flyaway hair that wouldn't stay put in back until I puddinged it up with Vaseline and mashed it and smoothed it against my lumpy skull.

Elder Stark got down on the carpet, planted his hands, and tortured himself through thirty shallow push-ups, followed by a single sit-up that he quit on partway through. I could tell he was nervous about his weight, but I hadn't looked hard enough at him in Bluff to figure out if he'd added any yet. It would come, though, I knew that much. At four a.m. he'd snuck out of the room and returned with a box of chocolate-covered raisins from the sidewalk candy machine. He ate them while sitting upright with his legs crossed, facing the busy but soundless television. Later on, when I woke again and looked across at him, his right hand was wearing the yellow candy box like a square cardboard mitten and he was snoring hard, with dabs of chocolate all over his big round chin.

Instead of breakfasting on barley cereal as recommended in the booklet we drove into Buffalo to a filthy diner so Elder Stark could get a caramel roll. Along the highway we saw four bill-boards preaching against abortion. They embarrassed me. Women in Bluff kept their pregnancies to themselves until they'd organized their situations. If they felt like they'd better wait to have a child, they were obliged to seek counsel from the Seeress, who had it in her power to dispense certain potent se-cret preparations whose ingredients hadn't touched men's hands.

A state trooper was using the men's room when we walked in. My partner greeted him too heartily, in the manner of people who fear policemen. Whenever we passed a cruiser on the road, he waved and smiled as though trying to look innocent, attract-ing long stern gazes from busy lawmen who might have ignored us if we'd ignored them first.

The trooper, who had no reason to say a word to us before my partner grinned his huge "Hello," asked us where we were headed. My partner said, "South. South, then east. We're zigzagging at first. Later, we'll straighten out, once things get clearer." This seemed to raise doubts in the trooper but not spe-cific ones, so instead of questioning us more he made a hard show of looking us up and down as though he were memorizing our appearances. I knew which features he'd write down in my box, besides my dusty-looking grayish teeth: a slick white scar at the corner of my right eye where my mother removed a mole once with a nail file, and a blackish left thumbtip damaged by a snakebite I'd gotten while haying on the co-op feed farm. Elder Stark's box would include his ears, near to double the size of normal ears and with several extra inner folds that made me wonder how the sound got through and if so, how it changed along the route. This was a serious, real thought of mine, especially a little later on, when it became evident to me from his actions that my partner was taking different meanings from words we'd heard at the same time.

At the counter we sat down next to an old man who was rubbing the edge of a coin across a card and hissing when he kept failing to win a prize. Though it was summer, the man had on a coat that looked like it was pretty expensive once, before the person it fit correctly gave it away to some helping agency or threw it down beside the road. Elder Stark, who knew about prize cards from somewhere, shook his head at the fellow and said to him, "This is my final theory on these things: every single one of them is blank. Nobody wins, not a drop of turtle spit." This seemed to anger the man and he moved down a stool, reaching back to drag his breakfast after him. Later, when we were standing up to pay, the man said to my partner, "This is mine: Christ won't come down until you nuts stop begging him. Damn it, I think he's afraid of all you goons."

"As a matter of fact," Elder Stark said, "we agree there. We don't care if he comes. There's enough down here already. Furthermore, we're not 'down.' From anything. We're 'next to,' we're horizontal. It's all spread out." He set his black briefcase on the counter and sprung the brass latches so they thumped the lid. Inside was a pocket edition of *Discourses* worth, we'd been told, five dollars and fifty cents, but free to anyone whom we deemed promising. We'd given out an average of two a day, with our mobile phone numbers written inside the covers, but we'd yet to receive a call from anyone. If we did get a call, we'd asked each other, how far were we willing to backtrack to meet the caller? Another unsettleable debate. The side I ended up on was: "It depends—but if it's more than fifty miles, let's press them hard to make certain they're sincere and tell them that they have to wait right where they are, no quick errands, no running to the store." My partner's side was: "Any distance necessary." If he hadn't taken his side first—the obvious and noble side—I wouldn't have thought up my picky, petty one. What nicked my hindparts about the whole dispute, though, was that I knew my partner, of the two of us, was the one least likely to go *ten* miles, especially not around a mealtime or if we had a fun station on the radio that might get scratchy or die out.

Elder Stark set the book on the counter like coyote bait, just beyond the old man's reach. The man eyed its cover but made no moves. I couldn't blame him—the cover put people off. Its title was done in a wavy silver script like something from an invitation to a fancy wedding of lady ghosts. The picture was a misty lavender planet with Saturnish rings and a Jupiterish eye— which was so close to a human-being eye that when I was bored in the van one afternoon I drew long lashes on my copy—and then a stretched-out slender tear. Lauer had promised us a new edition with a comet shower, no Cyclops planet, better letters, omegas in the corners, and a white satin placemark ribbon in the spine that the Seeress had rejected as too expensive but Lauer had sneaked around and found the money for (from a rich man who'd liked his stage show, probably). The books were on their way from China by ship, he said, but the ship must have had other stops. That nicked my hindparts, too.

"That's yours to keep," Elder Stark said. "Skim it. Browse it. Discourse Nineteen: The Ten Perennial Follies is where I'd start if I were you. It'll help you stop wasting money on sweepstakes cards. Or close your eyes and flip it open anywhere. That'll be your message. That's what we do. I'll show you. I'll get my message."

"That's pagan," the man said. "That's pagan divination. It's not one bit Christ Jesus. You're a hypocrite."

"I'd have to be Christian to be that. Should we try this?" My partner shut his eyes. He clenched them, really, bearing down for added believability. "The problem for me is I know this book stone-cold, every page, so when I flip it now—that way, don't grasp it, *hit* it—I can't be random. I try to, and I'm sure it looks that way, but once the inner mind has grown familiar—"

"I get it, kid."

"Read it now. Not out loud. Then let me guess it."

"Which part?"

"The message verse is always halfway down, precisely halfway, left page, the inside column. Tap my arm here when you're done."

"I'm done right now. It's short."

My partner pointed to his eyes to show again how terribly shut they were. The man and I stood waiting. The corner of his lip kinked up when he caught me looking at him. It seemed like he couldn't help it, habitual, a snarl from his moon-ruled wild-animal side. That's where his troubles came from, too, I sensed, as well as his sore-looking black-nailed stubbed-off fingertips.

I knew all about the fellow, suddenly. He'd lived with nice things and around nice people, but then—and it wasn't his fault, I had a hunch; it might have just been the food that he was eating—he'd turned into a boar. A sudden big-money prize might snap him back, though. That was exactly his thinking. I knew this man.

"I'm seeing two interesting competing verses. They're both pretty bold against the white. I have to choose, and I'm trying, but boy oh boy . . ."

Elder Stark's hands were on his head by then, up on the crown, the fingers arched and stiff and the two sets of knuckles facing toward each other so the hands looked like crabs about to fight. He relaxed them a bit and began to scratch his scalp, just lightly at first, but then scrubbing, digging in, down to the temples and back up to the crown, a full-strength attack on a deep serious itch—or maybe an attempt to raise an itch and make it worse until he reached his torture point. Everyone has one, and everyone's is different. The people who need to bleed before they reach it, and the people who still can't get there even then were the people I hoped I'd travel any distance for. It was just a hope, though; I hadn't done it yet.

My partner finally quit scratching about the time the waitress, who seemed so intent on proving that customers who'd finished eating and were using her diner as an arena for feats of mentalism didn't bother or distract her because she had so many pressing tasks, started to look bothered.

" 'As to what the crones assure the maidens,' " he said in his airy, swept-high quotation voice, " 'about how beauty fades, and must, and dry old Time unpinks the dewy cheek, the Discourser spoke thusly to Scribe Lucy: This too is a fib of False Esteeming Thought. Beheld all isolate, alone, and free of prejudicial overlay, the fair are fair forever absolute. Upon which the Discourser darkly reinfolded, undimensioned, and withdrew, resuming beetle form upon a petal.' "

"Wrong. So far off, it's ridiculous," the man said. He was a foul old hog on purpose now. He shouldn't have let the verse go on unfurling.

"Just read it out then." My partner seemed sick of the whole enchanted mood he'd tried to sparkle us into. He probably thought we were unappreciative.

" 'The cheerful fall is the highest sort of flight.' " The man closed the book. "So that's my stupid message, huh?"

"No," my partner said. "It's mine."

After we'd paid and gathered our literature and Elder Stark had shut and latched his briefcase, the scratch-card fellow seemed to mellow toward us.

"You're two good-looking boys," he said. "You should be out there chasing foxes."

"We plan on it," my partner said.

"So put on some jeans. Get with it. Buy some crank. The girls in these counties are crankheads. They're little freaks. The trick in Wyoming is show the chicks a party."

My partner laughed politely. I did, too.

"I've got the good stuff, the waxy, chunky stuff. A gram is fifty bucks. One gram's a lot. That is if it's the waxy, chunky good stuff."

"Thank you. No," I said. "But thank you, sir." I looked at my partner for backup but he gave me none. "Let's go. I'm going," I told him. I surveyed the place, table by table, stool by stool. No state trooper anywhere.

"I'll be right behind you," Elder Stark said. He patted his gut through his white shirt. "Those chicken wings. About to fly the coop."

I stood by the door and studied a newspaper through the scratched glass window of a paper box. The government had lowered a certain tax and raised another. I wasn't interested. I read the top half of a second story about a California kidnapping involving a male kindergarten teacher and the daughter of a cinema director. The little girl's picture looked like all the other ones I'd been seeing on posters and signs since leaving Bluff, and it made me want to go home immediately, before I spotted one of the lost children and was drawn into a complicated court case. The longer I spent here, the likelier it was that some act of heroism would be required of me, whose consequences might keep me forever. I'd changed my views about any distance necessary.

Elder Stark emerged from the diner and said, "Don't worry." He could see my concern and I could see his lack of any.

"You better not have."

"It was too much money. I just wanted to hear what the stuff supposedly does. Better energy and spoils your appetite."

"You can get both of those with poplar bark tea."

"For a considerably smaller outlay."

When Elder Stark sat down to drive, a grumble of trapped gas escaped followed by a long thin whistle of after-pressure. For Apostles, such noises weren't comical but ominous. I sympathized with his desire to foil his hunger with any chemical agent that came to hand. I pretended to concentrate on reading the atlas, turned the radio up loud, and allowed him to vent his fumes with dignity, eking out blessed relief in spurts that raised him from his seat an inch or so. We were brothers now, and I felt for him.


Central Wyoming was like hell without the flames, an underworld thrust up onto the surface. Treeless gray gravel-pit mountains, dry silt riverbeds, dump trucks heaped with mine tailings and slag, lethargically pumping gas rigs, crumbling buttes, and expanses of dead, abrasive-looking grass crisscrossed by sagging barbed wire with tufts of hair in it. There was no color anywhere but in the sky, and a lot of the time no color in the sky, just a uniform high layer of linty clouds that bled all the happy light out of the sun. A lot of Montana was plain and arid, too, but Wyoming was punishment for having eyes. Even the roadkill was uglier. In Montana the deer on the shoulders of the roads lay there intact and peaceful, with long curved backs, but here their bodies were blown apart in chunks.

"I'm reading through Lauer's Well-being Quiz again. It's impossible not to fail it," I told my partner.

"I believe that's very much on purpose. Reach behind you, would you? There's a bag. Never mind. I'm reaching it. You want some?"

I soured my face. I'd had my fill of the caterpillar-shaped orange crunchy things. I read out loud to my partner from the Quiz. " 'Are you ever aware of your own heartbeat?' Is that saying people *shouldn't* be aware?"

"I'm not. Not in the busy daytime hours."

"The Quiz says 'Are you *ever*?' Ever includes the night."

"That one would have to go against me then."

" 'In a dining establishment, when informed that only one portion of a certain menu item remains available for consumption, have you ever ordered that scarce item despite your keen prior interest in another item?' "

"I love how Lauer writes things. He lays it out for people, end to end."

"I can check 'No,' but I hardly ate out before. Just twice in Missoula when I needed X-rays and once in Spokane at a hotel."

"The hotel underneath the two raised highways? Right underneath where they crisscross?"

"It could have been. I was only eight," I said. "I went with my father for his police convention."

"It had to be that one. Apostles get a deal there."

My partner's eyes sharpened because a prairie dog that was

still twenty seconds or so ahead of us was up on its back legs and all alert, the way they get when they're about to sprint. They see everything but your gigantic looming car, it seems, and yet, when you really think about it afterward, you realize they must have seen you awfully clearly, because they timed their destruction so precisely. Once you've barreled over enough of them, not only do you not bother to slow down (their hot compact wizardly brains just recalculate, they wait a touch longer, and things come out the same), but you understand in a fresh, convincing way why science—microscope and number science, not AFA Etheric Science—will utterly fail and fail and fail.

My partner said, at the same instant it failed again, "That second question goes against me, too. I did that in Billings the other day. Remember? That chili con carne the place was so damned famous for? I was about to try salmon done in butter."

"Here's one I'm thinking you'll have a better chance with. 'When courting members of—' "

"That's fine. Let's stop. Go on and work out your own score, if you want. I know mine."

"You took the Quiz already?"

"I've *given* the Quiz." He reached out for the dashboard. "I'm dialing a new station. I know this one *sounds* like drumbeat rock and roll, but if you listen, the 'you' in all the songs, the person they love so much and can't stop cooing over? It's not a pretty girl."

I nodded. I'd already noticed and didn't mind. But my partner was more competitive. He minded.

"It's not so bad," he said, "when it's a woman singer, but when it's a man, a full-grown man, some fellow who maybe has a beard himself—"

"So dial a new one."

"This one's crisp and strong; I think I'll suffer. These big clear signals are tough to find out here."

For supper we stopped at a Sweety-Freeze in Casper that Elder Stark claimed to remember from a car trip he'd taken with his father when he was twelve. This journey—to Colorado to see a doctor who'd reopened his father's blocked left kidney—seemed to have been the high point of his youth, its gas stations and lunch spots and roadside lavatories a series of luminous mental monuments. He spoke of the trip so often that I felt bad for him, aware that his father had left his family soon afterward to work on a holiday ship in Florida as a stage magician, a vocation he'd been secretly preparing for in a locked basement room stocked with cups and scarves and playing cards. He'd never returned and he'd fallen out of touch, which was what generally happened when people left Bluff. Terrestria consumed them. They never wrote. We liked to imagine that they were miserable, and sometimes someone would boast of having proof they were, but in most cases there was just no way to tell.

"Try coffee," Elder Stark said when we ordered.

"I hear it makes you jumpy."

"That's overblown."

Apostles frowned on the caffeine alkaloid. We thought it promoted stones, or made stones harder. "How often do you have it?"

"Now and then. Whenever I need a surefire rapid purgative."

We prayed before eating our sundaes, but unobtrusively, still feeling conspicuous in our new outfits. They were based on Mormon missionaries' uniforms, except that we wore khakis instead of dress slacks and ties that weren't solid but had intriguing patterns. Mine was of bluish crescent moons and my partner's was Indian-based—arrowheads and tepees. Lauer had said that patterns put people at ease by giving them clues to your inner personality, even if the clues weren't accurate. The Mormon boys looked like pallbearers, he said. Still, if people confused us with them, fine, he said. They'd built up a lot of goodwill over the years that he felt we might as well take advantage of, which is why our lapel badges didn't name our faith. First get in the door, was Lauer's rule. You can talk about Lom-Bard-Ok-Thon later.

At a tippy aluminum table across the aisle from us four teenage girls in belly-baring T-shirts were picking at an enormous paper-lined basket of fried potato fingers glopped with iridescent-yellow cheese. Their flimsy plastic combination spoon-forks could only stab up a finger at a time. The girl who appeared to be the leader, the tallest and prettiest, with the lightest hair, nodded at Elder Stark's dish of swirled white ice cream.

"You know there's no actual dairy in that," she said. "It's totally animal fat whipped up with air."

"Sweety-Freeze is ice milk," Elder Stark said. He was an expert now—he knew his treats.

"Let it sit for ten minutes if you don't believe me. The stuff doesn't melt. It's lard." The other girls nodded. "Never eat Jell-O, either. It's made from cows' hooves."

"We're vegetarians," said another girl. "What are you two?"

I tried a joke. "We're starving."

I've never been good at jokes. They wilt on me. I feel them wilting even before they start to and it changes my voice a little, which hastens the wilting.

"Jehovah's Witnesses?" the top girl said. "Seventh-Dayers? Seventh-Dayers are *hot*."

"Because they watch their weight," another girl said. "They're way into fitness. They don't snarf lard for lunch."

The tips of Elder Stark's earlobes pulsed bright red as he set down a spoonful of chocolate sauce and pineapple. During our training course I'd heard it said that after his father left he developed a temper and was sent for a summer to El Dorado Farm, the Church's disciplinary youth retreat, where troublesome boys built fences, tore them down, and put them back up in the same place. The boys were allowed no red meat there, just fish and chicken, and supposedly they drank ice water all day to neutralize what Church healers called their "heat points." We all had our heat points, even normal children. Mine, a healer once told me, were in my groin.

"You tell us first. What are *you*?" I asked the girls.

"We're Wiccans. We worship nature," one said.

"How?"

"We run around nude in the woods," the same girl said. "Nude and completely shaved."

Her girlfriends cackled. The top girl looked angry and shushed them by pointing her spoon-fork. At the table behind theirs an old brown woman looked up from the job application she was working on. From the moment I'd noticed what she was doing, and how earnest and strenuous she seemed, I'd been feeling anxious on her behalf.

"Bethany's still a novice," the top girl said. "She hasn't learned respect yet. Excuse her language."

"It's her imagery, not her language," my partner said.

The top girl ate a cheesy finger. She fascinated me. I couldn't stop staring at her lipsticked mouth—at the perfect alignment between its wet red corners and the corners of her pumpkin-seed-shaped eyes, brownly outlined in pencil and bluely shadowed. Apostle girls used makeup, too, but without any flair or conviction, to mask their flaws. This girl, though, was a master of lavish effects beyond those required for basic facial smoothness. She belonged in a tent in a land across the sea, an amusement for warlords gathered around a fire. Looking at her I sensed for the first time that my return to Bluff was not assured, or at least not my happy, safe return.

"And don't try to tell us that Wicca is Satanism," said a girl who hadn't spoken yet. "We get that from our pastor and it's BS. Anything that empowers women, he hates. He knows that the planet's alive and that it's female and he knows that Jehovah is just some masculine fear god the Jews stole from the Persians to keep their wives in line. Read archaeology. Read history."

"We don't have any dispute with that," I told her. In fact, Mother Lucy had made quite similar points back in the early 1880s. The difference was that the Wiccans of the Sweety-Freeze were stern and resentful, while the first female Apostles were glad and buoyant. Could we correct these prickly girls? It felt to me unlikely. They were just children, children who wore paint, spraying big foggy ideas in people's faces to make the people wince and hold their noses. They weren't whatever that thing was they'd just called themselves. They were bouncy, flip-tailed little skunks.

I rose from the table and threw away my sundae cup, aware that my partner intended to stay and scrimmage. I'd tract a few dozen windshields in the parking lot, which also served a drugstore and a supermarket. We'd worked out a system for using our shrinking tract supply to what we hoped was good advantage. This system worked off the appearance of the vehicles. Dented ones and damaged ones, if the damage appeared recent and the car looked costly and new, were the ones we tracted first. Our reasoning was that their owners were shaken people who'd thought that handsome purchases would spare them the reversals and disappointments that people here seemed so paralyzed about. We wanted to hit them while they were still bewildered. Next were very old miniature dusty cars with lots of belongings crammed in their backseats and, ideally, lots of stuck-on decals whose messages and sayings didn't quite harmonize. The best example we'd found so far was a tiny Chevrolet that we knew wasn't manufactured anymore full of pillows and laundry and camping gear whose driver was eager to push the following three sentiments: "A Duck May Be Somebody's Mother," "Back Off, Asshole," and "Ask Me About the LifeZone Path to Health." What made such people so promising, we felt, was that they were so obviously confused yet also, it struck us, striving not to be.

I went at it in the Sweety-Freeze parking lot, spotting two nice but wrecked cars in the first minute. If Elder Stark wasn't finished when I got done, I'd drag him back to the van and turn us east. I'd been thinking the East was a better place for us. My impression from books I'd read was that people there had manners, traditions, guidelines, and good sense. In the West people made their lives up on the spot, with whatever materials were lying nearby and looked the most curious or colorful or easy to pick up. In some ways, that's what the first AFAs had done, and it didn't pain me to admit it, since I didn't feel these inclinations were necessarily harmful or inferior. I approved of them wholly, in fact. They'd made my soul. The problem was selling what these habits had wrought to people who shared them and knew full well what they led to, by and large. Piles of scratched-clean prizeless sweepstakes cards. Homesickness that gets worse when you get home. Endless soaring toy-rocket dreams and schemes that let out a sad, weak "pop" at their high climax point and then flake apart as they tumble toward some thorn patch that's also a hatching ground for baby snakes.

My sense of the more prudent eastern people was that they'd wised up to these perils centuries back and buried them pretty deeply in their cemeteries under big tombstones inscribed with somber wisdom about how not to stumble in the future. My other sense was that over the years the easterners had gotten awfully cocky and shed a lot of their ancestral vigilance. We might just be able to go in there with wheelbarrows and take them out in bales and bushel loads.

I was tracting a wee green Ford of the confused type when my pocket phone started buzzing inside my trousers. The sensation was just a few days old for me and still felt like a blast from the far future that I loved to research in the Bluff library, especially the domed cities beneath the oceans and growing our heads back if they got cut off. According to the more daring authors, in fact, we humans (people were "humans" in those books, which made us sound, to me, after a while, like something sleeker and kinder than we are) might have two other choices for saving our heads, or at least their inner contents. Carefully scoop out the brain and set it floating in a special brain aquarium or drain all the memories and moods into a computer with your old name on it. Both ideas sounded lonely, but maybe not if the tanks and computers were pushed up close together.

The future could take many paths, the books insisted, and might even vanish before it came if we badly imbalanced or despoiled Earth. Earth, the habitat of Humans. The words felt slightly greasy in my ears.

The buzzing stopped when I didn't answer the phone. The sound still jolted my dreamy thought side before it affected my hands and fingers. Lauer knew I had this problem. As quickly as phone electronics would allow, it seemed, the future buzzed again.

Lauer announced himself by saying, "Lauer."

"Greetings, Lauer. Person Two. The Child." This was how Mason Plato LaVerle would sound after he became a Human on Earth.

"Perverse phenomenon, just then. Not what the mind would rationally expect. Even though you were ready for my call then, there was a considerable lag. Was the unit right there in your hand?"

"I'm full of hot fudge and ice lard and I'm sluggish."

"Insulin overload from simple sugars."

Lauer was my model as a Human on Earth.

He asked me for our "location" in Wyoming and then why we hadn't "entered" Colorado yet, where "the population" was "denser and more affluent." I was used to his word ways, but "affluent" still nicked me. In the Church of my childhood, money stayed out of sight behind the things it bought, which weren't much to look at. Most were things to eat, and most things to eat were obtained with Virtue Coupons, which weren't even money, at least to my eye. But when Lauer let rip with his mansion, it cut a string in us. It released some new balloons. Women began to lounge around on sofas that were actually two sofas shoved into an L-shape, or even three sofas joined to form a U, reading catalogs issued by merchants we'd never traded with who dealt in fripperies we'd never needed, such as a wondrous clock one lady fell for that displayed information about the weather—the weather right outside her kitchen window, whose sill was where she'd put the clock! Bluff's men flew off in much puffier balloons. Street by street and block by block, they started building additions out of redwood, that showy lumber unwelcome in our midst since the time of the fire in the 1960s, when a mine foreman used redwood for a deck that obliterated his front yard and swept out to the border of the sidewalk. When the Seeress kicked the monstrous projection during one of her weekly Spirit Strolls, and when a young girl who'd spied the kick (my mother) larked through the co-op singing out the news, the deck reinfolded faster than the Discourser turning into an aphid on a rose, taking a class of lumber with it. Decades passed and everything was fine, but then, thanks to Lauer, our resident Human on Earth, redwood unreinfolded with a vengeance, billowing out in hillside-castle form and then popping up as gazebos and extra bedrooms and backyard sheds for storing an old sofa.

Sometimes I wondered if Lauer had sent me here to give himself a freer hand back there, maybe to erect a tall new guesthouse. I'd been awfully loose and loud around the co-op with my views about his redwood.

I had the phone up flat against my ear as Lauer praised the team of missionaries whose region was the Northwest and California for gaining a meeting with a young executive from an expanding computer firm. After taking the Well-being Quiz, the man had signed up for a twelve-week course of classes, to be conducted through the mail, in Edenic Nutritional Science. The missionaries had hooked him, Lauer said, by postering a natural foods store—a trick that he said we should try. He said that the people who shopped in these establishments were just the type we wanted as AFAs. This put me on edge. I'd thought the people we wanted were the people who wanted us. Or who needed us, but didn't know it yet.

I decided to hold Lauer back by talking more. I felt he'd forgotten the central truth with telephones. They only work in pairs.

"We met some Wiccan youth in a Casper sweetshop. I'm there right now. I'm in the parking lot. I just stuck our prettiest tract, the one on friendship, on the window of a scraped-up Volvo. That's one of the car makes we've been zooming in on." I summarized the system then, playing down the poor cars stuffed with rucksacks whose drivers might be headed for the nuthouse as cars we primarily tracted out of fairness, to balance all the dented Cadillacs. Lauer didn't comment. He didn't peep. I shifted to explaining about Wiccans. I built them up some, maybe quite a bit. My aim was to portray them as worthwhile prospects, good people who'd slipped a little in the sand but could easily be transformed into allies. I hinted that Casper was one of their new footholds, although they'd spread through Colorado, too.

"Give away many copies of *Luminaria*?" It was as if he'd just picked up his phone after letting it cool on a table for a while.

"Not boxes and boxes. A few. A healthy few. In a minute I'll take a copy to the Wiccans."

"Save that. Save that copy," Lauer said. Then he stopped. He didn't pause—he stopped. A pause means the person has something more to say.

"Can I be completely honest with you here?"

In the instant before I asked this question, before my mind sent the order to my lips and while I still had time to say some other thing, my higher mind—my Etheric, floating mind—reasoned out, composed, and signed a pledge never again to ask it in my lifetime, and not to ask it now, if possible. The pledge was swiftly delivered to my lower mind and its logic thoroughly explained (requesting permission from someone to be honest is really a way of accusing the other person of being so demanding or overbearing that you couldn't be honest all along—and eventually it always brings on a fight) and my lower mind agreed to take the pledge as well, and did. Which is the whole mystery. Right there. The reason we had a Seeress. And books. And a town in a place where a town did not belong.

Because I asked the question anyway, after both my minds had promised not to.

"Can I be completely honest with you here?"

My bafflement over violating my pledge brought on more rushes of Etheric Reasoning. There's a rock up ahead; if you don't watch out, you'll trip. The hazard's as clear as day. And then you trip. That's your mystery—but here's your error: glaring at the rock like it's the rock's fault. And here's your next one: kicking at the rock, because now you've decided it's *your* fault that you tripped and that you and your foot deserve a little pain.

Which entitles you to a dish of ice cream afterward, or a platter of fried potatoes glopped with cheese.

Instead you should have looked up at the sky and wondered at the fact that you have a foot.

My partner and the Wiccans needed me. I had their answers for them.

"No," said Lauer. "Let *me* be honest with *you*."

A biting lecture on perseverance ensued, but I didn't listen to most of it. I wanted to ask Lauer about Sarah, whom I'd dreamed had already found another man—a widower in his late thirties named Layman Markey who lived up the street from my parents and kept trim by lifting barbells on his redwood deck. His tiny blond wife had been killed two winters ago when a Highway Department sand truck hit her Plymouth, and Layman was living comfortably off the settlement—one of the only single men in town capable of buying Sarah her Saab. I'd noticed her watching him in the co-op one day as he was scooping bulk dog food into sacks, the muscles in his forearms like wind-carved sandstone.

"If the Church has any financial future at all," Lauer said, "it's as a human growth enabler."

"Elder Stark isn't eating right," I said.

"That's expected. That'll die down. I'd like to talk with him."

"He's with the Wiccans in the Sweety-Freeze, except I don't see them at their tables now. I'm in the parking lot looking at the window."

"Kids have parents. Try to meet their parents. Their parents might be professionals. Find out."

"I get a feeling their parents aren't around much."

There was a surge of static on Lauer's end, suggesting that he wasn't calling from Bluff, where the Church's First Council had forbidden cell phone towers out of a fear that their transmissions warped the ether. He might have been calling me from anywhere: while boarding an airplane, pacing in a hotel room, or waiting in the lobby of a TV station to give another inspirational interview. Five days ago he'd phoned us from a sailboat but hadn't specified which lake or sea. When I'd asked where he was, all he'd said was: "Nine miles out." This made me think it had to be a sea.

The static cleared and I heard him say, ". . . to Jackson. Jackson Hole. I'd rather have you there."

"How far is Jackson from Casper? It's still Wyoming?"

"Or maybe one of the Colorado ski towns. I'll be blunt: you're plowing barren earth. And the women you're meeting aren't of any consequence. Tell me about that aspect. I'd love to hear."

I lifted my downcast eyes from my cheap shoes, whose style, I'd realized the other afternoon, marked me as a young man to be pitied and only approached for favors like driving directions or change for a dollar, not growth enablement. Across the lot Elder Stark and the four girls were standing around an old white Pontiac sports car whose flame-decaled hood was propped up.

My partner leaned over the engine, reached his hands in, and grabbed ahold of something that didn't move but probably was meant to move. The girls seemed glum. They wanted to be somewhere. The top girl sat looking annoyed behind the wheel, a lovely bored sourpuss like on the dating shows.

"Snowshoe Springs, Colorado," Lauer said. "I'm looking at my atlas. It's four hours south. I spoke at a conference there once, at the big golf course. Lots of fine stores and second homes. Gentleman ranchers. Retired medical specialists."

"If that's your preference, sure."

"This system of yours for selecting cars to tract?"

"Yes?" So he'd listened. I warmed toward him a bit.

"This is the social, geographic version. The people who tend to cluster in prime locales, in the towns I've just mentioned, they constitute a network. Open one door, it opens other doors. Many, many doors. Along a hallway. Just move down that hallway and keep on knocking and don't get discouraged if most times no one answers. All you need is a fraction, a percentage. Go to Snowshoe Springs. Get out of Casper. All you need is half of one percent. But not of Casperites. Of Coloradoans."

"Do you ever see Sarah around? My Sarah? Kimmel?"

No answer. He'd covered his subjects. He'd drifted off again.

"I shouldn't call her mine. You're right," I said. I was acting like he was still there to bring him back.

"No," said Lauer. No to what, though?

"I had a nervous dream. She'd met a man."

"Life progresses predictably. I'm sorry."

"Sarah Kimmel's life or general life?"

"It's all one tide," said Lauer. "It's all one flow."

"Layman Markey?"

"Here's some sage advice. You're there, on the road, on your way to Colorado. Bluff is in Montana, far away. Be where you are. Let others be where they are. 'What should be, is.' Remember."

"What should be, is." Our great motto came out like a single word, as always. "So where are you right now?" I asked the Human. Besides on Earth. In a brain aquarium.

"In transit," it responded. "I'm in transit."

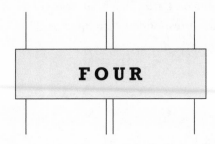

# FOUR

**The top girl did have parents,** as it came out—they just weren't in town that night, she said. They'd driven to Denver with friends to see a concert, of what sort of music the top girl wasn't sure, although I guessed from looking around the home—constructed from two identical chipboard half-homes whose joint was visible in the stucco ceiling as a long yellow splotchy line of water damage—that it wasn't the opera or one of the great choirs. The parents did appreciate their art, though. They'd hung it everywhere, on all their walls: photographically accurate paintings of Indian chiefs, misty sky scenes of migrating white geese, and above the toaster, a barbed-wire Jesus cross with a whittled twig Jesus glued to a barnwood plank. The art collection was reaching, in its way, toward some whispery spacious statement about courage, or maybe grief, or gratitude. Whatever the broad intent, it touched my bosom. Art, art of any kind, shows that folks are trying.

The top girl, named Sherri, and her followers (after some phone calls, the tribe had grown to six) were heating a pan of dark broth that they believed would grant them the power of invisibility, which they'd promised to demonstrate for us if we came home with them. Elder Stark had said "Lead on" for both of us and tried to convince me in the van, as we followed the Pontiac up a cracked state highway marred by swooping, scary-looking skidmarks that might have been the results of vain attempts to spare the lives of death-intent small beasts, that tonight was our chance to begin our mission in earnest.

"We've let ourselves get too inner, too snailed up. The people who cross our trail, it's for a reason."

"You had a 'prompt.' "

"I have them all the time." He rubbed his nose, which was red and drippy suddenly, and cleared his sinuses by loudly snuffling, though Apostles are taught that it's preferable to blow.

"You bought that old gambler's anti-hunger drug."

He didn't deny a single word.

"You eat ice lard for supper and now you're some sad drug crook."

"Illumined All-in-One," my partner said, as if he was setting out to really pray. But that was as far as he took it. Pretty weak.

"How much did you pay?"

"Not half of what it's worth. I feel like my head is finally the right size. I feel like it finally fits around my mind. Does that squeeze ever bother you? That lack of skull space?"

"Does it feel like it's wearing off?"

"I damned well hope not."

The Wiccan girls set out barbecue potato chips and opened a case of room-temperature beer that Elder Stark and I declined in favor of glasses of tap water with lemon slices. My partner did accept a cigarette, though, taking advantage of conflicting teachings on tobacco use, which Little Red Elk permitted for special ceremonies but Mother Lucy had abhorred. He stood in the doorway, exhaling complex blue clouds into the orange radiance of a bug light mounted on a pole beside the steps, and talked fancy doctrine with Sherri's sister, Karly, a thin brunette whose disfiguringly large breasts caused her to keep her arms crossed and hump her back.

"Who's trying this with me? Volunteers?" asked Sherri. She held out the hot pan with padded oven mitts and two of the girls bent over to sniff the broth, which had pine needles floating on top and smelled like drain mold. One girl backed away but another got a coffee cup, dipped it half full, and raised it to her lips. She couldn't quite do it, though. She poured it back.

"Come on, all you chickenshit witches," Sherri said.

"Yucky."

"I tried it last Friday. It's someone else's turn."

"I have to go pick up my stepdad from drunk-driving class."

Everyone but Sherri had some excuse. She, though, partook directly from the pan, tilting it back until nothing was left but grit. Afterward, she joined me on the sofa, where I'd turned on a show about two fashion models who'd been forced to survive in the Arctic for a month eating seal fat and sleeping in army tents. I was glad to have TV again. Its shapes and colors changed faster than those in nature and seemed to reach a deep layer inside my eyes that had gone unused since I was born. I suspected that there were other parts of me, other organs, other faculties, awaiting unreinfolding by Terrestria. I felt curious about what they were but my hope was they'd take turns emerging, not come in gangs.

"It takes a minute, you don't just vanish," said Sherri. "Also the moon might not be right tonight. Ideally, you want it either new or full."

"Your parents aren't Wiccans," I said. "They're Prince of Flocks types." I caught my old habit then. "Christ Jesus folks."

"That cross by the toaster? It was there when we moved in. They're actually nothing. Just fun-and-money people. My dad works on oil rigs, murdering the earth, and Katrina, my stepmom—really, she's just Dad's girlfriend; maybe they're legally married, but I doubt it; she came here one night for a threesome with my real mom but then, when my dad liked her better, my real mom left; we hear she deals Pai Gow poker in Reno now—just sits in the kitchen drinking Cokes all day and blows my dad's paychecks calling psychic hotlines. Like anything's ever going to change for her until she loses thirty pounds. And waxes."

"But you think there's more to life, don't you?"

"I sure wish."

"That wishing part of you?" I said. "Try to keep it a certain size. I'm not saying go get rid of it, just . . . keep it walking. Don't let it gallop and buck and toss you off." I turned on her one of the Person One hypnotic looks that Lauer said were irresistible.

"Was that from that Indonesian man on *Oprah*?"

"A woman named Lucy. Apostles call her Mother. She lived a life of quiet charmed attainment. She mastered the whole Hebrew language in one daydream. She reattached a farmer's pointer finger by holding it against the stump and humming. Mostly she taught the idea of smoother wishing."

"What did she think about the Bible?"

"Which?"

Sherri came to believe I'd told a joke, but it took a minute, and when she laughed it took me a minute to know why she was laughing: because she thought I'd been funny, obviously. The problem was that I couldn't remember how by then, or even precisely what I'd said. I laughed along with her, though, because it's pleasant. Things had grown very pleasant with the two of us, as if we were both Person Ones at the same time—or two Person Twos against everybody else.

"What about sin and redemption and all that?" she said.

"The Serpent? You mean the Serpent?"

"That's where it starts, I guess."

"What does?"

"Evil."

"Why? Which one of the evils? You mean the Follies?"

"Just explain it, okay? Don't make me poke around."

"I didn't mean to do that. I hate that, too. Like when somebody smiles just to make you ask how come? Is that what you think I just did about the Serpent?"

"Fuck the fucking Serpent. Let's just drop it."

"I think I just realized what Bible you meant back there. Here's the tale on that one. They wrote it backward, using opposites. Original sin? It's original redemption. That's the way it used to read, at least, before they had to put it into code. You know why they did that? I'll tell you."

"I believe you."

"You don't want the reason behind it?"

"I don't need one. It's a cool weird idea and it's neat you think it's true."

"Well, good. Okay. Can I tell you something, Sherri?"

"What?" she said.

"That was a pleasant gesture there. I like it when young women just believe me."

We'd drifted in across the sofa by then, drawn toward a mushy low spot in its center where the springs had given out. Not once had she looked away while I was speaking, and by the time I thanked her, our legs were touching, not with pressure but lightly, thoughtlessly, like the legs of two schoolmates sitting on a bench. Having never held someone's attention so thoroughly, nor felt it being offered to me so freely, I wasn't prepared for the tenderness it roused. A mission didn't have to feel like work.

Sherri let go of a question she'd been holding: "If you're saying there's nothing wrong with us . . . ?"

"Uh-huh?"

"Then why does it feel so fucked up?"

"Comparison. I'm this, you're that. I'm tall, that makes you short. It doesn't make you anything at all, though. Unless you have a stake in Fake Esteeming, like maybe you think you're the prettiest in town and think if you're going to stay the prettiest, that's a fair trade for believing that you're short. That's how it operates. It's a marketplace. I'll be the strongest so you can be the smartest and in return I'll also be not rich, because money is not what I care about. It's strength. And on and on and round and round."

Sherri had the Child look in her eyes. Not all the way, but it was creeping in.

"I get it," she said, "and it's cool, but why's it bad? It sounds like it kind of works out for everyone?"

"Not for the ugliest," I said. "It doesn't work out for the girl who's stuck with that one. Or the dirtiest. Or the biggest nincompoop. Or fish mouth and pig butt—"

"I know, it's really sick. Still—and I'm not being mean here, or stuck-up—there aren't a lot of those people. The bottom types. It's horrible, sure, and grotesque and sad and everything, but—"

"It's just the price we have to pay? One or two fish mouths,

[75]

a hundred Cinderellas? I'll be pig butt, you can all be . . . ? I'm out of examples here. You give me one. Something lots of people love to be."

"So did Christ have to die? It sounds like maybe not."

"Why does a Wiccan care? What are you, anyway?"

"I live in Wyoming. A lot of people care here. I have to talk to them every day at school."

"Can I maybe finish up on my thing first? On why it's not just bad because of fish mouth, even though that's really pretty bad?"

"I want you to. Go ahead."

"I'd like some beer now. Apostles drink sometimes. I'm parched. I'm dry."

"Maybe instead of a beer you'd rather kiss me? Get your mouth wet that way?"

"Maybe so."

"So go ahead and try. What's stopping you?"

First, there was the matter of Sherri's youth. Because I'd seen her drive a car, I guessed that she had to be at least sixteen, but age was hard to judge here, and I was antsy. Young women in Bluff could be dated by their hairstyles: bobs and pigtails until they reached eleven, bangs and ponytails until fifteen or so, and then a stretch of growing their hair out long until after the Frolic, when they tied it up, not letting it down again until they married, when they tended to experiment a little before their children came. Here, though, everything was flexible. I'd seen thirty-year-olds who dressed like they were twelve, in cheap plastic sandals and T-shirts much too small for them. I'd also seen twelve-year-olds who wore dark glasses and carried credit cards in leather purses with clasps and hinges that could have been true gold.

Sherri held out one hand and said, "I'm shimmering. That's

how it starts. If you slit your eyes, you'll see it." She rested the hand, palm up, on my left knee, and though its crosshatched lines were indistinct, showing, perhaps, that her life would not be long (the lifelines in my palms were not so promising either), the rest of the hand looked as solid as before.

"Do you have a girlfriend back home?"

"I did. Not now."

"You shouldn't buy shoes made of vinyl."

"I've determined that."

"You're sweet," said Sherri. "I like your thoughts. Your games. That one you tried when we first sat down together? Being short at first, then rising taller?"

This horrified me, if it was true. And it might have been true. I'd proved that earlier, when I'd asked permission to be honest.

I adjusted myself to Sherri's exact same stature, a fussier procedure than it sounds. Also, when she seemed to notice me doing it, she arched away a tad. Measurably so.

I'd meandered into some contest I couldn't win. All Lauer's fault. I despised that man sometimes.

My partner and Karly stepped in from the porch and joined the other girls at the kitchen table, where they were reading one another's tarot cards by the light of a stout red cookie-scented candle left over from some festive day, no doubt. He pulled up a galvanized trash can for a chair and said to the card reader, "Do mine next. I need one." Given who his mother was, he probably already understood his fortune and intended to discredit Wiccan by comparing his mother's predictions with the girl's. Still, I harbored some interest in their findings. My partner's life was so yarned up with mine now that if he was headed for something, so was I.

"Do you still want to kiss me? Remember, I'm a Wiccan."

"You'd be more invisible by now."

"Your call," said Sherri. "Your call, your fall."

Half an hour later, in Sherri's parents' bedroom, where most of the art involved circuses and whales, a powerful light beam washed the windows white. "The neighborhood watch," said Sherri. "Just ignore it." I couldn't ignore it, though. Too near, too bright. I put myself back in my pants, rezipped the fly, and sat up against the pillows in a position that made things look more formal, as though we'd merely reconvened our spirit talk in slightly softer, quieter surroundings. Through the wall I could hear Elder Stark and Sherri's sister discussing Geofibrillation, a theory propounded by Swift Aunt Patricia concerning slight hiccups in the earth's rotation that led to various civil wars and such that she was very concerned with at the time. The topic had first arisen at the tarot session and had absorbed Elder Stark and Karly so fully that the other girls had left the party.

The flashlight beam raked us again, then swung away. I watched its white circle trail across the yard, bringing out the texture of the grass, and then climb the side of a house across the way whose blinds were drawn but whose lights were all flared on.

"He's a registered sex offender," Sherri said. "That's why they bug him. He's cured, though. Got the surgery. All he does is eat pot brownies now and role-play on the Web. His gaming name used to be Grodel, but now it's Frantus. At least it was Frantus last month when I was Zyla and I fucking zworked him in the Zone. I neutralized his last Mixadril. With urine."

This was fierce deep Wicca, beyond far Neptune. This was Andromeda business, and not for me. I wondered what tarot deck these people used. Who were the figures? I knew they weren't the old ones.

Sherri rested a cheek on my bare stomach and gazed up at

me across my chest, whose muscles looked thicker than normal from my angle. I liked the whole picture, everything about it, and I wished that Sherri had shushed before the Mixadril. I petted the side of her head. I pitied her. The outskirts of Casper weren't the place for her, or for anyone, it seemed to me. I decided the neighbor had drawn her into zworking by slumping along the walks here looking hangdog about how lonely and shunned he felt and how he didn't deserve the surgery. (They certainly did have their laws out here, oh boy.)

She must have heard me thinking this. "If I was older, I'd make you take me with you. I hate it here. I hate my shitty friends. I hate doing spells. I hate my dad's fat girlfriend. I wish I was off in college in some nicer state. Where trees have leaves. With squirrels."

"It won't be long," I said.

"To me it feels like forever."

My stomach soured. A plume of acid rose and bit my throat.

"How old are you, Sherri?"

"Fifteen. Fifteen last week."

Sixteen would have been kinder on my gastric pipes. Fifteen burned. Fifteen last week burned holes. Something sizzled inside me—my pancreas, I thought. Sometimes I was able to feel it. My mother taught me.

"You drive a car, though." Wanting any balm.

"That's Mike's, from across the way. Castration man's. I'm his sweetie. He lets me borrow it. I sent away for a pretty great fake license. He says it's not fair that I'm stuck here when my folks split, and plus he has the bracelet until Thanksgiving. He can't really drive until then, unless it's medical. I buy his groceries. I pick up his prescriptions. Sometimes he flips me a monster oxycodone."

I looked down across my muscles at Sherri's face, which had suddenly lost its close-to-grown-up architecture. It was a moon now, full behind thin clouds, and though, like the moon, you could see it as a person, its features formed no fixed pattern in themselves. Whatever young-ladyness I'd seen in her I must have added for my own purposes. Now that mask was misting off. Even her skin, regarded honestly—seen with cold and legal eyes, not lust's whatever-I-need-here eyes—looked wetly plump and nursery fresh. And the harder I stared, the more babyish it got—not only the skin but the entire specimen—until its young freshness flipped over into ancientness and I was alone in a bad Wyoming bedroom with some kind of flippery sunless jelly porpoise that had just finned its way up onto the sand.

"I'm getting away." This was gallant, in such a place.

"Don't. I want you to teach me."

"I'll leave some books."

"I saw you with your phone. It has a number."

"Don't think that way, Sherri."

"So write it on my arm here."

My floating mind, my prompter, saved me then. No books, it commanded. Your number is in those books.

"You can't even fly but you always try," she said.

I interpreted this as grudging odd Wiccan permission to organize for a few seconds before I bolted. As I buttoned my shirt and pocketed my tie, rolling it up beforehand, which was pushing things, Sherri lay on her back in her slivery black crotch strip and sleeveless half T-shirt with the dancing elephant and stretched out her arms so her fingers touched the headboard.

"Look how long I am. I'm a tree," she said. "I'm a thousand feet tall, with roots and limbs and buds. I draw up the waters and bear them to the sky."

I opened the door to the hall and looked around for Karly and my partner. They'd gone off. I heard Wiccan love music playing, low and churning. I turned back to Sherri, who was sitting up now, brushing her hair out with her back to me as though facing a beauty mirror that wasn't there.

"The worst thing is that you upset the woodland balance. The stag hath had its pleasure and its romp, while the doe receiveth naught." She pointed her hairbrush handle at the window. "Look at that," she said. "You seeing that?"

I couldn't because Sherri blocked my view. I hoped her scripture voice had had its say. The notion that I'd romped was overdone. I'd scampered some, but so had she. She'd scampered all over me, in fact.

"The neighborhood watch guy is taking down your license plate. I hope he didn't peek inside my room and see your buddy with my little sister."

The word "little" overburdened my mind. Somehow I managed to fashion a departure by calling forth an immensely peaceful memory of standing in a buffet line at a Church lunch, loading my paper plate with three-bean salad. Everyone was there, my entire town, my family, even the Seeress, propped up in her wheelchair drinking red punch from a yellow paper cup. I was young, maybe ten, and was wearing a clip-on bow tie. My pockets were heavy with interesting rocks I'd found.

I was back in the van when I let the memory pass. My partner was at the wheel. We'd made it out. I seemed to recall him opening his wallet and putting money into Karly's palm as a sort of panicky last courtesy. Or maybe she and Sherri had required it. They'd been Andromeda's children at the end there, nothing Wiccan about them. Elder Stark's stance, after we were free, and set to be free of Wyoming in two hours, was that we should have known they'd change and that in many ways we had known, especially once they'd pursued invisibility. Since I hadn't recovered enough for a debate yet, I let my partner's side be the one and only side, whether it was true or not. I had to admit, though, that if he'd argued a different side, I would have taken it myself.

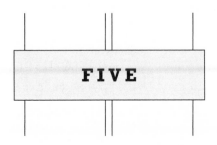

# FIVE

**Elder Stark was describing** the doctrine of Pre-existence, that life-out-of-time when the soul puts on its armors, chooses a body, a family, and a fate, and then plunges mindfirst, like an otter from a ledge, into the cold water of the world. His presentation was lyrical and beyond anything that I ever could have mustered, and he capped it off by miming a great dive, hands pressed together, head bent, toes curled, back arched.

"And so it begins: our swim back to our source," he said. He'd been taking his drug again; he had that fire.

The woman he was addressing was in a state, and we'd come to her house on the edge of Snowshoe Springs to sit with her and see her through the night. Two hours earlier, at dinnertime, Lara Shirer had swallowed thirty allergy capsules, drawn a hot bath, perfumed it with lilac bath salts, and climbed into it with a book, prepared to die. Instead she threw up and decided she wished to live. She dialed a crisis hotline but lost her nerve when an intermittent clicking sound convinced her that the call was being taped. Her second call was to our cell phone, whose number she'd gotten from a tract she'd found on her Audi that morning outside a downtown coffee shop.

"If I've already chosen everything that happens, why can't I see how all this comes out?" said Lara. "Do I try this again tomorrow, but with a gun? Does my mother drive up from Tucson with Dr. Grof and try to commit me to that same place she went where everyone has to hike six miles a day and sing in a big circle and take B vitamins?"

"It isn't like that," my partner said. "The moment a person's born a screen comes down. Absolute amnesia. Total blindness." He looked at me for backup on this point but I was busy with a washcloth, wiping up a splash of foamy vomit stained brilliant blue by the half-digested pills. I set the cloth in the sink, turned on the tap, squirted some liquid soap into my palms, laced my fingers together, rubbed, and rinsed. I dried my hands off on a purple towel and tried to refold it as neatly as I'd found it.

"If you plan your whole life but forget the plan," said Lara, "that's the same as no plan. What's the point?"

Lara didn't look well; she looked crazy. Her knees were tucked up tight against her chest, squashing her breasts out sideways into her armpits, and her head was tipped back against the tub lip, her hair hanging down in a sheet to the wet floor. Her eyes were little tar pits of melted makeup and in one of her nostrils a bubble of bright blood exactly the color of her fingernails inflated and contracted as she breathed. I wished she'd either inhale the bubble completely or let me blot it off with toilet paper, but I doubted she knew it was there.

"We only choose the big things," Elder Stark said. "Our relatives, our place of birth, our body. The smaller decisions are made in earth time. What will I eat tonight? Should I paint my bedroom? There's enough that's ordained to give life structure and enough that's left open to keep it interesting."

Lara's body slid lower into the cooling gray water. I was becoming impatient with my partner, who couldn't seem to see that what she needed was food and dry clothes, not a lecture on theology. Even to me, Preexistence was a muddle, another sign that the Church had spent too long talking only to itself.

"You see it?" my partner said. "You grasp it now?"

"I'd like to."

"That's good. If you'd like to, then you will."

I had to interrupt. "You must be hungry. Can I get you a robe? I think you're chilly, Lara."

"I won an Emmy once." Her words were faint, just trembling webs of phlegm. "That trophy out in the hall you must have seen? On the little mahogany pedestal? My Emmy."

My partner smiled and nodded, clearly ignorant, but I, for some reason, knew what an Emmy was. The seal around Bluff was loose. A lot leaked through. The other morning in the Billings paper I'd read the name Cher and a face had come to mind that I learned, from TV, was Cher's real face. I'd known she was a singer, too, but how? Solving the puzzle took a while. The faraway radio signals that whizzed through Bluff in certain rare weather conditions were a part of it—and a magazine I'd found fluttering by a road once—but the biggest part was a nicely boxed-up card game, Trivial Pursuit, that I'd rummaged from a trash can outside the co-op ten or eleven years ago. The oddity had dropped out of the stars, it seemed. I stashed the game, wrapped in a tarp, out in the woods, and I played it with myself for several months, until an owl that kept roosting and hooting there, directly above the spot in a dead pine, haunted me into burning it one evening. The cards had a coating that resisted flame, though, and many remained readable, just browned. I left them out there to rot and blow away, but I was still coming across them here and there as recently as a year ago. They'd scattered all over, beyond the woods, and I'm sure quite a number wound up in drawers and pockets. Once I spotted one wedged between two boards in the white fence behind Celestial Hall. I was afraid to remove it for some reason but someone else was unafraid. The singed blue card wasn't there a few nights later when I snuck back with a flashlight to check on it.

"You're an actress?" I said.

"I did a network soap. I quit because I got heavy and couldn't lose it, and then I moved here to ski and get my head straight. Then I met a guy. Now I'm suicidal. You're right, I might need a meal. Electrolytes. The last thing I ate was a pita chip with salsa after kickboxing on Tuesday. When was Tuesday?"

"Three days ago," my partner said.

"Then it was Wednesday," Lara said.

She gripped the sides of the tub and tried to rise but didn't get far until her second try. I could see from a pale indentation on one of her fingers that she'd worn a ring once, probably recently. I held out the biggest towel I could find as Elder Stark stood behind her in case she slipped. There wasn't much left of her but joints and knuckles—she'd gnawed herself down to the gristle—but once the towel went on I thought I could estimate where the flesh had been. My reconstruction convinced me she'd been a beauty once and could be beautiful again, perhaps, if everything were restored to the same place. Were such backtrackings possible, though? I had my doubts.

Lara went upstairs to dress while Elder Stark and I waited in her kitchen. We'd ordered a family-size pizza without the cheese because Lara had said she was sensitive to dairy products. To compensate for the loss in richness we asked for extra sausage and extra ham and added a double thing of Pretzel Puffs. We'd tasted pizza before, but only the yeastless, tomatoless variety prepared in accordance with Revealed Nutritional Science. We were disappointed by the prospect of having to eat our first non-Apostle pizza without its traditional main topping.

With nothing to do until the food came, we studied the photos on Lara's refrigerator, moving the magnets around to see the faces. I was right, she'd been very pretty once, with lively features and peppery dark eyes, but with something too condensed about her body. She had all the right parts and all were the right size, but they were positioned slightly too close together, as though she'd fallen from a height and been compacted by the crash.

Seeking a story, we puzzled through the photos—dozens of them that overlapped like shingles. One series seemed to have been taken in California and featured palm trees and houses with red tile roofs. Lara had had a dog then, a German shepherd, with a broad affectionate pink tongue that was always out of its mouth in some capacity, either to lick her hand or happily hang there as the dog stood tight at her side, its ears straight up. There were cars in these pictures, and men and other women, all of them slim and spotless and expensive looking. Every one of the figures, even the machines, glowed all over with promise and ability, and together the photos evoked a world so blessed, so soaked with careless glad good fortune, that I wanted to steal one and keep it as a talisman to ward off heavy moods.

Lara's bad change came in the cluster of pictures that included two people we took to be her parents. The woman we guessed was her mother liked to pose with something in one of her hands: a glass, a tennis racket, a cigarette, a plate of grapes, a cat. The mother's hair was always blond, but never the same blond, and though her skin was tan, it wasn't a healthy tan, won from sun and air, but a beige tone she must have acquired from a beautician, dull and stagnant and uniform. The man we supposed was the father rarely looked at her, though he usually stood dutifully at her arm, and he seemed to be shy about his face, which he kept tilted down or angled or in shadow. Lara seemed tense in the company of these people, her smile like a wire, her hands in fists. Some of the pictures depicted holiday feasts, with roasts and cakes and turkeys in the foreground, and I sensed they'd been taken by remote control, with the help of a timer, rather than by a person. The compositions were off a little bit, like scenes one might see through a hole cut in a wall.

What appeared to be the most recent series of shots was set outdoors, here in Colorado it looked like, and ranged from wintry ski scenes to sunny party scenes, all but a couple of them pairing Lara and a long-faced young man a good six inches taller than her and distinguished by a stunningly wide mouth always stretched in extreme hilarity, with a knock-you-back set of enormous jaunty teeth that maybe weren't quite as white or nicely spaced as he seemed to feel they were. His self-confidence was monstrous and all of his postures were Person One, the Parent. Next to him, Lara looked timid and unsettled, even in her cheerier robust time, before the gray crescents spread beneath her eyes and her breasts pulled apart to show a bony gap.

After learning all we could from the refrigerator, we started opening drawers and cabinets. We discovered that Lara collected salt and pepper shakers shaped like small wild animals—squirrels, primarily—and that she once threw a summertime party that must have drawn fewer guests than she'd anticipated. The shelves held a stockpile of paper plates with stars, firecracker-pattern paper cups, and plastic utensils with old-time bells molded in their handles. The Independence Day. I wasn't ignorant. The bell was the one they'd rung to warn the king to stay back in London with his hounds and jesters and keep his old claws off their daughters and their tea.

Still hunting, we learned that Lara liked to can, but only jams and jellies, no vegetables. The quilted glass jars were labeled "From the kitchen of . . ." and bore their production dates in neat red script. I imagined that they were intended as gifts for friends, but there were so many of them on the shelves—the bulk of them dated last October—that I wondered if Lara had suffered some catastrophe and found herself not widely liked as winter came on.

"Answer that," Elder Stark said when the doorbell chimed. He went on snooping while I paid the delivery boy with the last bill in my wallet that wasn't a one. Our budget was sixty dollars a week per person, but I'd been spending at twice that rate. My partner, I happened to know, was doing worse. When the pizza boy, not a shy one, said, "Hey, my tip," I gave him five quarters and he frowned. Then I dumped all my irksome pennies into his palm and shut the door on him.

Elder Stark was back studying the pictures when I returned. I called upstairs for Lara and opened the box. It hadn't been handled properly; half of the pizza sauce was smeared all over the waxy cardboard lid. I found a knife and scraped it off, spread it back on the crust, then licked the knife blade. A pungent, unfamiliar herb caused my throat to constrict and made my eyes run.

"Don't eat that," I said.

Elder Stark was somewhere else. He touched an index finger to one of the photos, shut his eyes, and turned his head away. "I see it. The whole situation. I see it all."

"There's a spice in it. I had a spasm."

My partner just stood there. With his right hand he touched and rubbed the photo. With his left he fingered the glands under his jaw as though he was checking for an infection. "He's here," he said. "He's with us, in this kitchen."

"We need to make more of an effort nutritionally. I said that before, but I'm going to keep it up."

"This Lara is walking in darkness, he's telling me. This whole town walks in darkness."

"Worse than Casper? How much of that drug do you have left?"

"I'm going upstairs. The woman needs to know. New powers are on the scene. She needs to know."

"To me, after Casper," I said to Elder Stark, "darkness is just a glass of chocolate milk."

He cracked his spine by twisting at the hips and the sound was like popcorn popping under water. He left me standing there with the cheeseless pizza, whose smell alone was choking me by then. I found this reassuring. There were some things out here that my system just wouldn't stand for. Revulsion, watch over Mason. My new prayer.

As I wandered through the house, I paused at the foot of a

staircase with a turn in it and tried to make out at a distance and through closed doors the tone of the conversation in Lara's bedroom. It rose and faded at intervals but always resumed with a new warmth. More doctrinal debates? It sounded too personal. It sounded to me like confession and consolation. Soon the voices began to overlap, but not impatiently, not competitively. "Humans on Earth," Lauer had instructed us, "fundamentally abhor apartness." We tend toward union. And we don't just want each other's company, we want to slide inside each other's muscles, pooling our bloodstreams, aligning our very skeletons. He was on a tear that day.

I went to find the Emmy. I passed a number of rooms that looked unused and seemed to have been furnished by different owners, or by one owner of shifting minds. There was a library with rust-red wallpaper, deep leather armchairs, and glassed-in bookshelves where I could imagine an educated widow lady writing a book about the London kings. The next room was cruder, with waxed plank floors. It held a spindly twin bed, an enameled tin bedpan in a wooden stand, and a church pew that ran the length of one whole wall and had nothing on it but a lone rag doll, its red-haired head collapsed onto its lap. The last room was another bathroom, perfectly clean and empty, no bath mat even, just a spotless stretch of purplish-black tile and a black tub and sink that looked like they belonged in an undersea future brain-experiment laboratory.

And then I saw it, lit by its own ceiling light: a golden angel with conical, pert breasts arching its back and holding aloft a globe. I picked it up. Was it insured? It felt insured. Its heft suggested high-quality materials, yet it still seemed cheap to me; a very elegant horseshoes trophy.

Elder Stark came down the stairs alone, no longer wearing

his hooded Hobo face. His brow was open and hopeful, rinsed of worry. I set the Emmy back on its display stand and wondered if Lara's sorrows, whatever they were, had begun with its acquisition. I felt they had.

"She needs a go-between," my partner said. "She's in love, and she's been mistreated. I can fix it. The man gets back to town a couple of days from now and I'm going to talk to him. By the way, she's baptized. I baptized her."

"Where?" Our baptisms weren't complicated or lengthy but they did require fresh clean air, not cooped-up indoor air.

"Her bathroom up there leads out to a small porch."

Three bathrooms in one house. I didn't approve.

"What color porcelain did she use in that one?"

My partner regarded the Emmy and ignored me. I could see tall ideas standing up behind his eyes. "This fellow of hers is a power. An Effingham. They own a lot of the Arkansas TV and over into Texas and maybe other states. Their ranch south of town has sixteen thousand acres and four hundred buffalo. They're people worth our knowing."

"Lauer is going to perish from a fever."

My partner's grin was so wide that it showed the inside of his throat.

"Lara still hasn't eaten," I reminded him.

"She told me to look in her refrigerator for a canned vanilla health drink. It's everything good in a pizza but in a can, she said. We can try them, too, she said. She bought a whole crate."

"It's like cold vanilla pizza?"

"No, I'm sure it's not, but I don't know. Why can't you just learn to try things for yourself instead of always making me go first and then explain them to you? I'm tired of it."

"That's just the foot we got off on."

"I'd like to switch feet."

"Fine. I'll be the tester. I don't mind. Go get us two cans. I'll describe the taste for you."

But when he came back with the drinks he'd almost finished his. Its sweet creamy whiteness was slicked all over his chin.

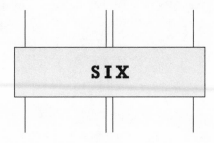

## SIX

**The campground** Lara recommended charged twenty dollars per day to let us park and connect our toilet to its sewer. I suspected the pipes ran directly to the river—all drought-exposed sandbars and shallow weedy sloughs—which was visible out the window above my bunk and gave off a stagnant smell of rotting lawn clippings. The deer that I saw come to drink there seemed stiff and slow, with none of the flickering nervousness of healthy deer, and on the evening of our second day there I asked the attendant if we could take a new spot, away from the water, closer to the hills. I immediately felt better, with clearer sinuses and a sense that my food was on the move again.

While we waited for Lara's boyfriend to return (he was off playing golf, we'd learned, in a Florida tournament hosted by a baseball player whose name I thought I recognized from the card game but found out from Lara wasn't who I thought he was, and was actually much more famous as a kidnapper who'd stayed out of jail through crafty lawyering) we made ourselves fixtures in Snowshoe Springs by renting bicycles from the campground office and riding back and forth along the length of the outlying commercial area and circling the fancy business district, which was mostly made up of art galleries, antique malls, coffee shops, and mountaineering stores where young men our age, who didn't appear to work, could be seen through the windows trying on boots and packs. Elder Stark seemed jealous of these fellows, particularly after he found out from Lara that Errol Effingham, her troublesome beau, climbed peaks in New Zealand when he wasn't golfing.

As we rode through the streets in the morning, we waved at people, especially the younger women, and once in a while one of them smiled back at us. Most of the women struck us as remote, though. Their faces were hard and windburned. They carried water bottles. Their calves showed carpentered edges as they walked and their throat muscles shifted sharply when they spoke, as if separately manufacturing each word. It was hard to imagine them pregnant, though many were. The fetuses rode up high in firm round capsules that gave the impression of being detachable from their mothers' bodies, like the seats that unhooked from the mighty eight-wheeled strollers they stuck the kids into after they were born so that they could be carried into restaurants and stowed beneath the tables.

"If the guy doesn't come back this Friday like she said, I'm ready to head off east," I told my partner as we cruised past the entrance to Snowshoe Alps, the main local ski resort, whose major buildings appeared to have been shipped over from Hansel-and-Gretel land. My frustration with Snowshoe Springs was real—its residents seemed unapproachable, cut off from us by their money and sporting interests—but the statement was also a test of Elder Stark's attachment to Lara, or his hopes for one. His motives in helping her make up with Effingham struck me as muddled and misleadingly declared. Which person he most wished to woo was also obscure.

"He's got an ailing father on the ranch. He'll be back on time. He has to be. The father's the one with the money, the way I hear it, and he's awfully demanding. The son's afraid of him."

"I'm only saying that if he gets held up—"

"What's your hurry?"

I couldn't say, exactly. Spending time in Snowshoe Springs felt to me like staying in a lodging whose rates I knew I couldn't afford. Somewhere a terrible bill was being prepared, and soon we would either have to run and duck it or take unpaid jobs ironing linens in the basement.

We bicycled to our favorite café and sat side by side on a denim-upholstered couch whose spongy, underfilled cushions made me feel trapped and forced me to lean farther forward than felt dignified to reach my breakfast on the small low table. I picked up the crescent-shaped chocolate-covered biscuit that I'd chosen from the bakery case and set it in my peppermint tea to soak. I'd expected the thing to be softer than it was, and the first dry, splintering bite had rattled me. I wished I'd had the money for a muffin stuffed with ham and egg and cheese, but the campground fees had pushed us past our limit on the credit card Lauer had provided. Until he paid it off next month for us, we'd have to live on cash.

"Those guys we saw buying ropes and cleated shoes today? I'd like to learn to do that," Elder Stark said. "Crawl up cliffs."

"We need to be earning. We're going broke," I said.

"Everything's right in place. We're fine," he said. Now that he'd become an open coffee drinker, Elder Stark was euphoric in the mornings. Hard truths about numbers couldn't cool him down. He sizzled until noon.

"My mother called last night," he said. "She gave me my weekly reading while you were sleeping. Sometimes I wonder if she's fooling me. It's always the same: It's cloudy, but it will clear. Trust a stranger. Beware a friend. This time, though, she was specific. She had good news."

I bit into my biscuit, eager to hear it. Pamela Stark was a golden figure in Bluff, known for her clockwork uphill morning strolls, her unmatched raisin buns, and the detailed files she kept on the dreams of leading Apostles, including the ladies of the First Council. She'd performed this role since age nineteen, when she'd correctly interpreted the nightmares of a bed-wetting seven-year-old boy to mean that a long drought was on its way and AFA farmers should rotate out of grains and into a mixture of hardy native grasses.

"She told me we're going to dine with men of fortune and win for the Church the great bounty of influence promised in the Eighty-third Decree. And it's going to be soon," Elder Stark said. "Not long at all."

"Anything about meeting wives?"

"Not this time."

"Your tarot cards in Casper. I never asked you."

"Unreliable," he said. He rose with his coffee cup. He loved free refills.

"Just for fun," I said.

"A sorrowful romance with a fair-haired goddess followed by ages of thoughtful wandering among a race of industrious sad elves. A Wiccan prank, I think."

"They zworked you."

"That man by the counter runs the natural foods store. He might let us post some literature on his board."

Elder Stark crossed the shop and turned the man to face him by touching his elbow, which seemed to startle him. Because of the man's shaved head, his lack of body hair, and his muscle-molding shorts and vest, which were the eye-frying orange of certain traffic signs, it was hard to judge his age. He looked like a being who'd voyaged back through time from a world that had overcome illness, pain, and conflict. As he listened to Elder Stark the only activity was in his eyelids. They'd flutter slightly, as if about to blink, and then retract so completely that his round eyes appeared to lose all depth and warmth. I'd seen quite a few of his type in Snowshoe Springs.

Elder Stark shook the store owner's hand and watched him leave, then went to the counter and topped up his mug by pumping at the lid of a steel thermos. He drank his coffee black, five cups per morning, which I guessed was the reason why he rarely slept these days and didn't appear to miss it or to suffer much. I envied his vigor and half wanted to join him, but it seemed important for one of us to maintain normal contact with the night realm, which *Discourses* taught was the lower mind's repair shop.

My partner sat back down next to me and said, "I think we've found an ally there. I think we've found a nodal leverage point." This was Lauer language. They'd been talking. Often.

"His store runs a popular evening lecture series. I volunteered to talk on Deep Digestion. He didn't say yes yet, but I think he will. He invited us to tonight's lecture for a taste of things."

"You act like we're going to be here permanently. We're supposed to go east. New York City. Washington."

"All the important easterners live here now. This food-store fellow's from Philadelphia. He moved here for the trout fishing, he said. The kid who serves the baked goods, he's from Boston. He's training for the Olympic bobsled team. His father makes all those yellow markers you see, for underlining books and documents."

"All of them?"

"That's what he indicated, at least." My partner gazed into the bottom of his mug. "I'm finally learning to talk to people," he said. "I never knew how shy I was before. The coffee helps, I think. That powder helped, too, but I had to pour it out. It made my scalp prickle."

"I'm proud. I'm glad. The problem is we still need money."

"This Lara has something a lot more valuable. Names and addresses," he said. "You'd be surprised."

"By what?"

"The sort of people that woman knows. There's a congressman in there. A U.S. congressman. He has a little horse farm up the hill here. And this Effingham bunch, they're the center of everything. They throw parties all summer long that people fly in for. The old man's a charmer, even though he's sick. He puts up tents. He hires national acts. That singer Cher you're always mooning on about?"

"I only mentioned her one time."

"She sang at his birthday party last September. I told Lauer and Lauer said, 'Stay put. Don't move. You're right where you need to be.' I'm with him there. A truss in the roof of Celestial Hall collapsed, and then it rained, and now a cave-in's coming. Things are tough. Yet you won't drink a tiny cup of coffee to loosen your tongue and get out there and get cracking."

I considered his words. I pictured the portrait of Swift Aunt Patricia dripping with rain in the lobby of the hall. I even imagined Sarah and her new man, whoever he was (I'd vowed not to inquire; I preferred that my bad dreams be vague), offering their first child for baptism in a temporary metal barn built to replace the grand structure of our childhoods.

"I apologize," Elder Stark said.

"I deserved it."

On our way out I spent almost three dollars on a drink that the counter kid claimed had such a kick that I wouldn't feel drowsy again until next week: a triple Americano. And though it was bitter and as thick as gravy and probably spelled a permanent end to normal, comfortable, wholesome eliminations, I resolved to be strong and to drink one every day.


About an hour before we were due to leave for the lecture at the natural foods store, Elder Stark took a call from Lara in the van. We'd been trying to clean it all afternoon, lying prone in the narrow central aisle flicking wet rags at spiderwebs and dustballs hanging just out of reach in the cracks beneath our bunks; kneeling between the front seats and using toothbrushes to scrub off the spilled chocolate-milk scum in the grooved floor mats; sitting bent over on the lidless toilet in the chimney-width bathroom spritzing 409 onto the urine-splattered and mud-scabbed tiles. We were tired and cranky by the time the phone rang, and the odors that we'd created and released by wetting the van's surfaces with various cleansers were as bothersome as the odors we'd removed.

Elder Stark held the phone to his ear and chewed his lip and did nothing but listen for a while, which led me to fear that a new crisis had erupted. A few minutes later, he broke into a grin, though, and he finished up the call outside, pacing in brisk circles around the campsite and—after putting the phone back in his shirt pocket—picking up a stone and rearing back and throwing it, out of sheer high spirits, it seemed, off toward the river a hundred feet away. He thrust one arm in the air when it splashed down, then turned to face the open sliding door and told me a wonder had occurred.

"I thought we had big trouble when she first called," he said. "She was flat on her sofa drinking wine and crying, talking a lot of gruesome, morbid nonsense about how peaceful it feels, supposedly, when a person dies by drowning, but then—she had a TV set in the room—some old movie came on that she'd played a little role in and she couldn't believe what a fine performance she'd given and how nice her hair looked. It perked her right back up. The next thing I know she's telling me she's hungry and could I quick get some Chinese food and come over there and maybe we'll read some doctrine afterward."

I biked to town alone. Inside the shop I found twenty or thirty people chatting in groups and milling through the aisles while an employee set up folding chairs in front of a wooden lectern with a microphone. The talk that night was on balancing the liver, a leading theme of Edenic Nutritional Science. Before it started, I read the announcements on the bulletin board. About half of them advertised places to get massages and quoted what were, to me, ridiculous rates, especially for a service that should be free. My grandmother had massaged me as a boy, paying special attention to the area where my skull met my neck, which in AFA anatomies was called the Royal Junction and was said to govern the flow of intuition back and forth between the brain and the body. I missed those sweet treatments. I missed the pinpoint grinding of those sharp old knuckles against my knots.

I missed a lot of things, but less often lately, and sometimes I feared that the people behind the memories ceased to exist when I didn't think of them. This nervous suspicion worked on me. To ensure Bluff's survival meant plunging into Terrestria, at least according to Lauer and my partner, but if I plunged in too deeply, home might vanish and I'd be stranded here. I could call my parents, I supposed, but they disliked telephones. A phone tied up your hands so you couldn't do more constructive things.

"I come up from Denver on weekends," a man was saying, apparently to me. I gathered that he'd already introduced himself. "I work in retail quality control. I handle a statewide team of mystery shoppers."

I asked him what those were. They sounded interesting.

"Say my client is Osco Drug. I hire someone who resembles a typical customer and send them undercover into a store with a shopping list. They note their findings. Are the displays attractive, are the floors clean, is there ample product on the shelves, are the employees helpful or are they nasty. I debrief the shopper, write up a report, and send it to Osco's headquarters, which does with it as they please."

I nodded. "Nifty."

"I haven't heard that expression in a while. Where are you from in Montana?"

"Bluff," I said.

"Very rural, I'm guessing. Low median income. Not many foreign luxury cars in town." His tone was one of professional interest now. "Any national chains?"

"Of what?" I said.

"Nearest Home Depot?"

"Missoula."

"Then that's your magnet city."

"We try not to visit it unless we have to."

"Clothing outlets?"

"Just the co-op," I said. "But mostly we only buy fabric."

"Raw fabric. Wow. For sewing, of course. Raw fabric for sewing garments."

"Right," I said, slightly confused. "I missed your name."

"Dale. You're in town on some kind of mission, I take it."

"Yes."

"I admire the daylights out of that. I'm a believer myself, and yes, I tithe—I *try* to tithe; I come up short some months—but you go all out, you sacrifice your *time*."

I told Dale that time was just time, that time was free. He seemed to think I was joking and started to laugh, but he ran short of breath. He closed his eyes and wheezed. The whole time we'd been talking, I'd sensed he might be ill, maybe even seriously ill. His reddish hair didn't match his olive complexion and it fluffed out from under his Colorado Rockies cap with a curious density and luster that made me think the cap and hair were one—a complicated cosmetic headpiece. Also, his hands shook. He kept them on his hips but every once in a while one slipped off and hung in the air for a moment, trembling. To bring the hand back to his hip he had to look at it.

"I think we may have a friend in common," he said. "Lara Shirer. She mentioned she'd been baptized by some young man who'd just showed up in Snowshoe, and by her description of him I'm guessing that's you. I hope for her sake it takes. I truly do. I hope she finds what I found."

"What was that?" I knew now that Lauer had misled us with his talk of the rampant godlessness out here. The problem, if anything, was rampant godliness.

"Two years ago," Dale said, "I contracted hepatitis, probably from sharing dirty needles. I'm only grateful it wasn't something worse. I was a human ruin, a toss-away. But then, on September eighteenth, at ten a.m., I lifted up my frailties before the Throne and was healed in an instant and filled with a new strength." He lifted his right arm and made a muscle that I pretended to be impressed by although I couldn't see it through his shirt.

"Back to Lara," I said.

"She runs with a fast crowd. I don't know how she keeps up."

"She doesn't," I said. "How well do you know her?"

"I know Errol some. I know Errol Sr. better. He got in touch with me about a year ago, after his diagnosis. He'd heard somewhere about my activities with AlpenCross and how it healed my hepatitis. We talked a few times, but he's a wary old snake—he thought we'd take all his money, probably—and nothing much came of it. Party invitations. A chance to hear Cher from ten feet away. Big whoop."

Someone tapped a hard object on the microphone and the people who were still standing moved toward their chairs while the people who already had chairs crossed their arms and settled in for the lecture. Dale shook my hand. His fingers and palm were cold and dry yet slippery, as though coated in the blue chalk that's used on pool sticks. Whomever he'd prayed to back when to save his health hadn't quite delivered, evidently, and I guessed that he knew this but felt the blame was his.

"You might want to try milk thistle tea," I said. "Three or four cups a day. Not hot. Room temperature."

"How long are you going to be in town?"

"Not sure yet."

"We've got a cool group here in Snowshoe that loves the Truth and also loves to get up in the mountains and hike and run around and climb and stuff. A few of us are here tonight, in fact. You're welcome to come hang out. You might enjoy it."

"We'll see," I said. "I had a little question."

"Fire away, man."

"It's Mason."

"Mason. Cool."

"These mystery shoppers. How much do they get paid?"

"For doing practically nothing, way too much. You're looking for part-time work?"

"Everyone please take their seats now," said a voice.

"I'll check my roster once I'm back in Denver. I'll see what I can do for you," said Dale. "If you'd like to, come join us for dinner after this."

The liver lecture, as I'd expected, confirmed my suggestion about thistle tea. I barely listened. I watched the audience, ranking the women according to a system that I'd been working out since age sixteen or so. I noted the looseness or tightness of their hairstyles, which I'd found to be an indicator of a woman's overall disposition. Tight-haired women tended, from what I'd seen, to be more patient, more yielding, and better listeners. They let a man express himself and seemed to gain feelings of security from a firm and confident approach. Loose-haired women, though, shrank away from forcefulness. They came off as warm and spontaneous at first, but in the end they lacked the inner discipline, the stable structures of instinct and belief, that would allow a man to seize and hold them. Sarah had worn her hair loose. I wanted her opposite.

From the tight-haired women in the audience, the users of clips, barrettes, and rubber bands, I picked out two who looked around my age and monitored their behavior during the talk. The taller and darker of the pair dwelt mostly in her spinal column. When the lecturer grew animated or made a stimulating point, she raised her shoulders to separate her vertebrae. When his words were dull, she hunched, bore down, driving her energy toward her pelvic cradle. According to the *Book of Osteograms*, Mother Lucy's posthumously published treatise on the spiritual aspects of physiognomy, this woman was a Verticalist/Expanded and leaned toward stubbornness and practicality.

In romantic terms, she matched best with men of the Radialist/Balanced family, whose well-developed shoulders and stout hips marked them as cheerful, rational, and steadfast.

This meant she wasn't the woman for me. My grandmother, a devoted student of osteograms (they'd helped her pair her daughter with my father) had classified me when I was just an infant as a Localist/Unpatterned, meaning that my Animating Essence roamed around freely through my skeleton and predisposed me to indecision, compassion, dependency, and disorganization. I wasn't told any of this until age twelve, but I sensed it well before then in my parents' insistence on order and routine in my smallest everyday acts, from the way I was directed to lay my head in the very center of my pillow to the way I was taught to drink a glass of water in six equal swallows spaced five seconds apart.

The other girl I was eyeing, petite but womanly, her hair clamped in place by a mousetrap-size black clip studded with rhinestones, was difficult to analyze. She was sitting one row ahead of me, at the end, wearing tall lace-up boots of lightly scuffed brown leather, tight dark blue jeans tucked into the boots, and a fitted tweed jacket with nothing under it but a shiny lace-fringed off-white slip that showed the deep, freckled crevice between her breasts. The small of her back curved so far inward that I wondered if she was doing some sort of exercise, and her legs made up close to two-thirds of her height. Her essence appeared to be centered in her hindparts.

After the talk, she went forward and thanked the speaker, who continued to look at her when she turned away, and then joined a group that included my new friend, Dale. I got his attention by picking up a pamphlet from a table beside the lectern and looking bored and forlorn while I read through it. I hoped he'd wave me over there but instead he came to me.

"Still interested in a little bite?"

I was. The restaurant was several blocks away. I walked my bike a step behind the others: the girl, whose name I hadn't gotten yet—a broad-faced, fortyish woman in black tights that emphasized the bulges in her thick legs—and an older fellow with a gray ponytail that had been brushed and conditioned to a high sheen. He stopped at a bank machine on the way there and collected a formidable stack of twenties that he casually stuffed in his back pocket as though he made such a withdrawal every night. My impression, formed on no clear basis, was that he hadn't earned the money honestly.

Dale said to all of us, "Dinner's on Lance, it looks like. Everybody order the prime rib." Lance shook his head in a humorous disgusted way and cracked, "It's expensive hanging out with slackers." He winked at me, trying to put me at ease, it seemed, and then turned and inserted himself between the females, throwing his ropy brown arms around their shoulders and tangling his fingers in their hair. The older woman leaned into the hug, but the girl broke away from him and walked on ahead. "I guess Pretty Betsy's on the rag," Lance said. Dale disappointed me by laughing with him.

We came to an intersection with traffic. Betsy hurried across it against the light, while the rest of us waited, bunched up on the curb. Dale said, "Lance was our AlpenCross team leader. He taught us to scale sheer cliffs with our bare hands." He made rigid claws of his fingers and scratched the air. "He said it would build our self-esteem—the liar. We love him anyway. He kicked our butts."

"The Father kicked their butts," Lance said. "Not me. The Father kicks our butts because he loves us. He wants us to grow, to test ourselves. And you are?"

"Mason LaVerle."

"That's a funky old-fashioned name. And you look like a funky old-fashioned guy. You're an old friend of Dale's?"

"We just met tonight," Dale said. "He's down here from Montana."

"Which part?" Lance asked.

"The part of Montana that time forgot," Dale said. "The part where they make their own shirts with needles and thread. I don't think he's ever even drunk a Coke. I'm thinking he might make an interesting mystery shopper."

Lance looked me over, my slacks, my awful shoes. I'd left my tie and my name badge in the van.

"At least not a *Diet Cherry* Coke," Dale said.

He had this wrong, but correcting him felt pointless. He'd settled on an identity for me that I'd only have to live with for an hour or two and which would probably earn me a free meal. I hadn't eaten since the coffee shop that morning and was starting to feel light-headed and adrift. I could reclaim my pride after the meal, but for now it seemed easier to go along with people. Plus, I might want that job with Dale. I'd never heard of work so easy.

Betsy was sitting in the middle segment of a leather-upholstered C-shaped booth. She was reading a one-page laminated menu whose back reflected a candle flame coming from a reddish glass globe. Lance and the woman, whose name I'd learned was Tania, took up positions on either side of her, leaving Dale and me perched out on the ends. A waitress set down a napkin-lined basket of dinner rolls, but no one took one. I waited and waited. The rolls smelled more homemade than real homemade rolls and soaked the insides of my cheeks with warm saliva.

"What are people's feelings about wine?" Lance asked.

The discussion went on forever. Real conflicts arose. Tania and Lance started out on opposite sides (red versus white) but managed, by stages, to reach a compromise that they then presented to Dale and Betsy, who couldn't agree on whether to accept it and ended up offering separate counterproposals (different versions of a certain type of red) that complicated the issue more than ever. Our waitress walked up in the middle of the discussion but stepped away when she saw how strained it was. I could tell she despised us, not as individuals but as a category. I wished I could tell her that I didn't belong to it.

A wine choice was made that left everyone looking grumpy. I decided that Lance and Tania were a couple—or perhaps that they recently had been, or were trying to be—but that they were also both more interested in Betsy than in each other. For some reason, her attention was the prize, and though they spoke across her, to each other, debating various appetizer ideas, their eyes kept returning to her pretty profile, whose only flaw was a slightly foreshortened nose with a small tab of scar tissue beside one nostril. She said nothing to either of them, just read her menu, running an index finger across the items while looking, to me, a bit bored by her own power. She hadn't asked me what my name was yet, or even given me a visible glance, but I wasn't sure it was a slight. I was the only mystery at the table, the only person she hadn't yet charmed and mastered, and maybe she was saving me for later. That, or she was just tired of being adored.

I tested my theory by ignoring her and questioning Dale about his faith. The more he explained it, the less sense it made. He believed in the Bible but only in the one Bible, as though God had retired a couple of thousand years ago having said everything he wished to say. He believed that the murder of the Prince of Flocks won the world forgiveness but that people still had to ask for it as well—they still had to speak the magic words, like children. He believed that we went to heaven but came from nowhere and that our physical bodies were glorious but also needed to be overcome, preferably by exhausting them in the mountains.

"And all of this inspires you?" I said.

"Deeply."

"You left out the spirits all around us. You left out animals, old folks, little kids."

"Except for the spirits, those things all have a place, I guess."

"And you think of yourself as a sinner first and last?"

"A sinner whose cries for help have gained him mercy."

"What if I told you that you can save your breath?"

I was arguing with half my brain; the other half was tracking Betsy, whose thought rays I could feel angling my way even though Lance and Tania had pinned her down with what sounded like an aggressive invitation to attend a new round of AlpenCross events, which I got the feeling people had to pay for. I heard Lance use the word "accreditation" and mention something called "level four self-mentoring," then talk about certain "surreal glacial cirques" with "natural prayer sites that will knock your panties off." This last expression cemented my view of him as a nasty specimen covered in a tarry spirit-essence similar to what grasshoppers excrete. My partner, in his discerning Hobo mode, would have spotted this substance the moment he first met Lance.

My show of indifference to Betsy was reaching its limits. It annoyed me that she'd let Lance slide in so close to her and speak to her so exclusively. I was about to excuse myself and leave when she set down her wineglass, abruptly cut Lance short, and launched, without any preface, into a story about being harassed that morning by a crew of menacing highway flagmen east of town. She'd found herself in a string of cars, she said, that had been waiting for ages to follow a pilot car over a pass with just one open lane. The flagmen waved the cars ahead, but just as she was passing them a shirtless young hard hat stepped out and slapped her hood, then stepped around to her window once she'd stopped and said into his radio, "Got her, boss. You're right, she's even cuter closer up."

This story, at first addressed to Lance and Tania, was opened to the whole table as Betsy went on, as though in response to some invitation from Dale and me, who were, in fact, still talking theology. I indulged this masked play for attention only briefly, so Betsy would notice when I resumed ignoring her. Then I started cutting up my steak. I dipped the rare chunks in the blood pooled on my plate, trying to look like a rugged character. Betsy's description of the randy flagmen—some of whom, or so she claimed, had trained binoculars on her from down the highway and, when they saw her spot them, had pounded their chests—convinced me that she had a weakness for beastliness, even though she pretended it repulsed her.

Still acting for her benefit, I tossed back the wine that I'd so far barely sipped at, then attacked the taboo rolls, tearing open their steaming yeasty hearts and wiping up more of the steak blood with the pieces. I swiped my chin dry with my linen napkin, then crushed it up and dropped it onto my plate instead of into my lap. Then, for the first time that night, I looked at Betsy.

"Good story. Excuse me." My voice was hard and rude.

"You're leaving? Just like that? No name?" she said. It seemed I'd done well.

"Don't worry. I'm coming back."

In the men's room, trying to wash my hands under a motion-activated faucet that only gave water in skimpy three-second bursts, I permitted myself a memory of home—a good one, the very best of all, of Sarah and me reclining in the dark hayfield, the chaperones off chatting at the picnic tables, the other young voices sifting through the grass, and stretched above it all our peculiar heaven, swarming with secret benevolent entities—and I told myself that for other, future Apostles to ever have a chance at such experiences I had to push ahead with what I'd started tonight. Even if Betsy was just the first of many and not the eventual mother of new Apostles whose blood would sustain us for generations afterward, she represented a start in the great search.

She'd ordered dessert, a slice of layered ice-cream cake, and was splitting it three ways with Lance and Tania when I sat back down in the booth and squared my shoulders. I watched their three forks cross, vying for the gooey parts. She was acting as if she'd forgotten all about me, as if sugar and chocolate were all she needed now.

"You're the three little pigs," I said. Not nice, but true.

The women stopped eating but Lance cut a new forkful, gobbled it up, and then sucked the dripping tines. Tania patted her stomach and said, "I need to watch it," while Betsy just glared at me, her plucked eyebrows arched, her nostrils flared, her tiny scar stretched taut. The most beautiful faces have some ugly in them.

"I've been meaning to ask you something all night," she said. "Why the Iowa sofa-salesman outfit?"

"My great-grandfather was an Iowan. Good guess."

"But was he in the sofa trade?" she said.

"You mean my shoes. No one likes them. And I don't care."

"Actually, I mean the whole ensemble. Mostly the short-sleeved dress shirt. My uncle wore those."

"Because he sold sofas in Iowa?"

"In fact, he sold mattresses in Massachusetts."

"That job has a ring to it."

"What's *your* job, anyway?"

The banter had come automatically so far, from a part of myself that I hadn't known was there and that life in Bluff had never made me use, but now nothing came. Nothing clever. I'd run dry. Elder Stark and I needed to start seeing some movies.

"I believe that the main job of people like Mason," said Lance, a pellet of ice-cream cake clinging to his chin, "is walking the streets spreading Pagan heresies and cadging free meals from vital young Christians like us."

Dale, Lance's craven disciple, softly chuckled.

My anger at them revived my snap. "Men who turn their faith into a business owe all of us a steak dinner now and then."

A fat grin from Tania, a choked-back snort from Dale, and from Betsy a slanted, cool, appraising look that I met with a calm, unapologetic stare. The candle flame between us seemed to dim as the energies behind our faces maneuvered on another plane. The Seeress, in a tape-recorded talk entitled "Love Me or Love Me Not" that my mother liked to listen to whenever she was fighting with my father, taught that relations between men and women unfold on two levels, the Thonic and the Matic. For Betsy and me that unfolding had begun. On the higher, accelerated Thonic level, our souls were rehearsing a roster of possible outcomes—a casual friendship, a troubled but passionate marriage, a happy marriage, a cordial but final goodbye—while down on the lower, trailing Matic level our nerves were responding to the flow of dramas with twinges and twitches of sadness, hope, apprehension, pleasure, and the like. Whatever was going to happen to the two of us was happening already, experimentally, but so were all the things that wouldn't happen, and the trick was to feel each one as it swept by and not to fight the feelings or try to hold them. We had no influence. Fate deals only with fate. But because we'd already lived through what would come for us, if only obscurely, we'd accept it when it did.

The waitress broke the moment by bringing the check. She set it by the candle, in a neutral spot. As had happened with the dinner rolls, no one but me seemed affected by its presence. Lance redirected his AlpenCross pitch at Dale, while Tania waylaid Betsy with a question about a new hairstyle she was thinking of trying. As the minutes went by the slip of lined green paper seemed to float up off the table and deepen in color. In my pocket were fourteen dollars in fives and ones and a hard lump of change that I feared was mostly pennies.

The waitress stopped back and informed us that her shift was over in exactly five minutes, then left again. Somebody had to act.

"Fine, then," said Betsy. "Let's make it my turn." She flopped her quilted cloth bag on top of the table and unbuttoned the strap that kept it closed. Out came a pen, a lipstick, another lipstick, a black plastic compact, a notebook, a packet of tissues. She was still digging through the stuff when Lance said, "Stop it. Don't be ridiculous, honey. Let Big Daddy. I was just trying to create suspense."

Before he could reach for the cash wad in his pocket, I covered the check with one hand and dragged it back to me, then turned it over, faceup, in my palm. I tried not to let my expression reflect the total. I doubted it did, since the number was so large—just shy of two hundred dollars—that I found it incomprehensible. I fished in my slacks for the emergency credit card, then twisted around in my seat to hail the waitress. Dale and Lance slid out and left without a word, followed by Tania, who patted my shoulder. Only Betsy and I remained. I held up the bill and fluttered it.

"Leave me your number," said Betsy. "I have a car. I'm working a lot now, but I'll be freer next week. You can't afford that check, can you? That's okay. You're proud, that's what counts. I like proud, foolish men."

Whatever had already happened was beginning.

# SEVEN

**The next day** at lunchtime we biked back to the coffee shop, having already been there at eight that morning so I could drink my triple Americano, and sat around waiting for Lara to pick us up and drive us to the Effingham ranch. At her house the night before, while eating Chinese food with my partner and watching the movie she felt she'd looked so lovely in, she'd summoned the courage to telephone Errol, who, it turned out, had flown home early without informing her. There were tears, Elder Stark said, and Lara hung up on him, but later, as they viewed the movie again, which Lara had recorded on a disc to serve as a handy emotional pick-me-up, Errol called back and they spoke for almost an hour, Lara telling him about her baptism and how she forgave him for various offenses, and Errol, as Lara reported it to my partner, confiding in her about his pain over his father's deteriorating health. Their talk concluded with

Errol inviting Lara and anybody she wished to bring along to a small afternoon party at the ranch thrown to celebrate Errol Sr.'s purchase of his five hundredth buffalo.

Still waiting for Lara, and drinking another black triple Americano while Elder Stark read a story in the paper about a bomb threat to the Grand Coulee Dam, I took a call from Dale, who said he'd gotten my phone number from Betsy, who had yet to contact me herself. Dale gave his location as "ten thousand feet" and told me that he could speak for just a minute or two because he was using Lance's satellite phone. Together with nine other AlpenCrossers, he said, they were about to walk down into an ice cave where the group liked to gather once a year to sit in the dark and fast and pray and sing.

"I was thinking about your employment needs," Dale said. "I have a slot next week in Boulder for someone to mystery shop a jewelry store and a mondo-giganto home improvement center. The normal rate's two hundred dollars plus gas and lunch, but the best I can give you is one-fifty, considering."

"Considering it's only my first time?"

"That," Dale said, "and the danger you just won't get it. You're not really very retail savvy, I have a feeling, and you certainly aren't anyone's target market. Though maybe that will turn out to be a plus. You haven't been desensitized. You'll notice things."

"I'll do it. I need the money."

"Bueno."

"Can I ask you a few questions?"

"No," Dale said. "This call has cost twelve bucks already."

Elder Stark looked up from his paper when I was finished. He'd lunched on a caramel roll and a coffee milk shake and, as had started to happen every time he whacked his glandular balance with too much sugar, his throat was as red as a cardinal's and his eyes seemed streaky and glazed, like a glass washed in hard water.

"I found a quick way to earn," I said.

"That's helpful. Unless it cuts into your duties. You'll tell Lauer?"

"You've been talking to him too much. He stirs you up. He doesn't understand our situation here. How expensive it gets, how busy people are, how dumb the Well-being Quiz is. He's on some cloud. He thinks we can stand in a supermarket parking lot and line up fifteen conversions by noon, bring in twenty subscriptions to *Luminaria*, and win the hearts of two darling banker's daughters who can't wait to move to Montana, drive junky cars, pray in a building with a caved-in roof, have three kids apiece, and eat trout six times a week. He's dreaming."

"Disaster. Defeat. Collapse. Paralysis. I want you to listen to yourself."

"I shouldn't drink two of these. One's enough," I said. "What's sad is I can't even go until I've had it."

My partner folded back his newspaper to show me a picture of the president, whom I could now recognize from any angle even though three weeks ago I wasn't sure I knew his face, saluting a long line of soldiers in desert camouflage. Behind them a helicopter with similar coloring hung, massive and still, a few yards above the earth. The sky above was Xed with jet trails, some of them sharp and fresh, some old and puffy. The soldier in the middle of the line was a tall handsome Negro and the one at his left shoulder was a young lady.

"This picture is why Lauer's not dreaming," Elder Stark said. "This is why they'll flock to us someday."

There was something in his presentation that I couldn't argue with.

"This Effingham helped get that man elected. Lara told me.

The father taught him to scuba dive. They own a company that built a tunnel forty miles long through a mountain in Armenia and they also own a plant in Thailand that makes half the fire extinguishers in Asia. That TV channel that shows restaurants and hotels all day, and that other one that shows car races? They're theirs. Now to me, to *my* mind, *that's* a dream."

I had to concede this point as well. I sighed and turned my hands up. Short, shallow lifelines.

"And yet we're going to meet these people later today," my partner said. "We're going to drink punch with them from the same bowl. I'm going for a refill. One for you?"

I shook my head. "I'll never get my teeth white."

"Give that up," my partner said. "The Hobo told me your teeth will never change."

Lara showed up at the shop an hour late in flowery cowboy boots with silver toe caps and a short western dress embroidered with striking scorpions. One good Chinese meal had softened her face. She'd also done something appealing to her skin: she'd turned it all brown since I'd seen her, wheat-toast brown, except for a spot in the hollow of her throat. I didn't mention it to her. There are parts of myself I can't see in mirrors, either, especially on the right side of my face between my earlobe and my jaw, where my partner would often tell me I had to shave again. We think we know what we look like, but we don't. Only the All-in-One knows. It may not matter, though.

I stood to let Lara have my leather armchair but she was too antsy to sit down. She opened her purse, made of lizard skin like her boots and inlaid with wrinkled lumps of turquoise that looked to me like pieces of chewed blue gum. She gave me five dollars and asked for a green tea and a packet of sugar substitute, the yellow kind, because the other two kinds, the pink and the blue, she said, were known to build up in women's reproductive organs and pass through to the brain stems of their unborn children. That she cared about such a risk encouraged me. I put her age at thirty, give or take a year, and it was high time that she stopped concentrating on how she looked in a swimsuit or in her underwear and turned her focus inward, to her womb.

We stopped at an automated security gate that Lara said she knew the code for, but when she lowered the window of her Jeep and punched in the numbers on the little pad, the gate stayed put. She tried it three more times and I could feel her mood sink with each failure. "They changed it on me," she said. She sounded devastated. She chewed off and spat out the window a bit of fingernail that looked like she'd taken great pains to grow and manicure.

"It might not be aimed at you," my partner said. "People think everything's aimed at them. It's not."

"You sound like a therapist. They changed it on me. I guess they expect me to talk into the thing there and state my name and the purpose of my visit and all that shit that their *yardmen* have to do."

We sat there in the idling Jeep. I worried that Lara was considering ramming the gate, which hardly looked sturdy enough to protect a family of such prominence or the possessions they'd probably accumulated. Its purpose was probably just as she suspected: to flatter a privileged group of code-holders and to humiliate everybody else.

At last Lara relented. "Ricardo?" she said, facing the box-shaped steel microphone. "It's Lara."

"Full name, please," the device said.

"Is that Ricardo?"

"No," the box said.

Lara looked at Elder Stark. "Not Ricardo. They must have let him go. He's been with them for twenty years. I'm disappointed. These aren't the same Effinghams I fell in love with. There's a major decline going on. I'm sorry, Elders."

The road to the house, once we finally reached it, was paved in sparkling, mica-flecked dark gravel that appeared to have been mechanically raked and smoothed. We drove through a curving uphill corridor of full-grown aspens, a number of them marked with fluorescent-pink ribbons tied around their trunks. Maybe the aspen doctor was on his way. I looked through my back window at sloping wide pastures that ought to have been full of children flying kites, but the fields were pristinely empty, no horses, no cattle. I asked Lara where the buffalo herd grazed and she waved toward a mountain with scooped-out rocky flanks that must have been three miles away from us.

"Off near the eastern base of Candace there. That's where they had them last. They're always moving them. Soil conservation reasons. They tramp the dirt down. They pulverize the stream banks. Plus, their meat's tough. It's a show herd. A trophy. Take that, Ted Turner! He started this bison fad."

"A neighbor?" I said.

"Ted Turner. If you don't know, I'm not explaining. I envy people who don't know all that junk."

"That mountain there is named Candace?" Elder Stark said.

"Eff Sr.'s first wife. The one he actually loved."

"So it's really only a pet name. It's not official. It has another name."

"I guess it must. Not that anyone remembers it."

About every quarter mile along the road there were signs reminding visitors not to drive faster than twenty-five and to watch out for deer or tractors or livestock. I didn't know how much money these people had, and I wasn't certain I'd understand the figure if it were quoted to my face, but their power to set their own speed limits impressed me. Judging by how many signs they'd strewn around, it impressed them, too.

Up, up, up, and still no house, no buildings. We passed a side road with a cable across it that Lara said led to a private landing strip capable of handling Gulfstream jets, a name that meant nothing concrete to me but whose sound conjured lovely, thrilling, far-fetched images that would reemerge in my dreams for weeks to come. I suspected my partner was in a similar state as we drove along listening to Lara explain the Effinghams' sprawling, private fairyland: so dazed by wonders, improbabilities, oddities, prodigies, and mythic inklings that it felt like his very brain was being remade. At one point, as we were crossing a wooden bridge spanning an acres-long chain of man-made trout ponds featuring almost identical grassy islands, I noticed a serpentine rivulet of sweat running down his left temple to his cheek. It was a struggle, taking all this in.

"The rules," Lara announced. We'd sighted the house by then, large, but as not large as I'd anticipated, set off against a pine-blanketed hillside which had been cleared in one spot for a steel tower supporting several satellite dishes facing in different directions at different pitches.

"Number one, don't drink too much. I don't even know if you do drink, but if you do just realize they'll push it on you all day long as though you'll wound them if you refuse, but in actual fact they find drunkenness repulsive and after you leave they'll stand around the game room repeating all the dumb-ass things you said and imitating your walk, your gestures, everything. That's their great secret pastime: caricature. Eff Sr.'s worse than Little Eff, but the daughter and her weird husband are worst of all. I've seen them eviscerate various Kennedys, Bob Redford. It's vicious, juvenile, ugly stuff."

My partner thanked Lara for the advice, then pointed, evidently for my benefit, at four enormous wire pens standing on a pair of unhooked semitrailers. "Guess," he said. "You'll never guess. Lara told me about them last night. They're for an animal."

"Leopards?"

"Be serious."

I had been. Leopards seemed possible here.

"For wolves," said Lara. "They reintroduced twelve of them last spring, the only pack in the entire lower Rockies. And they did it against federal law, with no review, no oversight, no hearings—just up and did it. It'll change the whole ecosystem in a year or two."

"But wolves eat buffalo calves," I said.

I knew wolves. Montana had wolves—in the country near Bluff, in fact. One night behind my house after a rain I was shining a flashlight in the grass, looking for fishing worms, when I heard a rustling noise followed by an unnerving raspy yip-yap. I swung my light at it. Two new silver coins, big fifty-cent pieces, not little dimes, hung in the darkness just beyond our garden. I exaggerated the next day and said I'd seen the wolf, not merely glimpsed what might have been its eyes, and my father recruited three friends to help him track it while all over town worried mothers hugged their toddlers. I awaited my punishment, just like in the fable, but that evening the hunters found an intact footprint in a stream bank near the girls' school. My lies were wiped away, and I credited the All-in-One. Now, thinking back on the incident, it struck me that it probably formed the whole basis of my faith. Sermons bored me. Scriptures baffled me. When the schoolgirls presented me with a thank-you card depicting me with a shield and angel's wings, protecting them from a bristling black beast, I felt I'd incurred a permanent solemn debt.

And here I was in Terrestria, still trying to pay it.

"They wanted wolves because wolves are rare," said Lara. I'd been thinking, she'd been talking. "And if one trophy eats another trophy, fabulous. It's life's tragic circle, and all on their own property. That's a trophy in itself."

Lara parked in a roped-off square of meadow at the end of a row of other cars and trucks, most of them newer and nicer than her Jeep and quite a few of them bearing those license plates that spell out words and phrases with letters and numbers. RU SXY. IH8 2 W8. I'd never seen one of these until two weeks ago, and it had taken Elder Stark and me a whole afternoon to master their code. They provided much amusement at first, but it only lasted a couple of days, and then it dropped off to nothing. Now they bothered me. Their jokes just weren't clever, surprising, or funny enough to be worthy of permanent display.

The house was still a good quarter mile off. To visit the Effinghams at home, a person really had to want to, and after hearing Lara's description of them, I wasn't sure that I did. I was doing it for my partner. He walked in front of us up the cobblestoned path, which climbed, by means of several sets of steps, a succession of terraces planted with native wildflowers whose names were given on wooden plaques mounted on metal rods beside the walkway. My partner paused to read every one of them, no doubt because he felt he was expected to. "Indian paintbrush," he said enthusiastically. The stuff was common, we'd seen it all our lives, and his show of excitement over it embarrassed me. I'd never seen him act this way before, so desperate to accept and be accepted. Normally he just stormed along, completely himself.

"Rule number two," Lara said in a half whisper, because we'd almost reached the pink-striped party tent. "No gawking, no staring. I don't care who it is. Bill Gates, Mick Jagger, I don't care."

"We won't know anyway," I said. "Don't worry."

My partner's face soured when he heard this. He gave me a look.

"Though we might," I added. "You're right. No one likes being stared at."

"That's not it. *They* could care less. They're used to it," said Lara. "It's how it makes *you* come off. Some starstruck nobody."

"All are equal in the All-in-One. That's how we Apostles are raised," my partner said. I knew by his voice he was going to overplay this. "The queen of Spain, the first man on the moon, the jack of diamonds, it's the same to us. We don't look up at people, we don't look down."

"Healthy," said Lara. She didn't believe him either.

Because it wasn't raining or all that hot, the party tent served no particular purpose other than marking the location of the food and drinks. Of the forty or fifty guests who'd come before us, most were standing in the open air, perhaps to avoid the smoke and fumes from a stupendous iron barbecue pit whose dual rotisseries turned boulders of flesh too large to have been obtained from regular cattle. I noticed a lot of cowboy hats, but only two men who actually looked like cowboys. Both had the outlines of snuff cans on their back pockets and both were talking to pairs of older women. The men's faces looked tired, and I assumed they worked here. None of the other faces looked even slightly tired. Not even in Bluff, at the Service of New Spring Morn, had I ever seen such a brisk-eyed, wakeful crowd.

Lara led us under the tent and dug up two freezing bottles of orange pop from a cooler packed with snowy shaved ice. For herself, she ordered something from the bar, violating her own rule. The bartender was a kid of maybe twenty in a starched white shirt, an agate bolo tie, and a black leather vest too short for his long torso. All the helpers that day were dressed like him. He poured, stirred, added a lemon wedge, presented. Lara tasted, then handed back the glass. She made the flustered kid start over. When I realized she was a baptized Apostle now, the first Terrestrian so privileged, I found myself doubting the wisdom of our mission. Maybe it was better to die off than to dilute our standards for membership.

Lara winked at us and strode away, headed in the direction of the house—a long, low structure of timber and adobe designed to follow the contours of its site. I took the wink to mean Lara would be back soon. Elder Stark and I loitered with nothing much to say, gazing past each other at other guests who, when they noticed us looking at them, smiled or tipped their heads as if they knew us, then calmly turned back to their conversation partners and forgot about us for all eternity.

"Over to your right there, by the hitching post. I think she's an Effingham," my partner said. "Paula, the daughter. A Cleveland baby doctor."

The stout, mannish, middle-aged lady my partner was talking about changed my ideas of what heiresses look like. They were dumb ideas anyway, backed by no experience, and I couldn't imagine where they'd come from—perhaps from the same realm as the face of Cher. The woman had on no jewelry, she wore her hair short, and she stood in her putty-brown shoes as if cemented to them, with none of the swaying supple lightness of the other female guests. Her hand gestures were precise and technical, the movements of her mouth were quick and beaverish, and she seemed to be saying something quite serious to the attentive young couple in front of her.

"Excuse me," my partner said.

"Don't just barge in there. She might be giving medical advice."

"We've already wasted twenty minutes here. Lara was supposed to go find Little Eff and bring him down and introduce us all. They're probably quarreling."

"Please don't call him that."

"It's his nickname. Little Eff."

"I just don't like it for some reason. Especially not from your mouth."

"You should leave."

"I'm waiting for the meat. I'm hoping it's buffalo."

"Go back to Bluff. You're a pebble in my shoe. Tell Lauer you want your pretty Sarah back, take out a loan from the co-op for a house, apply for a job at the talc mine, save your Virtue Coupons, and go down with the rest of them. You hurt my feet."

"I met a neat young woman last night. She told me she'd call." A disturbing thought perked up then. "Why would I have to ask Lauer for Sarah back?"

"Because you just might have to. Protocol. Because he's a power there now. The Church is changing. They're lovely, gentle, wise old ladies, but as a leadership team they're faltering."

"You looked away from me when I asked my question."

"Because I'm impatient. I need to meet an Effingham."

I let his dark bulk brush past me and finished my pop. The moment I did, a uniformed girl appeared and asked if she could take my empty bottle. Around me was a deserted ten-foot circle of absolute social uninterest. I needed new shoes. I also needed to speak with Lauer—that, or never to speak with him again. I'd always assumed he met women on his speaking tours, sleek young Terrestrian corporate executives who shared his Human on Earth concerns and led the same hotel-banquet life that he did, and that he'd return someday engaged to one of them. His cologne made me think this; its spices evoked damp bedsheets. Why Sarah, then? Perhaps to please his mother, but Madeline Lauer had been dead ten years, approved for a Mercy Passing by the Seeress when prayer and diet failed to shrink her tumors.

Sarah held nothing for Lauer, nor Lauer for her—except for the money to buy her a Saab, perhaps. But what if I was wrong? "What should be, is." As my grandmother explained it to our family the winter she lost three fingertips to frostbite when the furnace in her little house broke and she fell and cracked a hip while trying to light it, "Accepting life's imperfections is not the secret. The secret, dears, is to understand life *has* none. How could it? We've nothing to compare it to. We can dream something up, of course—some pretty *maybe* life where fingers are very hard and indestructible—but that's pure mischief, darlings. Fingers freeze. It's one of the things they like to do sometimes."

I found myself beside the barbecue pit, admiring the stately rotation of the bison quarters. I wasn't alone. A man in his early or middle sixties, strangely stiff in the waist as though he wore a girdle, and standing with his chest and shoulders bent forward like someone wading upstream in a fast river, had stationed himself at the backs of two male cooks who were basting the meat with liquid from foil pans and banking and spreading the coals with metal pokers. The old man's face was fiercely supervisory and it registered every action of the cooks with a flutter of tiny muscles or a quick wince. He spoke no orders, though. He managed through simple presence. The cooks seemed to move their basters and wield their pokers in response to intuitions about his wishes, and occasionally one would stop short and change direction like a hunting dog who's heard a whistle.

"Whether the ultimate taste is worth the wait depends on the animal," the man announced. He was talking to me, though he hadn't turned his head. "The one we've got here was a plodding big old guy. He liked to find a cool spot and snooze all day. Either his age will make him dry and chewy, or his incredible sloth will make him tender."

"I suppose we'll have to see," I said.

"*You'll* have to see. I can't eat it anymore." In his voice was a braided thread of irritation and something like despair. "I could mush it up in a blender and take a spoonful, but even then I'd bloat up like a hog."

I'd guessed the old man's identity by then, and it puzzled me that the host of such a party and the owner of such a colossal property would find himself alone with someone like me. We watched the roasts turn and waved away the smoke and our solitude there seemed to gradually draw us closer and ease us toward further intimate disclosures. I glanced behind me to check on Elder Stark, but both he and the Effingham daughter had been absorbed by the growing crowd. Once again, some of the guests smiled back at me, but with a subtle new wary curiosity. My friendly proximity to Errol Sr. clearly had made me an object of speculation.

"Does all meat affect you that way, or only buffalo?" This was a personal question, but he'd started it.

"Solid food in general," Eff Sr. said. "My gut is in bloody revolt against its master. It's no way to die, I can tell you that much. Why are you here? Who invited you?"

His bluntness shook me, but a look at his eyes suggested that what he wanted was simple information, not to frighten me. My grandmother's second husband was the same way. He'd run the talc operation for decades, overseeing tons of machinery and scores of men, and he lived for honest answers to straight questions. People got just one chance to offer them fully.

"We're traveling missionaries from Montana who met your son's friend Lara Shirer recently and are helping adjust her higher and lower minds. She felt for some reason that we should meet your family. When I say 'we,' I mean I have a partner. His name is Elder Elias Stark. Our church is the Aboriginal Fulfilled Apostles and we preach that the worthiness of soul and body is intrinsic and innate. We approve of many, many things."

"Unusually comprehensive. That's appreciated." Eff Sr. held out his right hand and when it gripped me I detected a willed attempt at firmness undermined by a basic cellular frailty whose nature and causes a trained Church Healer, or perhaps the Hobo, might have been able to diagnose right there.

"Enjoy my place today. Have lots to drink. It's time for my baby food," Eff Sr. said. "My job here is finished. This buffalo is done."

I waited until he'd gone off a couple of yards before I said thank you and goodbye. Without turning, he slowed his steps and waved me nearer. When I caught up, he clasped one of my forearms and gave me a good portion of his weight, the portion he couldn't carry by himself. I didn't make him ask me; I walked him home.


The gathering at the tent, I soon found out, wasn't the true party, the party that mattered, but a luxurious diversion staged to keep Snowshoe's prominent residents occupied while the *real* party happened inside the house. This party was smaller and more informal, its food just a platter of crackers and smelly cheese and a bowl of fruit salad that was mostly watermelon, and its drinks cans of Coke and beer from the refrigerator, but the fact that the Effinghams themselves were there made it more prestigious, I'd discover.

Not that any of them were having much fun. Paula, the daughter, who'd come up from the tent after fulfilling her obligations as ambassador to the general public, sat on a stool at a long butcher-block counter and placed cell phone calls to her hospital in Ohio. (She preferred to be addressed as Dr. Vance, I learned.) Her husband, Connor, who had the white teeth I sought but probably would have wrestled me for my hair, since his was just a dusting of thin gray fuzz adhering to a badly sunburned scalp, was amusing himself at the table with a red pencil and a book of word games. Errol—Little Eff—came in and out through a set of glass doors that led to a back garden where four or five guests whom I hadn't been introduced to yet were talking quietly under a big umbrella. The only point of his visits indoors, so far as I could see, was to ask an immobile, armchair-bound Eff Sr. again and again if he needed anything—a glass of water, another pill, his *Wall Street Journal*, a dish of applesauce. The father acted annoyed by his son's doting, but I sensed that he also expected nothing less from him.

My part in this scene was to wander around the room—an immense combination kitchen–dining room–living room from whose exposed and lowered wood ceiling beams hung a museum's worth of copper kettles, birch canoe paddles, tin mining lanterns, iron coyote traps, and bamboo fishing poles—and ask whomever I happened to be closest to where this strange thing had come from or what that thing did. Now and then son-in-law Connor would call for help with one of his word puzzles, and we'd all pitch in, but the rest of the time I felt bored, confined, and stunned.

Until Lara and Elder Stark appeared. Her head poked through

the door first and when she saw me there, at home with the president-electing Effinghams, holding a cola from their private refrigerator, and, at that particular moment, being congratulated by Eff Sr. for helping to solve a word problem that Connor had been struggling with, her face seized up with anguish and hostility. The look didn't last, though. Errol had just come in again, and when Lara spotted him she turned all twinkly.

"Hi, everybody. Hi there, Mr. Eff," she said. Then, to Errol: "Hi, where've you been hiding?" I gathered that she hadn't found him earlier.

"Nowhere. Here and there. Come in," he said. He seemed startled and a little depressed.

"I have a friend," she said. She opened the door the whole way. My partner bowed. Not a deep bow, but a bow. There were stains on his shirt that I assumed were bison grease.

"Who is that young man?" Eff Sr. demanded. He knew who it was because I'd pointed him out to him, so maybe the idea was to teach Lara a lesson about popping in without knocking properly.

A silence took hold. Poor Lara looked terrified. She started to back away. I was thinking about how to save things when my partner said, solemnly, deliberately, and—as events would show—not unpersuasively:

"Someone who can help, sir. Elder Stark. I've come from Montana to help you eat again."

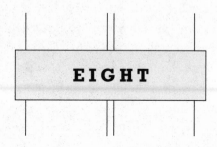

# EIGHT

**A few mornings later** Betsy met me at the van. I'd suggested a rendezvous at the coffee shop, but there was somebody who worked there whom she was trying to avoid. She didn't give any details, but I suspected she meant the son of the yellow-marker tycoon. He was the only employee near her age and he had, I'd heard, quite a history with the girls in town, who were said to admire his bobsledding ambitions. I'd learned that "Olympic hopefuls" were common in Snowshoe, and that the community had more "medalists" than any place of its size in the whole country. Indeed, Elder Stark had done some checking around after Betsy finally phoned me and discovered that she was a former snowboarder who'd quit the sport at twenty-one when her best friend was chosen for the Olympic team and Betsy wasn't. I didn't plan to ask her if this was true because I didn't want to make her feel bad.

She showed up at our campsite in a silver Ford Explorer waxed to the luster of a Christmas ornament. My partner was just leaving on his bike, bound for one of the mysterious appointments that had been occupying his afternoons since the party at the Effingham ranch. We hadn't spoken much since then. He wore his Hobo aura around the clock, studied *Discourses* late into the evenings, and spent hours on the phone with Lauer, who was lecturing in Japan that week. It was hard to imagine what could justify such costly international hookups. When I'd asked him if we were paying the bills, he'd answered curtly, "The funds exist." His schemes had dissolved our partnership. When Betsy's Explorer appeared, he biked right past it, incurious and fixated. I hated him.

"I'm sorry I'm late," she said, though she wasn't late. She'd said that she'd come at ten and it was ten, at least according to my watch. Hers, I saw, was running ahead of mine by a minute or two, but a minute or two wasn't late. Except for her, I'd learn.

"That's where you've been living?" she asked. "I'm sorry."

"Don't be. Don't always be sorry for everything."

"I am, though. That's just how I am. I want to see this."

I'd prepared for her visit by consolidating our boxes of books and our bales of tracts and pamphlets into a big solid cube at the far rear. The van looked as neat and spacious as it ever had, but there was no hiding the odor of Elder Stark's cheeseburger-and-burrito-related night sweats. They clung inexpungibly to the layer of carpet—a low-pile, faintly textured orange material—that started midway up the walls and covered the ceiling. The van had come off a lot outside Missoula, and the salesman had told Lauer little about its history other than that its last owners had been arrested for something and forfeited the title to the police.

"I think sometimes I'd like to live like this. The gypsy life,"

Betsy said. "But maybe not." She leaned down over my bunk and fluffed my pillow, then tightened the sheet and smoothed it with both hands. There were rings on both ring fingers that I hadn't noticed before: thin white-metal diamond-encrusted bands. "It is what it is in here. It makes me sad, though."

"We do just fine."

"Not sad for you. For people." She opened one palm and held it on her cheek and lowered her eyes to the toes of her suede boots. "Ugly things actually hurt me. It's a problem. Sometimes an old car will go by, let's say a station wagon, with the kids crowded into the back and half the windows blocked by all the family's clothes and junk, their moth-eaten blankets, their crappy pots and pans, and the mom and the dad aren't talking to each other, and maybe one of them's smoking, and I just think: I'd rather be dead."

"Than have to live that way?"

"Than even to have to see it."

I let Betsy stew in her mood for a few seconds before I said, "You don't know—they might be happy in there."

"That's even worse. That hurts me even more."

Eventually Betsy raised her eyes, inhaled, exhaled, then forced herself to smile. It took a moment for the smile to stick. "You have to replace those poly sheets you're using with one hundred percent cotton. Promise me."

"We're short on money nowadays."

"I thought Dale hired you to mystery shop?"

"He was supposed to call me with instructions."

"Dale's an airhead. He fried his brain on meth. I'll call him at his office. I'll handle it."

I thought Betsy meant tomorrow or the next day, but she was already unfolding her little white phone, the exact size and shape of a well-worn bar of soap. The whole conversation took about two minutes. Its results were conclusive: Boulder, Thursday morning, Betsy would drive me, dress like "someone normal."

"I think I need to get out of here now," she said.

Outside, as we leaned against her car and talked about how we might spend the afternoon—Betsy suggested a short hike and a trip to a mall to buy me some new shoes—she became distracted by our tires, which she said weren't black enough. I didn't know quite how to take this comment, so I did as I often did: I apologized. She told me it wasn't my fault; most people ignored the color of their tires.

"It's me," she said. "I'm a freak. Things bother me." She walked to the back of her Ford and opened the tailgate, brought out a spray can of something and a rag, squatted down next to the van, and set to work. Her squat pulled away the waistband of her jeans from her lower back, disclosing a dark heart-shaped notch I couldn't help staring at.

She wouldn't let me assist her, so I asked questions. "How old are you?" I had to get this settled.

"Twenty-six."

"Any sisters or brothers?"

"Two and one. Mimi, a nurse practitioner in Portland. Jenna, a paralegal in Santa Fe. Mark, who's gay, an electronic imaging specialist supposedly living in Washington, D.C., but probably in an AWACS over Syria. All three are married, Mark the longest. Parents divorced twelve years ago. Father a luxury-car dealer in Denver, and Mother a massage therapist here in Snowshoe. Everyone scattered, absorbed in their own lives, too busy to call each other except on holidays, and financially okay but panicked anyhow. The Decline of Civilization, chapter seventy. Look: your tires are black now. I feel better."

"So what do *you* do?"

"Nothing. I don't work."

"Where do you get money?"

"I made a little a few years back and saved it. Most of it's gone now, but I can get it back because I recycle. I recycle money."

"How does that work?"

"I spend it on things that hold their value and don't really cost much in the first place. Vintage fashion items, mostly. When I'm broke, I sell off my collection, and then, when I'm bored, I start building it back up. But I hate myself for it today, so please don't ask. Admit it—clean black tires change everything."

We drove to a trailhead in the national forest and hiked in the aspens for the next three hours. Betsy carried a pocket-size case of watercolors and a spiral-bound sketchbook whose plastic cover was decorated with a B, in glitter. Her painting style was wispy and suggestive. A bird in flight was two linked curves for the wings and a couple of swoosh marks for the wind behind it. A river was just its ripples. Because Betsy kept stopping to capture the essence of things, often very small things—a curled dry leaf, a beetle's molted husk, a shard of violet bottle glass—we never achieved much momentum on the hike. It was also hard to talk. I probed for information about the Effinghams, figuring that everyone in Snowshoe probably gossiped about them from time to time, but Betsy said only that she'd heard their wolves once during a camping trip with AlpenCross. Then she spotted an agate she wanted to paint. When she finished, I asked if her AlpenCross involvement had satisfied her spiritual longings. She told me no, it had extinguished them. Finally I tried to join her in her artistry by pointing out a cluster of purple berries swarming with infinitesimal fleas or aphids. "Wow," she said. But she didn't bother to paint it.

By the time we returned to Betsy's car my calves ached and my hopes for us had dwindled. She struck me as a beautiful sealed envelope, stapled, glued, and double-wrapped in tape.

Her life, or what little I knew of it, consisted of ironing wrinkles, masking blemishes, patching tears, and shining dullnesses. Our interactions on the Thonic plane were manifesting on the Matic as an empty dry sensation behind my tonsils and down into my throat. I suspected that Betsy was feeling something similar.

"Maybe," she said as we drove the road toward town, "it's not so crucial to buy you shoes today."

"No," I said.

"Maybe some other time."

"These shoes are fine."

The aspens thinned and houses appeared. Maybe I'd read this evening, or call my family. Maybe Elder Stark would get back early and we could make peace and visit our first movie theater. The one east of town had seven different screens, and all the titles I'd read on the marquee seemed equally intriguing. I'd let him pick.

"Let's bag the mall. Let's just go home," said Betsy.

I settled back into my seat, looked out my window. "Good idea," I said. We passed the coffee shop. The bobsledder was standing in the front window. He raised one arm as if about to wave, then stopped himself, perhaps when he saw me. Betsy and he were probably quite well matched, a pair of accomplished winter sports enthusiasts, and time would reunite them, I had a feeling.

"Tired?" she said. "You look tired."

I just shrugged. Was this a shortcut to the campground? I'd never been down this street before.

"I hope not too tired to rape me," Betsy said.


Betsy lived in the basement of her mother's house, a triangular redwood structure with tall bay windows built against a brushy eroding hillside where the sidewalks of Snowshoe's downtown neighborhoods turned to narrow dirt paths, then petered out. Cars shared the driveways with boats and campers and motorcycles—thousands of dollars of gear for every household and most of it looking forgotten, barely used. I'd stopped wondering on my fourth or fifth day out where all the money came from in Terrestria—from nowhere, apparently; it simply *was*—but the ways people found to waste it still dazzled me.

Inside, Betsy turned on a yellowed ceiling light, revealing dozens of stacked-up plastic grocery sacks knotted shut and containing what looked like clothing. "My thrift-store addiction," she explained. The piles left little space for furniture other than a queen-size mattress and box spring resting without a frame on the bare floor. Betsy asked me to excuse the clutter but there wasn't any clutter; the bags appeared to have been placed by a trained mason.

She crossed to a little half bathroom, shut the door, and a moment later I heard water running, followed by the high annoying whine of what I supposed, though I'd never heard or seen one, was an electric toothbrush. It sounded painful.

We sat on her mattress and ventured a first kiss that began with such force it had nowhere left to go and had to be abandoned and restarted. Her front teeth, which had looked smooth and glassy at the restaurant, had two tiny chips that kept rasping against my tongue tip. Her mouth and her breath were absolutely odorless and her saliva reminded me of mineral oil—slippery, tasteless, and neither warm nor cold. I suspected that she was the cleanest human being I'd ever touch, and this scared me for some reason. I feared it might spoil me for anyone else.

We stopped to rest after ten or fifteen minutes and regarded each other's faces from inches away, our chins rubbed raw, our lips all gnawed and puffy, and in her eyes (I could only guess how mine appeared) was a misty, vague, anesthetized detachment that convinced me she was seeing a composite of all the men she'd ever done this with.

"I want you to be mean to me," she said.

"How? In what way?"

"Whatever way you feel like."

"Mean like cruel?"

"Like my feelings don't matter. Only yours do."

I translated this into Casper Wiccan terms. The doe was asking the stag to romp unchecked.

I tried to satisfy Betsy's wish, aware the whole time that meanness on request isn't meanness at all, but kindness carried too far. I squeezed her left arm above the elbow until all I could feel was the pulse in my own thumb. I turned her face to one side by pushing her cheek and dragged my teeth down her neck from ear to collarbone. Still, I sensed she was frustrated with me. I hadn't uncoiled, I hadn't blasted through. To want this, she must have had it before, I realized, and I wondered from whom, and how recently. This froze me.

She pulled away and said, "I want to play now. I want to play dress up with you."

"I wasn't mean enough."

"That's okay. It's hard when you still don't know someone," she said.

She started untying and picking through the sacks. "There's a shirt somewhere here I want you to try on. I found it last year at a Santa Fe Goodwill and thought it might suit this man who I was seeing, but he said it was too 'cowboy,' too 'Roy Rogers.' It's vintage. It's funky. Me, I think it's manly."

"This is the collection you were talking about."

"The idea is to make it a business in a year or two, maybe a storefront or maybe through the Web. I only buy classic stuff in top condition. Those slippery seventies rayon disco shirts. Those wild old bell-bottoms with high tight waists. It's crazy, the prices people pay for those, but it also makes sense because they're hard to find; you have to hit every thrift store, every yard sale. Last year I went from Arizona to Oregon—I put twenty-three thousand miles on my car. The problem is when the stuff is gone it's gone, though, so I really can't take the time to sell it off until I've got most of what's out there."

"You think that's possible?"

"I can feel it—you're about to preach," she said. "Yes, I know, it's no substitute for God. It's stuff. It's only stuff."

"That's what the All-in-One is made of, actually."

"Not spirit?"

"That, and everything else."

She found the shirt and held it by the shoulders, her thumbs and forefingers pinched together like clothespins. I reached for it with insensitive cold hands. All the kissing had driven the blood from my extremities into my lower middle region, causing a pressurized, tense, unsure sensation that felt like it might lead to diarrhea unless I managed to discharge it by luring Betsy back to bed. The two urges felt so similar sometimes, like one fundamental urge divided.

The human body is strangely made and sometimes it pays not to think about it too closely.

I slipped off my dress shirt and changed into the new one, confused about why Betsy found it so extraordinary. I'd grown up wearing shirts exactly like it: pearl snaps, colored piping, pointed pocket flaps, and a design of braided thorns and roses embroidered across the chest and upper back. I fastened the cuffs and smoothed out some of the wrinkles and imagined that I was sixteen and back in Bluff, strolling in the evening with my pals, aware that off over the hills and down the highway there was a world that didn't even know us, or knew of us vaguely and didn't care about us. We knew we were missing something by living there, but they, the outsiders, were missing something, too.

"You look like yourself now," Betsy said. "Stand up."

I showed myself off.

"I want the back view."

She adjusted the collar, fiddled with the yoke, and picked off a couple of lint balls from one sleeve. I still regretted my failure to harshly use her, but it seemed that we were getting along much better now. She picked out a belt from a snaky tangled bunch of them and gave it to me with a pair of western pants whose legs were flared to fit over big boots. The bronze buckle was star shaped, like a sheriff's badge, and it weighed as much as a can of Coca-Cola. I snugged it tight and hooked it through a hole and posed like a gunfighter, legs apart, knees bent.

"Bang," I said.

"Bang is right. Bang, bang."

I felt it now. A sternness came over me. I motioned for her and displayed my antlered head. She stroked it with her hands, and then in other ways, and then I pushed her down onto the sheets and used it to toss her around and bash and batter her. It was more than a romp. It was closer to a stampede. My hooves came into play as well. All of my staggish parts did, at various times.

Afterward, when she got up to brush her teeth again, Betsy said, "Interesting—you're good at that. That was really just your second time?"

I rose up on my side, with a fist against my jaw. As I closed one eye to clear a stinging sweat drop that had rolled down from my hairline across my temple, I reached between my legs to readjust things. There was still some potential there, though it didn't look that way. In a voice that I couldn't have managed an hour earlier—resonant, full, from the sweet spot of my diaphragm—I asked her to bring me back a glass of water. When she returned and gently passed it to me, and then watched as I drank it, seemingly concerned about whether it pleased me and whether I wanted more, I knew that, at least for the moment, I owned this girl.

"Cold enough?" she asked. She meant the water.

"Yes."

She seemed happy.

I'd made a person happy.

# NINE

**The day the Seeress predicted** her own death, I was impersonating an average customer at the Boulder, Colorado, WorkMart, a store so vast that the people who stocked its shelves had to travel in electric carts equipped with steadily beeping warning horns. Its parking lot was half the size of Bluff, with two or three times as many vehicles, and after we parked there, I lingered in Betsy's Explorer and prayed to the All-in-One for comprehension. The dimensions of the rectangular beige edifice looming before me, its endless rows of doors sending out a stream of puny hunchbacks monstrously overburdened with crated dishwashers, cartons of tile, toilets, poplar saplings, unassembled bunk beds, hoops of hose, and inflatable vinyl swimming pools tested my sense of spiritual symmetry. I'd always assumed that a balance was intended between human beings and their things, but at WorkMart it seemed that our purpose on this earth was to lift, transport, and set back down stupendous loads of metal, wood, and plastic. This felt backward to me, but backward in terms of what? I had to remember: no False Comparisons.

Betsy had dressed me for the outing in a short-sleeved blue shirt with a penguin on the breast pocket, off-white corduroy trousers, and canvas tennis shoes. She picked my hair into points and froze it that way with a waxy white cream. The costume made me conspicuous to myself and invisible, it seemed, to everyone else. Just inside the store, a middle-aged worker with the low, globed forehead of what my grandmother called a "simple soul" detached a shopping cart from a nested line of them and pushed it my way without a glance of welcome. He didn't seem to register my "Thank you," he just repeated the favor for someone else.

"That's kind of them, to hire a man like that."

"All the stores do it nowadays," said Betsy. "I think it might be a federal law. McDonald's is especially big on it."

"I think it's very thoughtful."

"Pay attention here."

My task was to record and quantify, using a checklist that was folded in my pocket, my reactions to the WorkMart "shopping experience." Dale had given me a list of items to buy and a number of questions to ask the staff. As I hunted for the lighting department, the right front caster of my shopping cart kept sticking and skidding, turning the whole thing cockeyed and forcing me to wrestle it straight again. "First demerit," Betsy said. We stopped beneath an array of chandeliers, many fitted with brass or wooden fan blades, and a gleaming profusion of ceiling fixtures. Unable to see what kept them suspended there, I pictured a disastrous, shredding rain of slivered frosted glass and knife-edged metal. For a building so high inside, so wide across, and so overcrowded with tier on tier of inventory—table saws stored thirty feet above the ground!—its construction seemed ominously feeble: an airy grid of beams and cables that barely looked capable of securing a circus tent against a summer storm.

"It's like a gigantic shell," I said to Betsy. "Should I put down for Dale that I don't feel physically safe in here?"

"That's you. That's not an everyday response."

"I bet if you asked people, the feeling's shared."

"Just try," Betsy said, "to imagine you're an American."

This stung. I was more American than she was. I'd grown up so deeply buried in this continent, so thoroughly landlocked, surrounded, and enveloped, that I still couldn't clearly envision its coasts; to me the oceans were pure poetic conjecture, no more tangible than asteroid belts. Before the autumn of my fifteenth year, when an elderly Mexican couple passed through Bluff peddling hand-tooled leather belts and boots, I'd never heard a foreign language spoken. My childhood pizzas weren't even true pizzas. As for the Church, its doctrines and its founders—Little Red Elk, most of all—owed virtually nothing to sinister old Europe, with its monks and crusaders, its relics and inquisitions. Ours was a fresh revelation of the New World, as native to this land as pronghorn antelope. The aliens here were the Terrestrians, confusing their transient, preening little empire with the mineral essence of the place itself.

Was Mason LaVerle an American? Nothing but.

Still, as I pushed farther into lighting, searching for a yellow-aproned worker to pester with my scripted questions, I found myself partly conceding Betsy's point. For the purposes of the job at hand, which I hoped to be paid for and to keep, I had to step out of myself, to wear new skin.

"Excuse me, ma'am. I'm wondering how to light a basement

workshop. It doesn't have any windows to the outside, it's twelve by fifteen feet in area, and, because I work with dangerous power tools, it requires full, bright, even illumination."

The woman set her hands on her broad hips and scanned the man-made heaven of dangling fixtures. "Fluorescent?"

"I was hoping you'd advise me."

"These right up here ones are more your fancy deals that go off your dimmers and such to make a mood, like say if there's wine and your lady friend comes over. You're more wanting plain. For sawing under."

My brain churned and labored. Betsy said, "Exactly."

"If this wasn't break, and it's only two a shift now, I'd go along with you myself, but maybe Dan can. If I'd seen the man any. He's not on station, is he?" The woman's head went back and forth, more to establish Dan's absence, it appeared, than to locate him. "Wall treatments, try. Named Dan. Or else he quit." The woman flapped an exasperated hand at us, or maybe at the entire operation, and headed off toward the store's mysterious rear, where I sensed most of its suffering was hidden. Betsy watched her go, rubbing a fingertip against one temple. I had a tiny headache of my own.

"I have to include all that under 'Service,' don't I?"

Betsy sighed for both of us.

"With her name attached, don't I? Her tag said Marna B."

"If that's the procedure, I suppose you do."

"They'll fire her, won't they? I don't think I can do it."

Betsy kissed me on the cheek.

"I'm a terrible mystery shopper."

"Thank God," she said.

We abandoned the shopping cart midway through our trek to the far-off lawn-care aisle, where Dale had ordered me to choose a riding mower, arrange for its purchase with a salesman, and then, at the last moment, to feign cold feet and closely observe the salesman's behavior as he tried to salvage the transaction. Was he calm and persuasive? Angry and aggressive? Resigned and passive? I'd dreaded this assignment, mostly because of the acting skills it called for. Now, though, having decided back in lighting to dispense with strict honesty today, I looked forward to a revised version of the drama in which I'd pretend to discover I'd lost my wallet and would promise the salesman I'd return tomorrow. I'd award him the same score no matter how he dealt with me: ninety-one points out of one hundred.

"So you're definitely thinking John Deere," the young man said after I'd sat on seven different models, cranking their wheels and fiddling with their gearshifts. "The fity-one hundred or the fity-two?"

"It's a four-acre yard with a pretty fair slope," I said, "and most of it's in the shade, which means wet grass. Under certain conditions it's an outright marsh. Also, my wife works nights and sleeps all day, so the quieter, the better." These details weren't in the script; I'd made them up. Knowing the scene would end happily for everyone had liberated the artist in me.

Without explaining why it suited my needs, the salesman recommended the fifty-two and untwisted the wires that attached the price tag to the neck of the choke knob. I started patting my pockets. A problem arose: I'd neglected to hide my wallet. It bulged in my back right pocket, its natural place, where the salesman had likely already noticed it. I shifted to another plan. I brought out the wallet, smiled, opened it, frowned, frowned harder, and said, "No credit card."

"You misplaced it?" the salesman said.

"I think I must have."

"Nobody stole it, I hope."

"I hope not. *Damn*."

"You want to call the company? You can give them your password, they'll authorize the sale. You really ought to alert them anyway, in case someone's out there charging on your account. Here, use this." He handed me his phone.

"I don't know their number."

"Call up information. Visa or MasterCard?"

"I remember now: I left it on top of my dresser. What a dunce." I held out the phone for the salesman to take back.

"Just call the company and use your password. The mower's yours."

"I'm sorry, I can't right now. I'm already late for something."

The salesman's brow pinched.

"First thing tomorrow."

"I won't be here tomorrow."

My inability to sustain my story—I finally just said the mower cost too much and that my old one could last another year or two—brought on a bitter lecture from the salesman about the economics of his job. He worked on commission, and this was his peak sales hour, meaning that I'd cost him quite a sum, he said, by taking up thirty-five minutes of his time with no intention of buying anything. If I thought about it, he said, I'd stolen from him. I'd stolen from his wife and child, too. "That's selfish," he said. "That is so incredibly selfish."

"Oh please," Betsy said to him, stepping in. "Cool off. Come on, Mason."

"*Look* at me," the salesman said.

"We have been," said Betsy. "We're going home."

"Don't ever come back here. You picked my pocket, *dickwad*."

I was walking away when he said this. I halted, turned. Betsy released the elbow she'd been tugging at.

"You're going to regret that you weren't nicer," I said.

The salesman held out his hands. "I'm shaking all over."

"I'm a person who can tell the future. In five or six days—I see it clearly—your employer will call you back into his office, show you a certain report he just received, and inform you that you no longer have a job here. Unless you apologize to me."

I counted silently to five. I'd intended to go to ten, but it was pointless: the salesman kept up his mock shaking, unrepentant. I took Betsy's hand and left him standing there, alone with the fate he'd chosen for himself, and for the next hour, from kitchenware to flooring, I terrorized WorkMart's sales floor, sparing no one. Afterward, in Betsy's car, I signed my report and clipped it to an envelope. "Done," I said. "They got what they deserved."

"You changed in there," Betsy said.

"I did my job. You're right: I have to think like an American."

"I didn't mean *all* the time."

"That's how it sounded."

"I like you sweet, though."

"You said you liked me mean."

"That was a very different context."

I'd forgotten this about women: so many conditions. A man shouldn't take them to heart, and yet he does, because he doesn't want to be alone. The woman fears loneliness, too, but she can't help herself, though she knows her conditions may drive the man away. That's why, secretly, she feels relieved when he resists her now and then.

"The service at WorkMart is awful, and I said so. That's what mystery shoppers do," I said.

"You're playing tough now to show me I don't scare you. Which means I must, or else you wouldn't bother. I think it's cute," said Betsy. "How cute are you?"

This wasn't the sort of question a man should answer. I

stared out the bug-streaked windshield at the store and pictured it collapsing in a dust cloud that would spread over all of Boulder and block the sun. Someday it would happen; it felt inevitable.

"If I scare you, it must mean you like me," Betsy said. "Well, I like you too, so don't worry."

"Because I'm cute."

"No," she said. "Because you try so hard."


At lunch I rewrote my report to make it kinder, since being employed by WorkMart was its own punishment. We set out for our second stop, a downtown jewelry store, but on our way there my phone rang. It was Lauer. I had to cover one ear so I could hear him. He said he was on a plane above New Mexico and was using his phone in violation of United States government regulations, so he had to speak quietly. When he hung up, I tried my partner's number but couldn't get through. Then I told Betsy we had to turn around.

"What's wrong? You're crying."

"It's just my eyes," I said.

"I know it's just your eyes. They're full of tears."

My explanation consumed the whole drive back, although there were ten-minute stretches when I said nothing, just rubbed the knees of my corduroys and drifted, sometimes backward into childhood and sometimes forward to a future that I suddenly found hard to picture. I understood that no one lives forever, but there are certain people whose power and presence so thoroughly penetrate your view of things that contemplating their absence feels as strange as imagining never having been born yourself.

Even before my brain was capable of forming and storing

lasting memories, I must have seen her face a hundred times: the small pointed ears like tightly closed tulip blossoms, the fine but dense white hair swept back in waves, the pink upturned nose with the oddly snipped-off tip and the X-shaped wrinkle at the top, the round girlish mouth, and the knobby, prominent chin that looked almost manly when seen in profile. Strangely, her weakest feature was her eyes, which were tiny, close set, and dull in color—not quite green or blue but not gray, either. Though she didn't wear glasses, I wouldn't have been surprised if she needed them—the reason, perhaps, that when she spoke to people, she would always ask them to come closer, until they were near enough to feel her breath, which was teakettle hot and smelled faintly of black licorice from the anise seeds she liked to chew.

For years, I knew her only from a distance, as the short human figure between the towering floral arrangements at the far end of Celestial Hall. Before her arthritis forced her into her chair and confined her to the front porch of Riverbright, she delivered her talks standing upright, with her arms crossed, as though she suffered from a constant chill. Hearing her speak was like watching a magician draw an endless ribbon of yellow scarves out of his clenched fist—astonishing. She never used notes and rarely paused to think; her long singsong sentences sprang forth fully formed. Until I was tall enough to see her easily above the rows and rows of nodding heads, I liked to listen to her with my eyes closed while resting my head against my father's side between his rib cage and his belt. His organs gurgled and shifted with her words. "The All-in-One does not require our praise any more than the rivers and trees require our praise, nor does the All-in-One demand obedience, offerings, tokens, gifts, or sacrifices. The All-in-One seeks neither flattery nor increase but only the satisfaction of our companionship."

I quoted these words for Betsy. "Sweet," she said. Seeming to sense that I wanted more, she added: "And nice if it were true."

When I was nine, in the heart of a cold winter that had kept my family inside the house for months, restless, bickering, and chronically sick as the result of my mother's rash decision to heed the warnings of a Terrestrian radio doctor and have us all injected with flu vaccine, the Seeress appeared at our front door one night while my parents were washing the supper dishes. I was lying on the sofa, trying to make myself vomit into a canning pot set on a towel beside me on the floor. After two days of nausea so acute that even seeing bright colors made me gag, vomiting would come as a relief.

I felt a draft from the kitchen, then heard her voice, pleasant, composed, and utterly unnerving. I flung off my wool blanket and sat up straight. I napkined my chin clean, but, without a mirror, I couldn't be sure I'd gotten all the saliva left there by my unproductive retching. I felt around with my finger, found a wet spot.

"Mason?" my mother called. "We have a guest."

The Seeress insisted on drinking the tea we served her at the kitchen table, from everyday china. My mother offered her a slice of huckleberry tart, but she declined it, citing a "funny, belchy tummy." This comment helped put us at our ease. My mother finally let herself sit down, my father stopped scratching his thumbnail on his belt buckle, and my own hands stopped shaking enough to lift a spoon and stir a little honey into my tea. The Seeress apologized for intruding, and then explained the reason for her visit.

"I was strolling home this morning from my hair appointment and I noticed a purple spot above your house. It was faint, you'll be happy to know, not fully developed, but any purple at all concerns me, naturally. I should have come by immediately—forgive me."

My mother set down her full teacup on her saucer. It rattled and spilled. My father touched her arm. She took his hand and squeezed it and looked away. Over the Seeress's shoulder, through the window, I watched a magpie land on a slim tree branch that dipped and rose and dipped under its weight. A second bird landed and the branch stayed down.

"It was faint, as I said, so there's no reason to fret, dears. We caught it early, with time to spare, I'm sure." The Seeress eyed us each in turn as she helped herself to a warm-up from the teapot. She picked up the creamer and dribbled in some milk, her hand a fragile-looking claw, but steady. Her gaze had come to rest on me. "Tell me, child. Describe it for me, please."

Was it possible the old woman was mistaken? Her sighting made no sense to me—how could a stomachache cause a hovering purple spot? I feared insulting her judgment, though. I began with my first symptom three days earlier: a pang of revulsion brought on by smelling an orange, usually my favorite fruit. The Seeress asked me if the offending whiff had come from the skin or the flesh. "The skin," I said. This seemed to mean something to her—she pinched her lower lip, tugging it slightly between her thumb and forefinger in a way that exposed her crowded brown bottom teeth. I continued, point by point, mentioning my discomfort with vivid colors as well as a peppery taste behind my tonsils that intensified as sleep approached but vanished in the mornings.

"Peppery?" said the Seeress. "Not silvery? This is vital, child."

I thought about it. "I don't know what silver tastes like."

"Like this," she said. She tilted her head, reached up with her right hand, and unscrewed an earring made from an old coin. She presented it to me balanced on an index finger. "On the back of the tongue, where it's rough. The very back."

I turned away for modesty's sake, opened my mouth, and did as I'd been told. I tasted nothing at first, just noted the neutral hard coolness of the coin. After another second, it numbed my tongue. The numbness spread up the insides of my cheeks and through my gums and back to my esophagus, which was still sore and raw from all my coughing and hawking. At my back I could feel the warmth and pressure of everyone's concerned attention, and I wondered for how long the Seeress expected me to hold the earring in place. The test seemed pointless.

And then the cramps came, a rolling succession of whole-body seizures that caused me to rock backward in my chair and brought my pale, shocked father to his feet. He caught me from behind somehow, but the next contraction pitched me forward so violently that he lost his grip. My forehead sledgehammered the table and caused, I was later told, a stream of liquid to spout from the jostled teapot and splatter the Seeress, ruining the lace collar of a dress that had belonged to Mother Lucy herself once. I missed this disaster, though. All I saw was black.

The cleanup had begun when I came to. The Seeress and my father stood aside as my mother pushed a white bath towel across the table and what must have been two quarts of greenish sludge threaded with bright red blood sloshed off the edge into a galvanized bucket. Chalky shards of china littered the floor, and my mother, in slippers, was careful not to step on them as she carried the bucket to the bathroom and poured it loudly into the toilet. I heard distinct plops and isolated splashes—the stuff must have been quite chunky. I patted my belly. It was hot through my shirt and noticeably sunken. The nausea was gone, though.

The Seeress said, "Pancreatic, but caught in time. I'd like

you to rest now and sip molasses water, as strong and sweet as you can stand it." She extended one arm and opened a closed hand: the magic earring. The thing looked wet, besmirched, and her willingness to touch it made me love her. "We thought it was lost—you gulped it down," she said. "But it came back to us, Mason, and so did you. No more deathly purple at the LaVerles'. All is lovely blue again."

Betsy steered with one finger as the Explorer topped the ridge east of Snowshoe and nosed back down into its aspen-covered heart-shaped valley, speckled with the first house lights of early evening and softened by a fine magenta mist that looked like the vapor released by wealth itself. My tale of the time my life was saved had diverted her attention from the road. When a deer tiptoed out of the trees and crossed the center line, missing our hood by only a few yards, she not only didn't brake, she barely looked up.

"What exactly's wrong with her?" she asked.

"She said it didn't matter. She called the whole town together on her lawn for a lemonade social and just when it was ending she rang the bell that hangs on the side of her wheelchair and announced that she'll be gone by the next moon. People fainted. Not just women, men. Her nurses had to go around with smelling salts."

"Interesting."

"Sad," I said.

"But picturesque. The bell, especially. I liked the bell."

Betsy's tone was shifting in a direction that suggested I'd overwhelmed her with thoughts and scenes only an Apostle could understand. She'd done her best, though. She'd sighed convincing sighs. I lifted a twist of hair from her white neck and let it fall back in a way I hoped felt pleasant. Inside, I grieved. Or so I thought. This would be my first death when it occurred, my first real death, and maybe the pain I felt was anger, panic, or deep self-pity, not grief at all. In Bluff, we didn't inspect and name our feelings the way they did here—they came and went, unclassified—and maybe this limited us somehow. Our books, our parents, and our leaders spoke with a single voice about the unity of every creature in its creator, but I'd begun to suspect the All-in-One existed differently in different zones, and our zone had little in common with the others.

Soon it would have no presiding spirit, either.

The camper looked empty when Betsy and I pulled in. I didn't invite her inside—the place was filthy. Ever since being accepted by the Effinghams, Elder Stark had lapsed into a state of haughty dishevelment, entranced by everything about himself, including his own filth. I wondered if he'd heard the news yet and decided he'd probably heard it first, since Lauer and he were in league now, as close as crooks. Had he wept? Had he broken down? I knew he'd say he had, of course, but I doubted I'd believe him.

Betsy parked. I sealed the dishonest mystery shopper report inside its pre-addressed brown envelope, gave it to her to mail, and opened my door. A cloud of the delicate black-and-olive mayflies that had been hatching on the river all week swarmed into the car, and Betsy grimaced. She didn't start swatting, though; she restrained herself, even when some of the bugs climbed into her vents. This girl who enjoyed it when others were mean to her—at least in certain situations—didn't practice meanness herself.

"You'll be okay tonight?"

"I will," I said.

"I had a weird psychic flash a few miles back, but I didn't want to interrupt you. You should know that about me: I'm psychic, Mason."

"I expect that in women. It's assumed."

"You might not want to hear it, though. Do you or don't you?"

"I'll tell you afterward." It was a peevish remark, but I was tired, eager to lie on my bunk, alone, in silence.

"All right, then," Betsy said. "This seer lady?"

"Yes?"

"I said it wrong. I'm sorry. This Seeress?"

"Betsy, it's been a long day . . ."

"She'll be the last."

I swung my right leg out the door and onto the ground. "I'll be in the coffee shop at eight or so. And remember to send that report. I need the money." I spoke curtly, in clipped phrases. We traded feeble waves, I shut the door, and walked toward the van, aware with every step of Betsy's displeasure at my seeming dismissal of her vision. In truth, I'd grown weary of visions generally. Everyone had them, no one ever checked them, and even the few visions that proved true conferred no advantage on those who'd had or heard them. The Seeress was the lone exception. Though other Bluff sensitives were just as gifted, and some, including Elder Stark's own mother, were capable of feats she couldn't match, such as reading words from the dead in gnarled tree bark and finding lost pets by peering into their food bowls, the Seeress possessed a quality that vaulted her above all of them: judiciousness. She kept her beholdings close; she didn't scatter them. She intervened with hunches and predictions only when great outcomes were at stake: the fate of the Church, the survival of a marriage, the death of a child. Her visions mattered.

I undressed to my shorts and slid in under my blankets, clawing them up tight against my chin. Snowshoe cooled down fast at night; the valley just couldn't hold its heat. I lay awake and waited for my partner, but after an hour the nonsense thoughts began that ease the mind into deep sleep. A wolf running loose in the kitchen aisle of WorkMart, upending blenders with its swishing tail. The wedding of a doe and a bull moose with a lighted brass candelabra instead of antlers. Betsy in a wheelchair on a riverbank, coughing up little brown toads into a handkerchief while old Errol Effingham squatted in diapers beside her, the missing moose antlers sprouting from his gray head.

Visions perpetual. Visions on top of visions. The Seeress believed that visions were natural objects, as common and ordinary as stones or sticks. Taken individually, she told us, few of them were worthy of much attention; it was the material that formed them, and which was released for reuse when they dissolved, that deserved our wonder and admiration. Because, finally, this was all our world was made of: decomposed visions. Not atoms—bits of dreams.

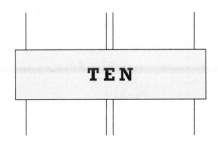

# TEN

**My partner stayed away all night.** I called him in the morning and got a message, longer than I thought a phone could hold, which jumped around in a way that frightened me and sounded at times like a child's letter home from some sort of camp or institution. "I'm heartbroken, and I realize you are, too, but we can't let our moods interrupt our mission. I'll try to be back by Friday, but until then please don't call this phone again. And don't drive up here, especially not with Lara. You might want to stay away from her, in fact. I know she's an Apostle now, but, well . . . The ranch is grand, a blessed place. Last night we watched two wolves from the back deck and I had the privilege of meeting Ronald Howard, a widely admired cinema artist. He's also a very funny, very kind, surprisingly philosophical gentleman. I gave him my pocket edition of *Discourses* to take back to California, so cross your fingers. He read a few lines after supper and seemed intrigued. Stay busy down there and don't brood about the Seeress. She's ninety-seven. It's time. Eff Sr. says 'Howdy.' Today I'll get to see buffalo up close."

The ramblings seemed to end there, but just as I was hanging up I heard: "This is a secret, Mason. I hope you're there still. Lauer says he's heard succession rumors and that it might be my mother. She's disappeared. He's guessing she's up at Riverbright, secluded. I don't know what I think about this yet, and I wish I could call you and discuss it, but all the guests here have to check their phones with ranch security. Even Ronald Howard. You'd be interested in the chat I had with him, but I'm bending the rules by even recording this. The guard is here beside me, listening. Thank you, Luis. Luis is Roman Catholic. I told him I had solemn religious business, but he could be fired for this favor, so I'm stopping now. Luis can view twelve different cameras from his booth here, but he tells me there's one he can't see that watches him. I think I noticed the screen in Eff Sr.'s bedroom, but it was all dusty, so I think we're fine. I'm learning a lot about the world up here, and I think I may be helping, too. Little Eff says his father's color was much improved after I gave him the tincture of powdered lichen described in Little Red Elk's *Prairie Pharmacy*. I wish I could contact my mother. I miss her voice."

My partner sounded lonesome and not quite sane. Considering his strange surroundings and the momentous gossip he'd just heard, I found this understandable. I set down my phone on the metal sidewalk table where I'd been drinking my daily Americano and sent a little tapping prayer his way. Tapping prayers were brief and wordless, an inspired invention of Mother Lucy's meant to accommodate nine Hungarian immigrants who showed up in Bluff in the early 1890s as the result of a story about the Church that had appeared in a Budapest evening paper for reasons no one could explain. The Hungarians, who spoke no English, were taught to touch their left hands to their right temples and tap them, telegraph-style, for thirty seconds while smiling in the direction of the sun and imagining their loved ones' faces. The tapping sent magnetic ripples through the ether that were of benefit to both sender and receiver.

I stirred more honey into my bitter coffee and looked up and down the street for a white Jeep. I was waiting for the very person, Lara, whom I'd just been instructed to avoid and no longer wanted to see in any case, because suddenly there was just so much to think about. She'd come by the van at a quarter after midnight, awakened me by rattling the door, and kept me up for another forty minutes with stories of her mistreatment by Little Eff, whom she referred to in a single sentence as a "passive-aggressive emotional cripple" as well as "the only man I'll ever love." Her charges against him were vehement but vague, expressed in a language I didn't understand. He'd "sexually invalidated" her. He'd "subverted" their "underlying romantic contract." I asked her if he'd ever hit her. "In what sense?" she replied. I begged her to let me rest then. I promised to meet her as soon as I got up.

Now I was considering escape routes. I sealed a lid on my cup, unlocked my bike, and walked it toward an alley between the coffee shop and a bakery specializing in dog and cat treats where I'd once tried to buy a doughnut by mistake. A block away I spotted long-haired Lance craning his neck out the window of a pickup that he was trying to park between two sports cars. Though the space looked plenty large, Lance pulled out and reapproached it twice, possibly concerned for his truck's paint, a smoothly luminous obsidian finish that couldn't have been achieved with normal spray guns and might have involved dipping the whole vehicle in a massive tub or vat. I doubted he'd seen me, but I waved in case he had. Snowshoe Springs was shrinking by the day.

I mounted my bike at the entrance to the alley, then saw that its outlet was blocked by a delivery van. When I turned back around, they were both there: Lara *and* Lance. Their postures indicated they knew each other but said nothing about whether they liked each other. Through some odd coincidence they were dressed like twins in red zippered sweater jackets, loose black pants covered with odd-shaped pockets and enclosures, and those thick-treaded hiking boots that pick up mud and then leave it behind in W-shaped chunks.

They said they were hungry and, to be agreeable, I said I was too, though I'd eaten a carrot muffin at the coffee shop. Through a series of tense suggestions and compromises that reminded me of the steak-dinner–wine debate, we ended up getting breakfast at a restaurant deep in the mazelike artificial village located at the bottom of the ski hill. The restaurant's decor seemed European—paintings of lakes and castles, cuckoo clocks—but the food was Mexican. Lance convinced me to let him order for me.

"The huevos," he said. "Guacamole on the side. Lara? Get something solid. It's on me."

"Sourdough toast, no butter," she told the waitress. "Decaf double soy latte."

"You're not in Malibu. Bring her poached eggs and tomatillo salsa."

Lara wrinkled up her nose. Perhaps to mask her fatigue from staying up so late, she'd brushed out her hair into curtains that hid her cheeks and bangs that hung down almost to her eyebrows. The strip of face that remained looked spooky, furtive, like a feral cat peering out between two hay bales.

As we talked and drank coffee and waited for our meals, my mind kept tugging me away to Bluff and thoughts of Pamela Stark, my partner's mother. Through what sort of alchemy could a neighbor lady be transformed into the Seeress? Or did the office consist of nothing more than a staff, a mansion, and a title? Maybe it was just another job. I felt the mystery draining from my world and resolved to resist the process.

I turned to Lara, who'd been holding a glass shaker of ground cinnamon over her coffee cup for several seconds, apparently worried about adding calories. "You still haven't told me how you know each other. Through AlpenCross?"

"Further back than that," Lance said. He nodded at Lara as though asking for her permission to relate the whole story, part, or none. Her hair blocked my view of her reaction. It must have been a strong one, though; she flipped over the shaker, slapped its bottom, and let the cinnamon stream into her coffee until it formed a floating brown pyramid that, after vigorous stirring with a spoon, flattened to a brown sand dune but wouldn't dissolve.

"She'd rather we talked about something else," said Lance.

"Actually," she said, "I couldn't care less." She bundled together three sugar packets and tore them open as a unit.

"Lara's my ex," Lance said.

"Correction. *An* ex."

"True. But by far my favorite."

"Whatever," said Lara. She sipped her coffee, which she'd turned into sludge. It coated her lips and teeth. She sucked them clean.

Lance's story lasted until the check came. Lara didn't interrupt him once, just went on experimenting with her breakfast until the hot-sauce bottle, the salt and pepper shakers, and the dishes of sour cream and chopped tomatoes ringed her plate like the moons of Jupiter. The commotion and the mess she made confused me as to how much food she swallowed, which may have been her plan. Her life looked like torture. She treated its simplest tasks—not just eating, I suspected, but bathing, dressing, sleeping, and socializing—as awesome, monumental contests that could end in just two ways: absolute defeat or joyous victory. But should she flee or fight? She couldn't decide.

Her marriage to Lance was brief, I learned: three months. They met on a weeklong wilderness rafting trip. He was guiding, she was paying. She'd brought along four TV friends from California, including a young musician she'd fallen in love with, but he gashed open one of his legs on a sharp rock and was helicoptered to Denver the first day out. Four days later, Lance and Lara were engaged. He quit his job, returned with her to Hollywood, and found work as an exercise coach—a "personal trainer." He missed the rivers, though. He missed the mountains. Then Lara's soap opera was canceled. She sold her house at an enormous profit and moved with Lance to Snowshoe Springs, intending to rest, relax, lose weight, and resume her career in six months or a year. The wedding, solemnized by a Hopi holy man ("My fault," said Lance. "I was full of New Age bullcrap") took place on a cliff top that Lance said I could see by looking through a window across the restaurant. I squinted and strained. "It doesn't matter," he said. "It's shaped like a dove; a miracle in granite. AlpenCross wants to buy it as a retreat but we'll need a big donor. Complicated deal. The family that owns it never sells land."

Lara glanced up at Lance from her latest project: ripping a soft tortilla into strips and wrapping them around chunks of avocado smeared with refried beans.

"Fine, then. No secrets. The Effinghams," Lance said.

The name set his story on a different course. He folded the

tale of his troubled marriage to Lara into a recent history of Snowshoe. The town had "sold its soul," he said. Starting fifteen or twenty years ago, the old family ranches he'd grown up around had been nibbled away at by rich folks from the coasts interested in lots for winter ski homes. As real estate values doubled and quadrupled, the ranchers' heirs grew flush with cash, which, in imitation of the newcomers, they rapidly squandered on cars and trips and luxury goods, amassing debts that required further land sales and sometimes provoked disastrous family feuds that led to liquidations of whole homesteads. Then the romances began. At drunken parties that ran throughout the ski season and later, after the golf courses went in, throughout the other seasons as well, local men paired up with visiting women, local women ran off with visiting men, and divorces, breakdowns, and suicides ensued—so many of them that the town acquired a nickname among the opportunistic Denver feelings doctors who moved to town by the dozens: "Snowshoe Strange."

"I'm not shifting blame, because sin is real," Lance said, "but Lara and I, we didn't have a chance here. Communal damnation—there's really such a thing."

Lara punctured an egg yolk with a fork and Lance cut his eyes at her. She didn't speak. She looked like she might speak later, but not now. She sprinkled the ruptured yolk with grated cheese.

"I fathered a child with another woman," Lance said. "A San Jose Internet executive. Lara'd like you to have the filthy facts, apparently."

She seemed to agree because she finally ate something. Ate, chewed, and swallowed it. A shred of lettuce.

"Her own indiscretions we won't go into," Lance said.

Lara shrugged at him.

"Okay, then. A certain then-married man whose wealthy father had just had several large colon polyps removed, thereby piquing widespread interest in the disposition of his estate, was soaking one evening in a natural hot springs when a certain restless married female happened along by sheer coincidence, shed her clothes, and climbed in next to him. Powdered narcotic stimulants appeared. Complaints of marital misery were traded. The following morning a private jet departed for either Las Vegas or Miami Beach—its destination still remains a mystery—and when it returned to Snowshoe five days later, two couples had been dissolved to form a third." Lance pushed away his empty plate, streaked with sauce where he'd mopped it with tortillas. "You look uncomfortable, Mason."

"I guess I am."

"Because my favorite ex refuses to talk. It makes people tense, like they're waiting for an eruption. An old only-child attention-getting ploy."

Lance had it wrong, though. The problem was my youth. At some point in the middle of his speech, I'd folded my hands on my lap and grown aware—keenly, overwhelmingly aware—of the defenseless softness of my skin and the tenderness of the underlying nerves. Time had battered Lance and Lara, encasing their spirits in crusty, windburned shells, but I'd developed no such coating. The world Lance described, so ravenous and faithless, so saturated with schemes and plots and traps, struck me as fatally inhospitable. Chances were I'd manage to survive, but how, exactly, and at what cost? I felt myself aging even as I wondered this. I felt the crackly dryness setting in.

"That it hasn't worked out must hurt like holy hell," Lance said, reaching for the breakfast bill. He brought out a checkbook, much to my relief, and signed his name, though the checkbook's cover read "AlpenCross." When he entered the figure in the ledger, I saw that the account held quite a sum: seventeen thousand five hundred and fifty dollars.

"Who's up for a hike?" Lance asked. "Buckhorn Falls, four miles. A little light cardio to start the day. Sunblock, fresh water, and trail mix in my daypack. Maybe we'll come across a calving elk."

At last Lara spoke: "I still believe in love. I always will. It's my blessing and my burden."

Our waitress, who'd come up beside her, said, "Ditto, hon." They shared a long look, then the waitress took Lance's check. Lara watched her walk off with moist pink eyes.

"You need to get right with the Lord," Lance said.

"Get fucked."

"There. The first step. The eruption."

"So hard you hemorrhage."

"Anally, presumably," Lance said.

Lara nodded. Then we all went hiking.


The boots Lance gave me to replace my dress shoes were tight in the toes but loose around the heels. After walking in them for an hour, up a switchbacking path of mud and jagged stones that was blocked every few hundred yards by fallen pines that the Forest Service had flagged but not yet cut, I could feel my heartbeat in my feet as well as the warm, oily ooze of broken blisters. Instead of pushing the pain aside, I did as my father had taught my buddies and me during a freezing fifth-grade camping trip and forced myself to dwell inside the agony until it started to feel normal.

Lara fell back about two miles up, telling us she wanted to gather wildflowers but looking like she intended to take a nap, and Lance and I picked up our pace, passing the water bottle back and forth until we were gulping each other's blended saliva. I hoped he lived as cleanly as he pretended to. I walked two steps behind him to watch his calves flex, a rhythmic display of focused power that seemed to reveal some obscure, essential lesson about the nature of motion itself. Spirit, according to *Discourses*, was a by-product of activity, like the reflection from a spinning fan blade, and our souls in the end did not reside within us but flowed outward from our movements. This conflicted with certain other doctrines, but such conflicts just gave us topics for debate.

I softened on Lance as we climbed through aspen groves whose mottled profusions of trembling leaf-shaped shadows and rich, humid layers of moss and mushroom smells brought on a feeling of storybook enchantment. His voice sounded more sincere in these surroundings, less distorted by pride and pain. He named the plants we passed, the types of rock. When a ladybug landed on the back of his right hand, he showed it to me, then held it near his whitish, wind-chapped lips and carefully puffed it back into the air.

"How well do you know Betsy?" I wanted to trust him.

"You've seen her since that night?"

"A time or two."

"She's everything I wanted when I was young and everything I distrust now that I'm not. I guess you can tell that I've answered this question before."

"Who asked it?"

"Lots of people. The girl provokes that. Why she stays down in the minors I don't know—she could be out there playing the big stadiums. She has the right build and all the moves." Lance snugged down a shoulder strap on his orange pack by tugging the end of a hanging black nylon tab. "I'd say steer clear, except you probably won't, and if you do, she'll come back so hard and strong . . . can you reach behind me there, the bottom zipper, and maybe you'll notice a medication organizer, see-through plastic, with little flip-up lids?"

He took his pills without water, five or six of them, his chin tilted up and his throat stretched long and tight like a pelican swallowing a minnow. He seemed to be able to track the pills' descent; he didn't look down until they'd reached his stomach, at which point he shut his eyes and mumbled something that might have been a brief, memorized prayer. The man had his layers, his levels; I could see that. AlpenCross was just a wrapping for them.

A hundred yards farther on, Lance said, "Bipolar. But maybe they don't have that where you come from. We didn't have it down here until five years ago. We barely had adult ADHD. I'm always a pioneer with these new things, at least as far as the greater Snowshoe area. I think they kick off in the San Francisco suburbs, or Cambridge, Massachusetts, around the colleges. You've slept with her?"

Once I'd caught up, I fibbed to him.

"Good. Your higher self might have a chance then." Still, the look Lance gave me was grim and pitying. There might have been envy there, too. Between his eyebrows. It was time that I let him play nature guide again.

We came out in a sandy clearing atop a ridge whose boulder-strewn, treeless shoulders sloped so far down that the ponds at their base looked like shreds of silver foil. Colorado wasn't Montana. It was steeper. More violence had gone into forming its terrain. And unlike Wyoming, which seemed spent and petrified, this place felt restless, charged. I'd never experienced such crashing sunsets, such surging, erupting dawns. Through my boot soles I thought I could feel a deep-down hum, conducted through the granite and the gravel, that was either the echo of a past earthquake or the buildup to a new one. No wonder people in Colorado kept moving, always running, skiing, climbing, racing. No wonder Lance had adopted his swift, long stride. The planet itself spun faster here, it seemed, and just staying upright required leaning forward.

Lance shrugged and dipped one shoulder and slid his pack off. He set it on the ground, untied a cord, and folded back its topmost flap, his movements soft, deliberate, and exaggerated. I could tell he was going for his Bible, since Elder Stark behaved identically toward his copy of *Discourses*—as though it was made of blown glass, and irreplaceable.

Lance held the book in one hand and read it silently, his body angled toward the thousand-foot drop, which was just a yard or two away. The Effinghams' private mountain loomed miles off, and a couple of times he gazed in its direction, trying, it appeared, to clear his thoughts so as to memorize some verse or phrase. I studied the backs of my hands; I couldn't watch him. Other people's devotions embarrassed me, perhaps because, like other people's kisses, they rarely looked genuine when viewed too closely.

He snapped the book shut as though he'd settled something, then tucked it up high and tight under one arm. He opened his stance to me and I stepped closer, into a warm updraft near the ridge. It smelled of green grass from the valley and in its currents star-shaped bits of seed fluff swerved and tumbled.

"I almost pushed someone off here once," Lance said. "I planned it, I pictured it, and weighed the consequences. I even carried out a little test run. The thing's still down there somewhere—a canvas sack stuffed with a good eighty pounds of rocks and dirt. That's how profoundly effed up I was back then, particularly in regard to women I 'loved.' What scared me off in the end was how the sack stayed nearly completely intact the whole way down and didn't shred or explode like I expected. It told me that they could identify the body."

I wasn't sure how to acknowledge these disclosures, delivered so flatly, with such a level stare. I made a rough sound in my throat, glanced down, glanced sideways. I shifted my weight very slightly to my rear foot but decided it made me seem timid and shifted it back. It came to me that I was being addressed not as Lance's friend or confidant but as a dispassionate student of human depravity—as a fellow theologian, really. First, he'd saturate me with ugly storytelling, and then he'd try to show me proof, in the form of the new, redeemed person standing before me, that AlpenCross's god was great and merciful, the only god truly worthy of my loyalty. Then, no doubt, he'd offer me a membership.

Fair was fair. I deserved this, I decided. But I resented the setting Lance had chosen. Elder Stark and I approached prospects in their homes, on the street, in cafés, in comfortable surroundings where they were always free to walk away from us. Up here, though, a person would have to fly away.

At first Lance proceeded as I'd predicted. To the crime of premeditating a murder he added a host of other offenses whose details filled out his earlier chronicle of Snowshoe Springs' decline. He'd peddled a drug known as angel dust, he said, through a regional ring of high-school students, one of whom he'd had a romance with that led to her commitment to a mental hospital. He'd been at fault in a drunken auto accident, which he'd avoided prosecution for because the people he hurt were Mexican peach pickers driving an unlicensed truck without insurance coverage. More recently—just five years ago, he said—

he'd enticed three young women to cooperate with a "perverted Web site" he'd created that allowed men from all over the world to direct the girls in various acts, individually and together, that were observable on computer screens. The girls had made thousands of dollars, Lance informed me, and he, their manager, had earned much more. When the prettiest one threatened to expose the scheme after being recognized and contacted by a man who, it turned out, lived just three blocks away from her, Lance panicked. This girl was the person he'd thought of killing.

"But the worst thing," he said, "was those felt like happy years to me. I drove a classic Mercedes convertible. I scuba dived in Antigua twice a winter. And—please don't tell Lara, don't ruin her illusions—this ridiculous 'Little Eff' she set her sights on, the guy with the tiny penis and the big jet, we partied together, in secret, several times, in international waters on his yacht. Models, video cameras, black tar heroin, this weird rich young Arab guy who traded platinum over his sat phone while getting his big toe sucked—those sailing trips were Sodom on the high seas. And I couldn't get enough. I gloried in it."

"At breakfast . . ." I said, my first venture into speech for ten or fifteen minutes.

"I know, I know. I made Lara feel bad for stuff that's far more innocent, but I'm trying to train her to take responsibility. Comparing her sins to mine won't minimize them. I know, though. It's unjust. It's inexcusable. I'm afraid it's a sick old dynamic I slip into and only by grace will it ever be relieved. And believe me, I pray for that daily. Hourly. I'll show you my knees if you want. They're black and blue."

Lance was speaking and thinking at a furious clip by then, his neck flushed streaky red, his gestures motorized. If his intention was to demonstrate how undeserving he'd been of spiritual amnesty, he'd already convinced me. He couldn't quit, though.

Reliving his degradation had struck some spark in him and it was glowing now like a blown-on coal. And his tales had grown outlandish. Platinum? He'd started to say "gold," stopped at the vowel, wet his crackly lips, and then reached out for something less common, more specialized. I'd seen it: momentum overrunning fact.

To help Lance, to bring him around, I said, "Miraculous."

He repeated the word, but his thoughts were clearly still shoving him further away, toward some ultimate dark drama that he might or might not have actually lived through but whose telling would let out the pressure inside his skull. Lara, who'd lived with him, must have seen this coming when she excused herself to gather wildflowers.

"Miraculous that you managed to turn back. A voice? Was it a voice, Lance?"

"I don't hear voices. That's never been a part of it."

"I'm sorry."

He glared at me. "People should think before they say things."

"What changed you? That's all, Lance. That's all I want to know."

"So you are or you aren't prepared to let me finish?"

This was grinding. This was work. My attention strayed out past the ridge and I envisioned my partner's patient labors with Eff Sr., who longed for the pleasure of eating his own bison and might give some share of his fortune for the privilege. If such payment were offered, maybe we should take it. Maybe our services warranted nothing less.

Lance removed his Christian Bible from his armpit and pressed it with rigid, crossed hands against his heart. The comfort this seemed to provide him was real and physical; his breathing slowed, his locked-up hips unstiffened. Next might come tears, if his body weren't so dehydrated. My own need for water felt dangerously acute.

"It's home, but I need to move away," Lance said. "I meet someone who's not from here and I see that. I'm faking it, man. I act saved, but I'm not. I have history here, and it's thick. It's thick and sticky. I go downtown, it's in half the ladies' eyes; I hike up here, it's below me on that ledge there. I came a whole lot closer than I told you."

"Thoughts are thoughts and that's all they are, Lance. Thoughts. Read to me from your Bible. Something calming."

He seemed to like this idea. He traced a finger down a densely printed concordance page. It was one of those scriptures with gold-edged, crinkly paper, and it rustled as he flipped through it. "Here we go now. This is from John. It's my new bedtime verse." He coughed into his fist, then looked at me. "One last little thing first. A favor."

"Only one."

"Now, exactly—I mean this, *exactly*; I need to *see* it; this helps me, I can't explain why; it helps unstick things—what did my little lost Betsy let you do to her? The usual, or past that? How far past that? My savior and I have a deal—he lets me ask these things. He knows how deep the hurt goes. Describe her outfit."

When I reached the bottom, alone, two hours later, Lara was in her Jeep, with music playing. The way she turned the car key and pushed the gearshift, gently, with minimal motion and no noise, felt like an indirect apology. She knew what she knew, and she knew that I knew now too, and that part of my knowledge was that she might have spared me but hadn't because of her greed for sympathy. When she looked like she might defend herself, or Lance, I raised a stern hand that she was right to flinch from. "He can walk home," I told her. "Lance needs a long, long walk." Later, as we drove into the campground, I spotted my partner's bike against the van and asked to be taken back to town and dropped there. I just wasn't ready for his stories. They'd breed with the others I'd heard and hatch new monsters, because there was no such thing as separation here, not once you'd started listening. Never listen.

# ELEVEN

**For most of the evening** and well into the night I sat propped against a pillow on my bunk while Elder Stark paced the van from end to end and recounted his visit to the ranch, which he called by the name of its brand, the Rocking F. From somewhere he'd picked up an insulated mug that held at least a quart of ice and cola and allowed him, by use of an elbowed plastic straw, to prod his sagging metabolism with sugar whenever his presentation slowed or wandered. The cola would darken the straw for a few seconds, followed by a creeping facial tightening that convinced me his body no longer wholly belonged to him but now responded chiefly to outside substances, of which the soft drink was probably just one. In the right front pocket of his suit pants I'd spied a small bulge that rattled when he moved and must have been a bottle full of pills. Twice he broke off his speech to use the bathroom, and both times the bulge had switched pockets when he returned.

"They take a lot of steam up there," he said. "I'd never done that before. It's interesting. The heat and the fact that you can't see each other's faces even though you're sitting side by side makes people very honest for some reason. Eff Sr. told me some things he probably shouldn't have—where his money first came from, for example. Foreign animal medical experiments."

I squinted at him to show I needed more.

"Apparently the government has rules about what scientists can do to animals, especially to apes and chimpanzees, when they're testing a new medicine or drug. Eff Sr. built laboratories in El Salvador where those laws didn't have to be obeyed. He flew in the animals straight from Africa, including some species you're not allowed to capture. He told me he had to bribe an actual king for them, I can't remember of which country. The king got angry once about late payments and had his army surround Eff Sr.'s airplane. It couldn't take off for six days and all the apes inside died of dehydration. That's when he finally closed the laboratories and bought his first cable-TV company, in Tulsa. He cried when he told me all this. His voice was cracking. Little Eff said he shouldn't feel bad because his laboratories helped invent a new bladder cancer treatment, but his father said he still dreams about dead primates. He wonders if that's where his stomach problems come from."

"The guilt," I said.

"The debt to nature. That's why he brought in the wolves. To even things out."

"With who?"

"The universe."

"The 'universe'? That's really how he talks?"

"Late at night he does. With me, at least. Around his son

he's quieter, more practical, but he says that I bring out his philosophical side. He's always had it, he told me, but he hides it. He has some private theories on world history he writes in a notebook stored inside a gun safe. Human beings have nearly died off twice, he thinks, once in the Bronze Age and then again around the year one thousand. Both times 'the Keepers' nursed us back. Some are scientists, some are businessmen. They're still around, but the common folk resent them. The Keepers protect them anyway."

"He dreamed this up all by himself?"

"He had some help. There's a famous dead lady philosopher he loves. He worked it up from dreams he had after finishing his favorite book by her."

"What's the book called? I'd like to have a look at it."

"Something like *The Keepers Quit*. Or *Samson Sits Down*. He was talking pretty quickly."

"So why do the common folk resent them?"

"Who?"

"These Andromedan types who rescued Humans on Earth. Human life on Earth."

"That's your facetious voice. It's not appreciated."

"I want an answer," I said. "Why don't the commoners like the Keepers?"

"Because the commoners are proud, I guess. They like to think they can take care of themselves."

"It sounds like the Keepers are even prouder."

"I guess they deserve to be," my partner said.

The tales went on, outlandish and disconcerting, accompanied by the racket from the campground, which had filled up with motor homes over the last few days and developed a lively social life. The license plates were from Texas and California, and most of the tourists were thin-haired older couples who enjoyed grilling hamburgers on the concrete pads set in the grassy strips beside the parking spots. One spot over from ours a bearded fellow who dressed in overalls and sleeveless T-shirts that showed off his densely interlocked tattoos of sea monsters, crucifixes, and thorny roses would uncase a guitar after supper and strum till dark, attracting a circle of listeners in lawn chairs. Though they'd only just met and soon would separate, they drank beer and wine and clapped and swayed and laughed, concluding their parties with hearty, tuneless sing-alongs. A few of the campers breathed through plastic tubes attached to portable oxygen tanks on wheels, and I sensed that almost all of them knew they didn't have much more time on earth. Maybe this accounted for their willingness to pitch in with strangers and form a neighborhood.

"The important part," my partner said, "is that I think I gained Eff Sr.'s trust. We studied *Discourses* every afternoon. It relaxed him, relaxed his colon. He's eating meat again. He told me he got more relief from our four days together than his doctors have given him in seven years."

"Does he want to convert?"

"We have to take it slowly. People want things from men like him. They make appeals. Save the orphans. Save the chamber orchestra. There's a fellow who started a church of the outdoors here—"

"I hiked with him this morning. Lance," I said.

"If he claimed to be friends with Little Eff, he lied. He told you about a boat, I bet. A yacht. Their grand old times together on a yacht."

"He said Little Eff stole Lara. They were married."

"People don't steal people, Mason. It can't be done."

My partner's loyalty repulsed me. He spoke like a paid defender, a hired aide, without any views or opinions of his own.

If it had been me who'd heard the monkey story, which stuck in my mind like a food scrap in a molar, rotting away in a place I couldn't quite reach, I wouldn't have accepted Eff Sr.'s tears. I would have walked off through the steam and slammed the door on him.

"This Lance is a pest. A parasite. A barnacle. That's what the Effinghams call his type: the barnacles."

"I've been thinking we need to leave this place," I said. "I've been thinking we'd do awfully well in New York City."

"That's not where the central powers are nowadays."

"That's *exactly* where they are, according to my reading back in Bluff."

"Those library books are from Missoula garage sales."

My partner stopped pacing and sucked his straw. It gurgled. He pried the lid off the mug and opened a window and slung the ice cubes out into the dark. The nightly campground sing-along had started and before the window was closed I heard the words: "*If I had a hammer . . .*" The passion behind them startled me.

"According to Little Eff you've met a woman here. The news is you're in love," my partner said.

This information surprised me, though it shouldn't have. The tattling elves of Snowshoe never rested. Betsy, however, wasn't one of them. At the end of our first night together she'd clasped my warm, flushed face between her palms and made me promise, eye to eye, to shield what she called her most prized possession: her privacy. She told me something awful had happened once that had turned half the town against her, including her mother, and though she insisted the charges were false and mischievous, she said she was still repairing her good name. My talk with Lance had convinced me that her fears were warranted, whatever their basis in real events. I didn't plan to ask; it didn't matter. On the Thonic level, a couple meets in innocence, and the twists and turns in the paths they walked beforehand are revealed as straight and necessary. Combination transforms—absolutely, if it's allowed to.

"Little Eff said he spoke to her father," my partner said. "They do business together occasionally. In Denver."

"What kind of business?"

"I counsel. I don't pry. The Rocking F sets high standards for its guests."

Elder Stark slid his belt off, hung it on a hook, stepped out of his pants, and unbuttoned his white shirt, proceeding backward, from the bottom up. Something had happened to his nervous system; his reflexes seemed scrambled, all crossed up. Things he used to do with his right hand, such as loosen his shoelaces or scratch his nose, he did with his left now, I'd noticed. He also blinked more, though never with both lids at the same time.

He sat on the edge of his mattress and combed his hair, which had finally grown out long enough to comb. His shorts had slipped low around his thickening waist and uncovered a track of pink welts from the tight waistband. "We're moving tomorrow," he said. "I paid the campground. Eff Sr. offered his guesthouse. I accepted. Lauer approves. He told me we've been called. No more pestering strangers, no more tracting. The Effinghams are our one and only job now."

"And he made this decision by whose authority?"

My partner settled his hands on his bare knees and looked up at the ceiling of the van. In its bubble-shaped amber skylight there were stars, blurred and enlarged by a film of greasy dirt. "You don't seem to understand the situation. The Seeress is about to pass," he said. "My mother's shut away with the First Council. The co-op's run out of flour, oil, and sugar because everyone's rushing to use their Virtue Coupons. The succession looks cloudy. Everything looks cloudy. There is no authority, Mason. We're on our own."

# TWELVE

**The guesthouse of the Rocking F,** which wasn't much smaller than the main house, had two separate wings, and in the second wing, behind a locked door we didn't have a key to and hidden by curtains that stayed drawn all day, a man whom we'd been ordered not to speak to was writing a book we were not supposed to ask about. In the evenings he stood in the yard with a cigar and stretched his neck and mumbled to himself, but otherwise we never saw him. His meals were delivered by a Mexican maid who also did his laundry and handled his mail, which was dominated by large manila envelopes. In the mornings, before the sun rose, he played loud music and engaged in some kind of exercise routine that shook the floors and walls, but after that he was silent. I guessed his age to be about forty, maybe forty-five, but I'd never seen him up close or in full sunlight, only across the lawn, at dusk, so it was hard to tell. Elder Stark thought the man was famous but had no evidence, just a vague Hobo hunch. I thought so, too. Only a great one could bear such isolation.

The comforts of the guesthouse embarrassed me. The sheets and the bedding were cotton, their labels said, but they felt like satin against the skin, and the mattresses rested high up on their frames under fluffy domes of quilts and blankets. On the beds, the sofas, and the armchairs fancy pillows were heaped on fancy pillows—so many that some of them had to be removed before a person could sit or lie. In the tall bathroom mirrors my body looked leaner than usual, my face more symmetrical, my eyes much clearer. The soaps and shampoos came nestled in a basket lined with perfumed pink tissue, and over the sink, arranged on the shelves of a green enamel cabinet, were old-fashioned shaving brushes, safety razors, cotton balls, and bottles of spice cologne. Using these items, I felt strangely ladylike, as though my appearance mattered to the world and grooming was a job of consequence. I took up whitening my teeth again.

On our second day there, after grinding our coffee beans and spooning them into a gold mesh filter to brew, my partner looked around the kitchen and said, "Mason, this is what's possible in life." He left it there, and I spent the next few minutes speculating on what he'd meant. Possible for us? For anyone? He couldn't have meant anyone. What bothered me was the finality of the remark, as though Elder Stark had beheld the end of history, the climax of all human striving, in a coffee machine.

We ate breakfast at the main house with Little Eff, who'd costumed himself for a movie about a day wrangling livestock on the open range. The red handkerchief knotted around his neck drew attention to his bony Adam's apple, whose contours when viewed from the side repeated in miniature the profile of his face. The thorn-scratched denim of his shirt contrasted oddly with his pampered skin, which was visibly saturated with lotion and reeked so strongly of vanilla that when I sat down beside him at the table I looked around for a tray of cream-filled pastries.

"I'll show you the lay of the place today," he said. "That way you can go out alone, unsupervised. My father offers his apologies. He'd ride along, but he's closing at noon central time on a Mandan Sioux casino contract. Normally he'd do it on the phone, but these Natives, they like to touch flesh when they make deals. They still do the pipe thing, too. It's fun to see."

"He's flying?" my partner asked.

"At nine, to Bismarck."

My partner frowned. "No travel. We discussed that. No changes in drinking water for a month."

"Xavier filled a few thermoses. It's covered." Little Eff uncapped a bottle of green hot sauce and shook some drops onto his pale gray omelet. He avoided yolks not for health reasons, he'd told us, but because of an incident at a Maine fishing lodge when he was twelve years old. The guide gave him a hard-boiled egg for lunch, and when he unpeeled it he found a big-eyed embryo complete with a tiny beak and stubby wings. Screaming and shaking, he flung it into the water, where it floated for a few moments before attracting a school of nibbling pickerel. Little Eff said the sight made him vomit into the lake and led to the guide's dismissal from the lodge. "My father raised hell. He overreacted, probably, but that's how this family works: we go balls out, especially for each other. It's called 'love.'"

We set out for the ranch tour in a long-cab pickup so new that its right rear window still had tape marks where the price sticker had been removed. Little Eff drove and I sat in the back, having lost a coin toss with my partner that I hadn't even requested—I'd told him I understood his need for leg room. Still, he insisted on being fair. His gesture seemed meant to prove to Little Eff that Apostles, like Effinghams, stuck up for each other, prizing unity above all else, but it appeared to go unnoticed.

We drove beside a dry streambed through tall grass that powdered the hood and windshield with seed and pollen. I could feel fallen tree branches breaking under the tires. Little Eff called the ranch a "comprehensive ecosytem" and described how his father bought the place for him during a ski vacation nine years ago. Little Eff was living in San Diego then, running a family-owned network of AM radio stations and suffering through a marriage to a young woman who played professional beach volleyball and couldn't bear children, she'd told him on their honeymoon, because of a drug she'd taken to build her muscles. "My liver enzymes were screwy, I had a gut, I woke up with cluster headaches every morning, and my wife, I found out, was still on major steroids, so crazy and pumped that she lost her driver's license for going sixty through a school zone, twice. She slugged me a few times, too. Then Dad stepped in. He flew me out here on the Gulfstream to our condo, sold the radio stations behind my back, annulled my marriage in seventy-two hours—a six-figure sum changed hands, that's all I know; the woman's in Maui now, dating teenage surfers—and gave me the deed to all you see around us. 'You're a gentleman now,' he said. 'No more coat and tie. Just give me a grandchild someday, that's all I ask.' "

Little Eff slowed the truck and reached in front of my partner for a pair of binoculars from the glove compartment. He'd spotted something. Steering with one hand, he scanned a far-off ridge of scrubby cedars, then passed the field glasses over his shoulder to me. "They're on a kill," he whispered. "Three of them. To the right of that big cleft rock, at two o'clock."

I fingered a dial, focused. Nothing there.

"The alpha's the one in the middle. Silver fur. In a minute, he'll smell us and run. His name's Napoleon. He ran off old Nosferatu last December and mated with Nefertiti. Got him now?"

I kept trying but it was useless; my eyes had started to water, blurring everything. My partner twisted around and scowled at me. I was disappointing our host, our lord, our patron. "By the rock," he hissed. "Two o'clock. What's wrong? You're blind?"

"Too late," Little Eff said. "They got our scent. They're gone. The sighting of a lifetime. That's a shame."

The mood in the truck cab flattened as we pressed on. Nothing else on the ranch could match the wolves, and though Little Eff continued pointing out various beauty spots and natural features—a steaming mineral spring, a herd of mule deer, an ancient tepee ring—he sounded bored, even depressed after a while. My partner asked questions designed to let him boast about the expense of his hand-built jackleg fences, the lushness of his summer pastures, and the abundance of eagles in his blue skies, but Little Eff declined to play his part, answering only "No kidding" or "You're right." His pride in the place seemed thinner than he'd pretended and dependent on the excitement of his audience, which had to start out high and keep on rising. We'd failed him, though, and turned him from Person One to Person Two. As we drove past a hillside with dozens of grazing bison, he unhooked a radio mounted on the dashboard and said, "I'm at Cottonwood Meadow. We need lunch." The hulking, snorting brown beasts went unacknowledged and carried on feeding, oblivious, prehistoric, turning their heads between ripping bites of grass to watch out for saber-toothed tigers and men with spears.

A ranch hand on a Honda ATV delivered a cooler of tuna-salad sandwiches, canned lemonade, and thawing Fudgsicles, which we consumed while sitting on the ground. Little Eff spread out his handkerchief for a place mat and Elder Stark quoted a sentence from Little Red Elk's journals that I couldn't believe he'd managed to memorize. "As food sustains our bodies, yielding up its vital elements as it wends its way through us to the soil, so do we sustain the All-in-One, into whose belly we pass and are dissolved, only to be reconstituted as the creative Etheric Understrata."

"You never use 'amen,' " said Little Eff. It seemed he was used to my partner's verbal unfurlings.

" 'Amen' means a prayer has ended," my partner said. "Our prayers never end."

"Who wrote that passage, anyway?"

My partner told him.

Little Eff said, "Bullshit. He had help. That's not their kind of vocabulary or grammar."

"It's an inspired pronouncement," my partner said.

"Inspired by whites?"

"Inspired every which way," my partner said.

I felt proud of him for once, both for his snappy answer and for his courage in planting our message in such unlikely surroundings, among people whose lives it could only complicate. He'd always been the one with vision, and who was to say that his dream of bringing home some fantastic bequest that might secure Bluff's future didn't contain a vast compassion, too. I watched Little Eff peel the wrapper from his soft Fudgsicle, hold it sideways, and lick away the drips. It hit me that he and his father and all their kind, the bosses, the rulers, the powers of Terrestria, deserved true knowledge as much as anyone.

"I'll be in town tonight," said Little Eff, "so you're on your own as far as dinner. Call the main house at four and make requests, they'll see what's on hand and cook it if they can. I think we got in some fresh king salmon yesterday. Edward's a fish eater."

Edward—the writer's name. I'd seen it on an envelope left for him on his doorstep by the maid.

"Will your father be back to join us?" Elder Stark said.

"Can I be frank? The man is searching. He's in a long-term state of mind. For decades he's been all business. It took a toll. Obviously. And not just on his organs. Since Mom died"—he sent a glance north, in the direction of the woman's mountain memorial—"he's had two marriages of ten months apiece, a dinner date with the president's first cousin that ended in a huge quarrel about Israel, and a night with a lady I met at the Bellagio back when I wasn't thinking very straight and hired to console him on his sixty-fifth birthday. He's lonely, he wants answers, and he wants peace. He wants to enjoy a Thanksgiving without cramps. And after all he's done for me, I owe him. I owe him whatever he wants. So I'm indulging you. Maybe you can feel it: my forbearance. It's not my custom to open the Rocking F to crude gypsy mystics angling for a windfall."

I set my half-eaten sandwich on my lap. Tension had caused me to squeeze it and mash the bread. My partner tightened his crossed legs and sucked his lips into his mouth. Off behind him the bison had gathered at a watering hole and were shoving and jostling for position as small nervous birds pecked their necks and backs for insects.

"So let's put it all on the table," Little Eff said. "It's almost July, a busy season here. We entertain friends. We throw functions. We host a gathering. I didn't expect you two fellows, but here you are, and as long as my father's amused, that's cool. A generous check for your cause? You might just get one. It's nothing to us, and we live to starve the tax man. You can do a few chores if you want to show good manners—it's in your best interest; Dad loves men who sweat—but otherwise I have just one favor to ask. Or is that one favor too many?"

We didn't answer him, or feel expected to.

Little Eff snapped the tab off his can of lemonade and drank it down in one long freezing swallow that he'd regret when he grew older, because such digestive shocks add up. "This favor I'm asking, Mason, would come from you; your friend here has his hands full with my father. It relates to a woman who's flying in next week—one I'm fairly serious about and plan to ask to stay the summer here."

I nodded my head.

"You're sweet on someone, too, I hear. Seen the girl but never spoken to her. Very pretty. And controversial. But that's just Snowshoe Springs. You'll probably hear yours truly slandered, too."

"My partner says you're friendly with her father."

"Former Olympic freestyle skiing god, Audi and Jaguar dealer, killer poker player, and someone who used to be able to get you anything as long as you swore not to ask him where he got it. We used to meet up in Las Vegas, at the fights. He taught me to how to lose money and keep my sense of humor."

"You're still in touch, though."

"I'm a Jaguar prospect. Rob makes his pitch, we do our little dance, he calls again six month later, someday I'll buy. Here's the favor, though. My lady friend doesn't know a soul here. She needs company. You know how women are. A pal. To shop with. She's the same age as your girl, so what I'm thinking is: a couple of double dates, a picnic maybe, and then, if I'm lucky, those two will hit it off and I'll have some time to myself this summer. Yes? Otherwise she'll get bored and she'll scoot off and I'll be forty-one and even balder. Richer, too, but that only goes so far now. This new generation, they want the hair. The package."

My partner sucked his Fudgsicle and eyed me. I gathered he was in on this. He'd already assured Little Eff that I'd cooperate.

"I'll call and ask her."

"I'm paying, of course. You realize that. My treat."

"Thank you. I'll ask her. When next week?"

"Next Friday. We can drive down to Aspen, if she'd like. Whatever tickles her."

"I'll ask," I said.

Little Eff picked up his handkerchief, shook out the crumbs, and tucked it in his shirt pocket, flaring out one of the corners for effect. He looked restored, revived. My partner did, too. We collected the Fudgsicle sticks, the cans, the sandwich bags, and dumped them into the cooler and put the lid on. When I saw that no one else was going to do it, I lifted the cooler into the truck bed, and Little Eff thanked me with a wink. He insisted I ride up front with him this time, and as we pulled out he patted my left knee and tilted his head toward the bison, which were resting now. I apologized to him for failing to see the wolves and he forgave me with a shrug. We were buddies suddenly, it seemed. I gave myself license to ask a question that had been welling up in me all morning.

"I realize Edward needs his privacy, but has he written any other books? I'd like to read one. I'm curious," I said.

My partner reached over the seat and squeezed my shoulder as Little Eff said, "I thought we made this clear. Edward's project is no concern of yours. As a matter of fact, it's no concern of mine. It's purely my father's affair."

"I'm sorry," I said.

"There are boundaries here. Respect them."

I said that I would.

"Good enough. Just arrange things with your girl," he said. A few minutes later he used the rearview mirror to address my partner in the back. "I'm sorry about insulting your Indian. We actually revere the red man on the Rocking F—my father especially. I was making a point about language, not intelligence. I'm really sincerely apologetic. Cool? Are we cool or not on this?"

"We're cool."

My partner nudged me from behind and I said it, too, though not as smoothly and naturally. I practiced the phrase in my head all afternoon, and when I used it at breakfast the next day to answer Eff Sr. when he asked me if I found the guesthouse satisfactory, he didn't correct me or give me a strange look, which meant I must have learned to use it right.

# THIRTEEN

**Little Eff's black Suburban,** driven by a ranch hand and looking like a cross between a hearse and one of the armored military vehicles that I'd been seeing on the news, arrived at Betsy's mother's house at six, an hour earlier than we'd expected and before either one of us was ready to go. Betsy was still in her bedroom in the basement altering a tiny pink children's T-shirt she'd bought at a Red Cross thrift shop for fifty cents. The shirt showed an elephant standing on its back feet, balancing a beach ball on its trunk. Though it barely covered her stomach, she wanted it shorter. She also wanted to trim the sleeves. When she'd told me she planned to wear it on our night out, I'd held my tongue. The beach ball, drawn with sequins, was positioned precisely over Betsy's right breast and stretched by the fullness there into an oval.

I was upstairs with Betsy's mother, Helen, whom I'd met for

the first time that afternoon and had taken an instant liking to because her strong voice, quick opinions, and springy manner reminded me of the ladies back in Bluff. For an hour we'd been discussing Helen's massage work—a vocation she said she'd taken up twelve years ago after her divorce from Betsy's father, whom she referred to as "the Huckster." She said she refused to speak ill of the poor man, and then went on to tell me that since their breakup he hadn't managed to keep a steady girlfriend and often resorted to prostitutes for company. She'd heard he'd caught a disease from one of them and been blackmailed by another, citing as her source the senior salesman at his Audi and Jaguar dealership, which, she said, he'd embezzled from to the point of bankruptcy. She sounded boastful telling me these things, as though her ex-husband's ill fortune was the result of a successful curse she'd placed on him, but something told me she still loved the man and awaited the day when he'd come to her for help. I asked her if Betsy still saw him and she said no, not that she knew of, but that she couldn't be sure because her daughter was so private. Did I know, for example, that she cuddled with stuffed bears? I admitted I didn't. "In her sleep," said Helen. "I creep down and watch her sometimes. She looks so cozy. Once in a while I snuggle in next to her and lie there for a while, to feel the heat. I miss her baby years. I miss the odors. Even the bad ones. The diapers. The sour-milk breath."

"Most mothers miss those," I ventured.

"She may have nursed too long. Four years is too long. I made a great mistake there. I'd like to see her settled soon, with children, but here she still is, no plans, no life, no structure. Maybe that will be your job."

"What?"

"The structure."

We returned to the subject of reflexology. Helen believed

that the feet control the body and tried to convince me of her theory by instructing me to remove my shoes and socks, pressing her thumbtips into my big toes, and asking me to monitor my heart rate, which she claimed to be able to influence through touch. It did slow down some after a few minutes, but I attributed this change to the valerian tea she'd made me drink after I'd confessed to feeling anxious about the coming evening. Little Eff's plans seemed needlessly elaborate: a two-hour drive to Aspen, dinner, dancing, and—he'd sworn me to silence about this part, explaining that his date, a woman named Hadley, had accused him once of lacking spontaneity and therefore deserved to be taken by surprise—a wee-hours ride back to Snowshoe in a helicopter, which would deposit us atop a glacier for a sunrise catered champagne breakfast.

"If the fellow's a friend of the Huckster," Helen said, responding to my description of the big night, "he overdoes things out of insecurity. They're little boys, that crowd. Big toys, small minds, and—let's be blunt here; anatomy is destiny—even smaller ding-a-lings." She formed a caliper with a thumb and index finger, holding them a couple of inches apart and then closing the gap by half, to maybe one inch. "I'm speaking literally," Helen said. "I've had these men on my table many a time."

I didn't like this line of talk. I never had. It was the utmost in False Comparison.

"Fortunately," Helen said, "that's not a complex you'll ever suffer from personally. According to my daughter. Well, good for both of you."

Private. What a very private girl. As far as snuggling teddy bears, not people.

"What was the Huckster's friend's name again?" asked Helen.

"Errol Effingham Jr."

"The buffalo family?"

"They have a wolf pack, too."

"A colleague of mine—she does Swedish and deep tissue—worked on his father a few years back, I think. Pockmarked buttocks. Suffers from colitis. My friend said he fancied himself a sage, a thinker. He gave her a pamphlet he'd written. On wizards, was it?"

"The Keepers?"

"I don't remember—some made-up silliness. My friend said the thing was unreadable, illiterate, but I've heard that about your Book of Mormon, too."

"I'm not a Mormon. I'm an AFA. An Aboriginal Fulfilled Apostle."

"Well, there's good in all of it," she said.

"I'd like to think so. I don't know."

"I don't know, either; it's something you're meant to say these days. Whatever you are, though, my daughter seems to like it, so I like it, too. She's my cuddly angel pie. Wounded inside, I suppose, but aren't we all? My grandfather used to take me for naked swims and check between my legs for chiggers afterward, but I still achieved healthy intimacy in marriage, so, honestly, what great harm could it have done? I think we exaggerate these matters now. Still, this obsession of Betsy's with dress, with clothing—it's a reaction to *something*, obviously."

"Or it could be an anticipation."

"Interesting."

"People react to the future, not just the past," I said.

"This is why she likes you, isn't it? A man of ideas. In a clean white shirt."

I thanked her for what I gathered was a compliment and delved into the Matic and the Thonic, Preexistence, Perfection, and the rest of it, aware as I spoke of a glimmer in the air that usually preceded a bad cold or an incapacitating headache. Helen opened the teapot and held the teabag by the paper tag clipped to its string, dunking it a few times to strengthen the brew. She emptied the pot into our mugs, which advertised Hair We Go!, a local beauty shop. I could tell I'd lost her interest. I abandoned my lecture and looked around for something that might inspire a fresh topic, but the large, undivided room held little more than Helen's massage table, a stained blue sofa, and an oddly shaped structure about five feet tall made up of carpet-covered arms and platforms, on the highest of which an orange cat was sleeping. There were three or four paintings, but of scenes so neutral—a moonlit sailing ship and so on—that the moment I took my eyes from them I completely forgot what they depicted.

"When Betsy moved home after college," Helen said, as though resuming an interrupted thought, "she worked as a model for a year or two. Locally, regionally, not nationally. I'm afraid there were racy undergarments involved, at least in a few of the jobs. I found one once. Plastic, it felt like, black, with straps and buckles. I bring this up in case you've heard it else-where." She fixed me with a flat, appraising look while blowing across her mug with tight, pursed lips.

"No. Not exactly," I said after a pause.

"Just in case you do, though," Helen said, "I hope you won't think she's ruined or unfit. As a potential mate, I mean. Because that's why you're here, I assume. May I assume that?"

"Yes."

"Because if not, I'll toss you out of here. I'm very protective. I'm fierce. A momma grizzly."

"I'm starting to see that."

"I've told her: 'Snugglebug, you make poor choices. Your longing for a father blinds you, Cuddles. It's time for a husband,

and I'm the one who picks. No more artists. No more tricky trash. I'm not going to pay another ten thousand dollars next time you need your lovely young bare fanny erased from the computers of the world.' "

I'd finished my tea but pretended to sip it anyway. I needed time, though I didn't know for what, and I wished for some reason that my feet weren't bare, that I'd never exposed my toes to Helen's fingers. It had brought us too close too early and we were stuck now. Helen carried the teapot to the sink, rinsed it, dried it, placed it on a shelf, and turned back around to face me with crossed arms and a look that seemed both angry and beseeching. That's when I heard rumbling in the driveway and saw the glow of headlights in the curtains. I reached down for my shoes.

"At two and a half," said Helen, "she started biting me. She wanted off the breast. She'd had her fill. It didn't work, though, because it didn't hurt. Even when she drew blood, it didn't hurt. Love is a powerful painkiller, I guess."

I unrolled one of my socks and pulled it on. My feet smelled of sweat and lavender massage oil.

"Take her," said Helen. "Get her out of here."

The Suburban's rear seats were arranged to face each other across a low table equipped with sunken cup holders and a central well that held an ice bucket. Soft music streamed down from speakers in the ceiling as Little Eff uncorked a bottle of wine and held it steady, wrapped in a white towel, while the Suburban rounded another curve. The tilt of the floor and the pressure on my eardrums indicated to me that we were climbing, but the vehicle's purplish dark windows blocked my view and prevented me from estimating our speed. A tinted-glass screen concealed the driver, too, increasing my sense of detachment and dependence as well as my nervousness about a crash that I wouldn't see coming and wouldn't have time to brace for.

Little Eff filled our wineglasses once we'd reached a straightaway and toasted "the freedom of the American road," clinking his glass against Betsy's and then Hadley's but merely raising it when my turn came, which I felt was a slight and, possibly, bad luck. The women sat hip to hip and smiled and chatted, their legs crossed at the knees, their shoulders squared, their spines held taut and competitively erect. I suspected that before they could make friends, as Little Eff seemed so confident they would, they'd have to resolve the fundamental matter of who was prettier, and by just how much. Little Eff and I would have no say here; their contest would be private, its rules obscure, and its outcome final.

I asked Hadley what she did, then wished I hadn't. Like Little Eff, she clearly did nothing. Nothing I'd regard as work, at least.

He answered for her. "She designs."

I sensed a request to change subjects and honored it by asking Hadley where she grew up, a question that interested me far more than my first one because, after watching her for the last few minutes, I doubted that she'd be truthful about her origins, just as I doubted that Hadley was her real name or her face was the face that she'd been born with. Everything about her seemed invented: her prolonged pronunciations of words from books that are rarely heard out loud (she'd said of the wine "It's fetching but somewhat nebulous"); the annoyed way she kept flicking hair out of her eyes that she'd put there on purpose by tossing her head; the draftsmanlike neatness of her too-straight nose, identically dimpled cheeks, and her plump, bowed lips; and even the punctual little breaths she took between her measured swallows of wine. With Hadley, nothing was casual or careless; she timed every blink, considered every sigh.

"My family traveled," she answered. I detected a challenge to probe further and a warning that I might not get far if I did.

I went ahead. "From where?"

"You mean our base? D.C. My father worked out of D.C."

"For the government?"

"One would assume. We didn't ask him."

"A spook," Little Eff said. "Her father was a spy."

Hadley said, "He lived a life of service."

"Of all the places you traveled to," I asked, "which was your favorite? Which did you like best?" I glanced at Betsy, convinced she knew the game now and shared my skepticism about Hadley. I expected a wink but got a scowl.

"Rome," Hadley said.

"Why Rome?"

"Because it's Rome."

"I love your jeans," said Betsy. "I love the stitching, especially on the inseams. Vintage? New?"

"Reconstructed vintage," Hadley said. "There's a shop in La Jolla. I have their Web address. The owner used to costume Sharon Stone. Nina Karloff, a magical old Jewish lady. Very serene, very centered. She does tai chi. That shirt of yours, by the way—adorable."

Betsy thanked her. "I also love your boots."

It was no use now; I gave up needling Hadley. The beauty contest had ended in a draw, it seemed, and the women had formed the tight, exclusive partnership of the uncommonly tasteful and attractive. For the moment, there was no opposing team, but later on this evening, chances were, one would emerge and unity might prove crucial. Growing up in a faith ruled by women had taught me something: they face the world in pairs whenever possible. The only exception is the queen.

I helped myself to more wine as Little Eff opened the glass screen and asked the driver to watch out for elk and deer along the highway and to turn up the headlights until we got to Aspen, even if they blinded other drivers. Something told me the driver would ignore him the moment the screen slid shut and that Little Eff knew this but felt that giving orders, however they were received, was a duty required of him by Nature—a duty I had a feeling he resented. From what I saw, he was a timid man inside who mostly just wanted to enjoy good things. But there was the name, and the money, and the position, and whether he liked it or not, they made him boss.

Except around Hadley, it turned out. She didn't like our table at the restaurant because it stood in a cold spot by a window that Little Eff had tipped a man to seat us near.

He'd told me I'd love the view. I did. It sparkled. It reminded me of a train set that a neighbor had built in his attic for a son with kidney problems that the Seeress had deemed incurable. The father, a plumber, sold his truck and tools to pay for the lavish miniature wonderland, whose layout, he said, was inspired by a dream he'd had. Toothpick log cabins whose chimneys leaked cotton smoke clung to the sides of papier-mâché mountains topped by snowfields of glitter-sprinkled plaster. Rows of streetlamps with firefly-size bulbs illuminated storefronts with foil windows that faced on winding pebble-cobbled sidewalks thronged with people in bright enamel coats. I felt cheated when I saw this masterpiece. I was nine and I knew that no such village existed on earth, but I wished that one did, and I longed to dwell in it. The fact that I couldn't hope to angered me, and it also angered me that the Church had lied. Because if Bluff was perfect, as I'd been taught, then why had the sick boy's father not built its replica? Why had he envisioned this other, better place?

Now I knew. He'd been to Aspen, possibly; or somehow the All-in-One had shown him Aspen. Aspen existed—I could see it from my chair. The very same streetlamps and even the same people.

"I'm chilled," said Hadley. "I'm shivering. Why can't we sit by the fire? Let's try. Let's ask."

"I'll trade places with you. It's warmer here," I said, reluctant to give up the view I'd waited so long for.

But Little Eff wasn't strong, or found no reason to be, and I ended up with my back to Aspen's nightscape, next to a massive stone chimney decorated with rotting horse collars and rusty rock picks. Colorado adored its olden days. It hung on to junk that we threw away in Bluff or salvaged for parts that might still have a use. The past hadn't died there and so it wasn't worth missing, nor were its worn-out scraps worth idolizing. For time to pass it would have to go somewhere, and where would that be? Time sits. We move, it sits. Sometimes it trembles slightly, but that's all.

The table switch had put me beside Hadley and Little Eff with Betsy. The noisy room made it hard for them to hear us or for us to hear them, but Hadley didn't mind, it seemed—her only interest, suddenly, was me. This interest felt almost genuine, unlike the rest of her.

". . . what I think you may not realize yet," she said, following an extensive interrogation about my background and my people, "is that you carry it with you, in your *mien*. See Errol there, and then the man behind him, the one in the collarless white linen shirt—the one with the woman whose highlights need a touch-up? See how they guard themselves, sort of leaning back, all smiles and chuckles but actually not listening because they're always scanning their perimeters? You, though, don't do that. You lay yourself wide open. Your hands, for example—I've never seen you close them. You're totally frontal, totally exposed. I could pick up my knife here and hold your eyes with mine and reach around very slowly to the side and *sssttt*, before you know it, slit your throat."

I poked my fork into a shred of quail meat glazed in a berry sauce rich with forest flavors. Softened by candlelight, Hadley's face looked natural now, broader, more liquid, less acutely organized. It soaked me up, but her words squeezed me back out.

"I think you misinterpreted my jest," she said. "My point was you don't understand your own appeal, the source of your own charisma. Its unprotectedness. Feel flattered, Mason."

"I'll try. I'm not so good at that."

"Then flatter me back. I'm great at it," she said. "I'm serious. Say something wonderful. But swallow first."

I was chewing my quail meat and trying to make it last because there wasn't much of it. Hadley fingered the stem of her wineglass with her right hand and pressed the other one lightly against her neck as though she were checking her own pulse. Somehow the touch released a puff of perfume as dark and woodsy as my berry sauce. I still had no idea who she was, but her claims about having traveled as a youth seemed plausible now. She made such quick transitions. In the car she'd been pert and angular, at the window table sour and pushy, but here at the fireside table she swished, she flowed. Maybe she wasn't the daughter of a spy, but a spy herself.

"You're a talented actress," I said, "with flawless features."

" 'Actress' meaning 'insincere.' 'Flawless' meaning 'ever-so-slightly sterile.' "

"You said you take flattery well. I guess you don't."

"Only when it's wholehearted."

"It was," I said.

"Naughty. Eek! But honest. I just love it. Now don't look down at your knee, here comes my hand."

And then, as promised, there it was. But not on my knee. Above my knee. And rising. Sliding at first, but then walking like a spider.

"If they can do it, why can't we?" said Hadley.

I aimed my attention at Little Eff and Betsy for the first time since the appetizer course, and what I saw proved Hadley right: my jugular could be cut without my noticing. First, they had a private bottle of wine, its label older and fancier than the common bottle's and the level of fluid inside it lower. Second, they'd moved the candle and the flower vase next to their plates, which still held most of their food but also their silverware and napkins, meaning they'd finished eating a while ago. Third, no light showed between them, not a twinkle. They were optically one object. But at least their lips were moving. At least they'd refrained from progressing beyond the talking stage. If there was a fourth thing, the table blocked my view of it, but I assumed there was, and so I left, passing the dessert cart on my way and not even bothering to tell the waitress to cancel the lemon cheesecake I'd just ordered because I knew Betsy seldom ordered her own dessert but liked to eat a few bites of someone else's. At the oak double doors, which someone opened for me, I realized I was still holding my dinner fork, but I had a momentum by then and a direction: out, away, and into the great train set.


At almost ten at night a surprising number of places were still open, including a coffee shop whose ponytailed countergirl forgave me for being seventy-five cents short of the price of the triple Americano she'd made for me and sweetened with the same brand of hazelnut syrup I'd found in the guesthouse kitchen three days ago and grown so fond of that I sometimes sipped it plain. I'd left my wallet at home, I'd just remembered, because, with Little Eff around, why carry any money of your own? As I fished up loose change from my pockets, so embarrassed that the countergirl blushed on my behalf, I learned the answer: to pay for your escape.

I walked the streets and found music along one of them—a string quartet in formal clothing playing a piece I'd heard in church once and thought had been composed by an Apostle. (I'd thought we'd invented the sewing machine, too, once.) I spotted a hat on the ground near the viola and, completely coinless, I backed away some, a few feet behind the paying listeners and next to an older man who looked bankrupt, too, but seemed to love the music more than anyone. His eyes were closed as he directed with his fingers. Some of his nails were black and others were missing, but his hands had lost no flexibility—his performance animated every knuckle. I wanted to speak with him when the playing stopped, to see if he needed help of any kind, but I felt bad about my coffee, whose purchase had left me with nothing to offer him except for a tract that was folded up in my back pocket. I'd spent my funds, my time, and my advice on all the wrong things and wrong people, I understood then, and in my shame I slunk off down a side street in search of a trash can for my paper cup.

I knew they were in the Suburban looking for me, and I knew they'd find me eventually, but I wanted to delay the strained reunion until I'd rehearsed my part in it and pictured in more detail what theirs would be.

From Hadley, sympathy and comfort, in any form or degree that I desired. Wherever Little Eff had found her and whatever his reason for flying her to Snowshoe, the two of them had no deep sentimental ties. People like them weren't capable of any. They skimmed and skipped and floated, they never landed, like birds in the time of Noah and the Flood. Hadley's work was no mystery to me now; it was simply the work she'd done this evening. She tried out interesting words, she showed her legs, she kept track of her hair under varied types of lighting, she created distractions, she chased the mood, she winked, she dissolved herself in the occasion. Maybe she was paid in money or maybe in the pleasure of being near it. Had Little Eff ever really thought of marrying her, though, or was she just someone to bring along to parties and occupy men whose women he had eyes for? I couldn't quite decide. They lived in a blurry world, those two, where clear, consistent intentions weren't required.

And then there was Betsy. I expected she'd apologize, but not for misbehaving, merely for mismanaging her vitality. Too much wine, too much commotion, too much noise, too much eagerness to please her host. She'd reduce her offenses to small mistakes, reduce the mistakes to innocent missteps, and then ask forgiveness for having done nothing, really. And I would tell her I couldn't grant forgiveness, and neither could I withhold it—I didn't have it. Forgiveness already took place. It took place first, on the Morn of Emergence, which other faiths call Creation. Forgiveness and Creation were the same act.

And Little Eff? I imagined he'd just shrug and then direct our driver to the nightclub by way of some shortcut the driver would likely not take. On the way Little Eff would tell us about the helicopter and the incident at dinner would be forgotten. I wondered now if there'd even been an incident. Apprehensions set loose by my conversation with Helen and fears left over from my hike with Lance might have conspired to reshape a scene of ordinary Friday-night high spirits into something sinister and sickening. I concluded as I walked farther that it was true: I'd worried this betrayal into existence.

I happened upon another group of street musicians who sang in close harmony while snapping their fingers and spinning on their heels. I'd never seen a living black face before, and suddenly here were three of them, ecstatic, showing none of the anguish that I'd been taught was the ineradicable legacy of their people's forced exile in Terrestria. Indeed, their ongoing mistreatment was often cited by leading Apostles as one of the chief reasons for our policy of social withdrawal. We wanted no part in a hatred which the Seeress had characterized in the pages of *Luminaria* as "a loathsome reflux heaved up from sour bellies poisoned by the acids of Comparison." It mystified some of us, including my grandmother, why the All-in-One had not thus far directed a single Negro to our safe harbor. She consoled herself with the notion that cruel Terrestrians had blocked the way of many who'd tried to join us but that one day the tide would be too mighty to frustrate. I asked her one time how she knew this. She answered, "Logic."

"It's nice to see them so happy, isn't it?" I said this to a young mother whose little boy had edged up close to the singers to mime their dance steps. She swiveled her eyes at me but not her head. She called her boy, who didn't turn, and then stepped briskly forward, grabbed his hand, and led him around behind the trio to listen from another spot. A man to my left who'd heard and watched, apparently, said, "She's too sensitive. Don't sweat it, kid. You bet it's nice. I'm glad they've got this outlet." We spoke a bit and I learned the entertainers were part of an annual festival of the arts meant to bolster summer tourism. The news disappointed me. I'd come to think of Aspen as a place where people gathered spontaneously, out of sheer enthusiasm, to fill the crisp night air with pleasant sounds.

"Here you are. I've been everywhere. My God . . ." Betsy clutched one of my elbows and tugged me backward, away from the crowd toward the window of a jewelry shop displaying rows of empty felt-lined boxes. The Suburban was nowhere to be seen, and the hairs that stuck to Betsy's damp forehead said she'd been running—facts my hopeful heart interpreted as evidence of a quarrel at the restaurant. Betsy, aware that I'd been schemed against, had declared her love for me and fled. The others had stayed behind and eaten dessert, hatching new mischief between bites of cheesecake.

I opened my arms but Betsy rebuffed the hug. "Something terrible happened. Errol got a call. Somebody croaked. Some weird, depressed ex-girlfriend. He hired a helicopter to fly him home and left us the car. The driver's getting gas."

"Her name would be Lara. She's dead?" I asked. "She's dead."

"She killed herself up at his ranch, at the security gate. She overdosed in the front seat of her car."

I could see it, and the moments leading up to it. Varnished pink fingernails punching numbered buttons, desperate to work out the code that raised the gate, and Lara's numb face as she finally understood she'd been barred for all time from a life among the Effinghams and their invented private wilderness. Betsy dragged me across the street and through a parking lot, describing in more detail what she knew, but I hardly listened; my thoughts kept clustering around Lara's first attempt in the lukewarm bath, when she'd gazed at me with mascara-smeared raccoon eyes as I wrung out her gritty vomit from the washcloth and my partner held forth on lofty Apostle doctrine. She was already dead, but we were starved for followers and stupefied by the elixir of our own heroism, and so we pretended words could resurrect her. As she slipped into permanent slumber at the locked gate had the newest Apostle beseeched the All-in-One or had she, as I somehow knew she had, appealed to some white-bearded deity from childhood more easily envisioned and comprehended? We'd brought Lara nothing useful and come too late, I saw, and this would be the story of our whole mission, which sprung not from compassion, as we'd told ourselves, but from bitterness over our own approaching demise. We wanted to drown with strangers in our arms, to take outsiders down with us and feel them struggle. We were lonely in Bluff. We'd made ourselves so lonely. We'd waited for more than a century for company, persuaded by Mother Lucy's divinations that columns of pilgrims would show up any day, compelled by our irresistible magnetism to abandon all they knew. It wounded our pride when the seekers never appeared, and so we went out to abduct some before we vanished.

Poor Lara was our first victim, our first sacrifice.

As Betsy and I climbed into the Suburban and settled in beside the knee-high party table cluttered with empty glasses, bowls of peanuts, and balled-up napkins soaked with spilled red wine, I vowed to myself that there would be no more—not by my hand, at least. Betsy leaned her head against me and I reached up to stroke it, but stopped myself. "Don't still be jealous and mean," she said. "Be kind." But I was being kind. And I was even kinder when I dropped her in her mother's driveway, declined her invitation to come inside, gave her my cheek to kiss instead of my lips, and told her I wouldn't be seeing her again. She took it badly, but she shouldn't have, and she asked if the problem was her "reputation." I told her no, that it was mine.

# FOURTEEN

**Elder Stark drove to town** to negotiate with the priest appointed by Lara's Episcopalian mother to conduct the funeral the next day. As proof of Lara's conversion to our faith and justification for his demands to speak during the service, approve the hymns, and perform a brief Aboriginal graveside ritual known as the Reinfolding of the Raptor, he carried with him three photographs I'd taken showing the two of them sitting in the coffee shop underlining verses in *Discourses* with red and yellow pencils. The pictures had been his idea, not hers, for an album he said he wanted to send his mother, and Lara had tried to worm out of them by claiming that a new face cream she'd applied that morning had inflamed her pores. My partner mocked her for being vain, and his bullying struck me as yet another symptom of the accelerating decline that soon, I expected, would place him at the mercy of the same Terrestrial medical doctors he blamed for savaging Eff Sr.'s bowels. When the pictures were printed, his skin looked worse than Lara's, which looked as bad as she'd predicted. She asked him to throw them away, but he refused, and he told me why as he left to meet the priest. "The Hobo wanted her picture. He badgered me. He wouldn't explain, he just said I'd understand."

I confined myself to the guesthouse for the day, needing a respite from the strong emotions that had overrun the Rocking F following the discovery of Lara's body. Eff Sr., who'd been enjoying a surge of vigor as the result of my partner's ministrations, had lapsed into a volatile funk, relentlessly abusing the hired help and announcing at breakfast the day after the suicide that this year's "gathering" would include a "frontier safari" in which five guests, selected through a drawing, would be allowed to shoot one bison each using a priceless rifle from his collection of historic American firearms. The ranch foreman, Xavier, when he heard the plan described, refused to participate, reportedly, and Eff Sr. canceled the event, but not before turning his fury on a cook whose spaghetti sauce he blamed for giving him heartburn.

Two housekeepers walked away with the fired cook. Within a few hours the house deteriorated into a chaos of overflowing wastebaskets and empty toilet paper rolls. My partner volunteered to pitch in and recruited me to help him. As we were making up his bed, Eff Sr. stormed in and accused us of snooping in his closets. Maybe he feared we'd seen the plastic covers that presumably shielded his mattress from nighttime accidents.

Little Eff's state had decomposed more quietly. The morning after the suicide, having been taught by my father that hard labor purges dark thoughts, I'd gone out to the barn, where Xavier was stacking bales of barley hay grown as feed for the imperiled bison. Little Eff wandered in around lunchtime wearing slippers and a white bathrobe whose unbelted open front revealed a pair of silky baby-blue undershorts and a large crimson birthmark near his breastbone shaped like a tortoise with all four legs extended. Numbly, with a distracted, mechanized apathy, he lifted a bale by its twine and set it down far from the stack, in the corner of the barn. He sat on the bale with one foot across his knee, produced a small silvery object from his robe, and proceeded to clip and file and shape his toenails for most of the next hour. He hummed as he worked—and I recognized his last tune as the rousing Apostle standard "All Hath Ability." My assumption that he'd learned it from my partner foundered when he began to sing out loud. "God Bless America," he sang, "land that I love . . ." When Little Eff finally shuffled back out of the barn, the nail clippings piled on an outstretched hand as if he planned to show them off to someone, I asked Xavier if the lyrics were correct. His answer galled me. I killed the afternoon watching what Elder Stark and I called "squealing shows," in which people whose lust for Comparison had caused them to grow discontented with their clothing and furniture were showered with new things they weren't yet sick of.

After my partner drove off to see the priest, I searched his bedroom for clues to his diminishment. If he'd wept over Lara's death, I hadn't seen it; all that pained him, it seemed, was her mother's disinclination to allow a traditional Apostle ceremony, for which he'd already reserved the services of a Grand Junction falconer. (Clutching in its talons a lock of hair cut from the crown of the dead person's head, a hawk or eagle circles the burial site while the mourners drop white feathers into the pit.) When the woman arrived at the airstrip on Little Eff's jet, which he'd sent all the way to the island off British Columbia where she'd been filming whales with her fourth husband, an Australian author and oceanographer, Elder Stark had presented her with the wreath of sage leaves worn by Lara at her First Avowal. She'd stuffed it into her cosmetics bag and damaged it when she zipped the zipper. He spat in her footprints as she walked away and told me that night that he wouldn't be surprised if she suffered a mishap at sea within six months.

Rolled up in a pair of socks inside his dresser I found three amber pill bottles whose labels cautioned against drinking alcohol or operating machinery. Eff Sr.'s name was on the labels, and one of the bottles was dated just four days ago, though it held only five of the thirty tablets prescribed. Since I doubted my partner would tell me what they did, I swallowed one dry and waited for a change I hoped would be shallow and short-lived. Terrestrian medications dazzled me. Their names buzzed and crackled with Zs and Vs and Xs and, unlike the powders and slurries I'd grown up with, they came in forms so denatured and compressed that their botanical origins, if any, were impossible to puzzle out. The tablet I took, pink and stop-sign shaped, scuffed my tender membranes as it went down and within twenty minutes brought on a placid listlessness I associated with the moments before death, when passions vanish and through thin gray mists the mind's eye discerns a hovering bird of prey. When it swoops, my grandmother once told me, wise folk bare their breasts to it in welcome, but when her own hawk swooped down late one night in the juniper sickroom adjoining our kitchen, she drew a wool blanket taut over her body and curled up under it like a porcupine, facedown, limbs tucked, exposing to the great beak only her vertebrae and quills.

Our newest Apostle had done much better, I'd heard, adjusting her car seat so it lay nearly flat, pulling up her short skirt, and tucking her Emmy tight between her legs. Elder Stark said the Snowshoe police had taken pictures that Little Eff had bribed someone to shred.

I was rolling the pill bottles back up in the sock when something thudded in another room. My sluggish drugged nerves didn't twitch. Another thud flickered the lightbulb in a ceiling fixture and shivered the floor joists. The sounds of smaller disturbances led me into my bedroom to a wall shared with the other apartment. The possibility that Edward, the writer, was being attacked voided my promise not to interrupt him. I rapped my fist against the paneling, got no response, then hurried downstairs and around to his back door. There was another crash as I shouldered it wide and burst through into his kitchen in a crouch like one I'd seen apprehensive soldiers use in a televised raid on a den of foreign evildoers.

Through an archway identical to one on our side, in Edward's identically furnished living room, I saw a floor adrift with torn brown envelopes, tables stacked with scrap-strewn dinner plates, a leather armchair draped in bath towels, and a desk with no drawers converted into a bar complete with a jar of olives, a moldy lemon, and a dozen or so liquor bottles, one of which had a burning candle stub jammed at a wax-dripping angle down its neck. The noises gave way to a depleted silence as I crept forward shouting Edward's name and gained a fuller view of his depravities, the strangest one being a uniform scattering of sunflower seeds across the soiled beige carpet, as though he'd been trying to plant an indoor lawn.

"I'm working. I'm turning the corner. Respect my process," a croaky, disheveled voice called down the stairs.

Seeds crunched underfoot as I went up. In the hall I cleared a pathway through a barricade fashioned from a box spring, a wicker hamper, a carved oak headboard, numerous dresser drawers, and a mountain of bedding that smelled of spoiled milk. The first bedroom looked normal when I flipped on the light, but the next one struck me dumb. It was empty except for a pillow on the floor, but its walls were covered, every inch of them, in several hundred scribbled-on white note cards like those my mother used for recipes. Fastened by thumbtacks, the tiled rows of cards showed no gaps or cracks. Inconceivable precision. My father had raised me to honor a job well done, and I stood there in awe, ignoring the breathing sounds issuing from the closet to my left.

I granted Edward the dignity of revealing himself when he felt ready. He wore gray slacks but nothing else, and his bare chest and forearms were marred by inky doodles and little blocks of minutely lettered text. He looked like a living truck-stop men's room wall, only hairier, with a sprinkling of pink moles. His navel was the smallest I'd ever seen, just a dimple in his starved pale belly. It served as the nose in a frowning round face he'd drawn under a crescent moon that also had features, including a nipple for an eye.

I pulled my sweater over my head and gave it to him. He put it on inside out and rolled the sleeves up.

"Tell him I'm making progress. He thinks I'm slacking. The manuscript's two hundred pages. You can see it. Tell him I've finished transcribing and started writing and ought to be done by Thanksgiving. *This* Thanksgiving. Tell him I won't take another dollar till then."

Twenty minutes of hushed, persistent coaxing like a person might use to rescue a treed house cat succeeded in leading him to my kitchen table, where I refused his request for strong black coffee and offered a mug of sweetened hot milk instead. Over the next two hours, in jumbled blurts and headlong rants, it all came out: the tale of Edward's literary enslavement.

It was his phrase, not mine, and along with other deft turns—"brutal caprices worthy of Pharaoh," "vivisectional vampire," "esoteric whimsies," "a positively Adamic grandiosity"—it convinced me that Edward's talent had survived the suffocating, humiliating labor of confining to orderly paragraphs and chapters the billowing idiocies of a rich man's dreamworld. What the project had devastated was Edward's sanity and a pride in himself that he told me filled him once, although I could see no evidence of it now.

The tale began five years ago, in New York, when Edward's book *Let Them Drink Coke*, about the rise of the global soft-drink industry, received a prize of one hundred thousand dollars sponsored by the Foundation for Moral Prosperity. Though Edward now viewed the foundation as "a tax shelter for Effingham monkey-blood money," he used the windfall to finance a new apartment and new car. He overspent, he later realized, and committed himself to payments he couldn't keep up with, particularly after his next book, *Bombs Away*, about the international nuclear arms trade, provoked a lawsuit by a Swiss uranium dealer whose wife, Edward claimed, was carrying on a love affair with the chairman of the book's French-owned publisher. Facing huge debts, he sold his Saab convertible (no good ever came of those cars, I'd come to learn), rented out his apartment, left his boyfriend (Edward paused at this detail but I reassured him that in Bluff such couples, though uncommon, were cherished as proof that authentic Thonic bonds can form without reference to Matic expectations), and moved in with his mother in Denver to write a novel whose plot he described to me as "a combination of *Huckleberry Finn*," a book my grandmother had read to me to help instill sympathy for Terrestrian

Negros, "and *The Day of the Locust*," which I resolved to read because its title sounded scriptural, like the product of one of Little Red Elk's vision quests.

"The only hitch in my noble plan," said Edward, "was that, since boyhood, I've been a pitiful liar, and fictional narratives lie in every line. For example, when something is said to take place 'suddenly.' In life, nothing ever happens suddenly, not even a drunken automobile wreck. The driver spends hours in a tavern first, and before that, of course, there's the painful adolescence that initially led him to imbibe. Which necessitates a description of the parents and their own flawed origins. It's endless."

I thought this through, but wound up disagreeing. I explained to him how time sits or stands in place, and that one moment is as good as any other to begin a new journey or end an old one. Things did indeed happen "suddenly," I said. There was no other way for them to happen. Life was suddenly after suddenly—so many suddenlys in such quick succession that people wrote made-up tales to stop their onslaught, to rest in the illusion of some smooth flow.

"You're either an upbeat nihilist," said Edward, "or an opportunistic bullshit artist. Either way, you remind me of myself. Of what I remember that self to be, I mean. I leased it to someone. They haven't yet returned it."

Edward's mother, a widow who cleaned motel rooms, kicked him out for stealing a pack of cigarettes from a carton she'd saved for weeks to buy. At the prize dinner Eff Sr. had invited him to visit the Rocking F at any time, so Edward bought a bus ticket to Snowshoe, obtained a decent clean suit at Goodwill, and presented himself at the guardhouse. Little Eff was somewhere in the high country hosting his annual society pack trip and Eff Sr. was at a Minnesota clinic, but Edward, by showing the guard his prize certificate, managed to reach the main house. He told a housekeeper he'd been hired to write Eff Sr.'s biography and, once situated in the guesthouse, he promptly went to work on its first chapter, a poetic description of the ranch itself. He couldn't lie, remember, and two weeks later, when Eff Sr. returned from his stomach operation, Edward politely reintroduced himself and handed over the scenic opening pages of his proposed *American Maverick: Errol Effingham's Long and Lonely Ride to Riches*.

The bluff succeeded. Impressed by Edward's bravado and delighted by his prose, Eff Sr. had his lawyers draft a contract that offered him a quarter of a million dollars to complete the book, which had been reconceived as a "personal memoir" bearing Eff Sr.'s name and no one else's. There was one condition, though, based on Eff Sr.'s annoyance with the way Edward had dissipated his prize money: the payment was split into equal halves, and the first half, due immediately, was converted into Effingham Systems stock that couldn't be sold, not one share, before the day that the second half came due. Until then, Edward would have free room and board and a monthly cash stipend of three hundred and fifty dollars, which Eff Sr. joked he'd have nowhere to spend because he planned on chaining him to his desk. If Edward desired female company, Little Eff would have it flown in on the Gulfstream. Edward declined this kind offer, but signed the contract.

That was a year ago. The book had changed since then.

"This business about the Keepers and Shadow Managers is pretty simple, essentially. The man has read two modern authors in his life, whom his soft brain found equally persuasive, and he's taken synthetic narcotics since he was thirty. First came *Atlas Shrugged*, that fabled 'objectivist' bible of individualism by a woman who I've heard was very fond of threesomes. Then came the works of Carlos Castaneda, the mock-anthropologist and pseudo-shaman who the old man's son was quite taken with in college. Mix those up with lots of Percocet and a loony hysterical Baptist mother who suffered from crippling libidinal blockages, and—"

"Have some more warm milk," I said. Edward's eyes were popped out an inch in front of his face and his lips were cracked from constant nervous licking alternating with stretching.

"The Keeper's obsession was a minor eccentricity. Then we got up to the laboratory years, to the thousands of apes he tortured with syringes or peeled back the skin from and rubbed with hair conditioner to test for allergens. That's the gentle stuff. I'm skipping the amputations, lobotomies, the CIA-funded torture experiments, and the organs they extracted and sent to space to check for chromosomal mutations. Which he was candid about, astonishingly. For about five manic hours. Then he stopped talking. I looked in his eyes and I saw the lights go out. When they came back on, the old crow was in a rage. 'Sell your stock. You're fired,' he told me. And that's when I sinned," said Edward. "When I transgressed."

I coached him to drink more milk by raising my own mug. He mimicked me, nothing but reflexes by then. His brain had abandoned ship. It swam alone.

"The stock was down sixty percent from where I'd bought it, so instead of running for daylight, I stayed and coddled him. I asked him to tell me more about the Keepers and about his opinions and ideas in general. Then I pretended to find them interesting rather than an abominable hash of incoherent paperback cosmologies, opiated hallucinations, and hardtack oilpatch BS like 'Don't go crying over a dry hole and don't go grinning over a gusher. Just keep drilling.' He thinks he coined that one, and I encouraged him to. I drew the line at 'A penny saved is a penny earned.' "

"And this," I said, "is the book that you've been writing?"

"Pretending to, while waiting for the stock to rise. Your friend, the fat one, is keeping him distracted. He listens, he shows interest, he asks questions. I'm no longer capable of that. I've devoted myself to watching the ticker. It almost broke through at twenty, but today it fell back to twelve. I started smashing things. I figure I can cash out before he notices and beat the bounty hunters to the state line, but there's not enough money left to buy an automobile. I'm a snob there. I like European and turbocharged. I'd rather crawl on my belly over cactus than drive the new Chevrolet Impala."

"Run away in our van. As soon as it gets back."

"Dodge," said Edward, "is worse than death, particularly in van form."

"Be serious."

"Tragically, I am. I'm forty-six. No partner, not a single trusted friend, my work's out of print, and I lack integrity. I demand compensation. I demand a BMW. Until I can buy one, I'll swear before the court that 'Try, try again' and 'Teach a man to fish' are the words of none other than our gracious host, the long, lonely maverick of the Rocking F."

"I'll drive you to the bus station in town. You can't let this man keep zworking you," I said.

"Is that the word for it?"

"It's my word for it."

Edward gazed past me, at an antique wall clock Eff Sr. had told me belonged to Buffalo Bill and had come down to him through a series of poker matches played in the game room of the Terrestrian White House on every tenth Good Friday since 1900. The matches commemorated the Roman soldiers who'd gambled for the possession of Jesus' garments.

"It's dinnertime," Edward said, "but there's no cook. We'll

have to raid the fridge at the big house. You go first. We can't be seen together."

I didn't know how to tell him that two hours ago I'd seen Little Eff out the window and he'd seen me. He had on boots and a swimsuit, carried a book, and appeared to be headed for the pool. His face, though it wore a white mask of anti-sun cream, betrayed an acute displeasure, which I'd ignored. I was decaying inside from postponed consequences. It was time to breach the dam and breast the flood.

"My partner will be back in a few minutes and you can sneak into the van and ride downtown with me. I think I have eight dollars for chicken strips. You can start out once you've eaten. I'll draw a map."

"To where?"

"To Bluff, Montana. My parents' house. You can rest there, you won't be followed. You can heal. It's close to Canada, if you need Canada."

"What I need is a BMW sedan, turbocharged, pearl paint, stitched leather seats. That, or a merciful point-blank execution. I could line up with the bison at this 'safari.' What a sadistic bloodbath that will be. Have you ever seen those leviathans go down? The impact ripples the ground like a damned trampoline."

"I heard he relented."

"Just to please his foreman, who quit last night because he has a family he'd rather not see cursed for generations. By tomorrow he'll find a less conscientious lieutenant, and by Saturday, when the pack-trip guests arrive, the cannons will be oiled and primed. I know this because I spied your paunchy partner cleaning the Gorgon's lever-action Sharps. It was custom-built for Teddy Roosevelt but lost in a card game to a Scottish earl who lost it to someone who lost it to Samuel Goldwyn, who didn't play fair and locked it in a safe which JFK paid the Mafia to crack, ensuring continued fine sport for future plutocrats."

"That clock there." I turned and pointed. Coincidence.

"Shotgun, clock, whatever. The maverick is sloppy on the details. Blame all the Vicodin he shovels down."

I knew this name—from the pill bottle I'd pilfered. The drug had worn off by then, or maybe it hadn't; maybe I'd just grown accustomed to the way it slowed down the suddenlys, stretched them, blended them. Maybe I'd changed forever, as Edward felt he had and I worried that my partner had. But that didn't invalidate Perfection. I was as I must be to do what needed doing, which, just then, was to stand up from the table, greet Elder Stark as he lumbered through the door, and lead a drooping Edward to the van.

"I'll need cash," he said when we got there. "It's in the microwave."

The bills, neatly rolled and secured with rubber bands, fit, just barely, in a shoe box Edward had used as a file for yet more index cards. I read one before I dumped them in a wastebasket. "Today I ate three hundred and eighteen seeds," it read.

On my way back out, as I was crossing the driveway, my partner waved to me from our front door, and then, when I kept walking, hustled over. "Illegal," he said. "Violation. That man stays put."

"He can't anymore," I said. "He did his best here."

"He's a paid amanuensis."

Everyone now was speaking Andromedan. Elder Stark raised an arm to block me—I strode right into it. I gripped the arm by the wrist and tried to lower it as he punched my rib cage with the other one. In Bluff, the old ladies forbade all fisticuffs, and when fights broke out anyway, they were clumsy, symbolic affairs in which the combatants sought to prove with sour looks and surly swaggers that they would have hurt each other terribly if they'd grown up elsewhere and been allowed to. This punch had aim and acceleration, though, and his next two blows met its high standard. They brought me down. I kicked at him from the ground, but had no leverage, and he calmly sat astride my heaving chest, pinned my arms to the ground behind my head, and brought his damp red sugar-blemished face so close to mine that I couldn't see sky around it.

"The roof of Celestial Hall collapsed," he said.

"That's been coming for a while now." I tensed my arms and yanked them free, but only for half a second. It exhausted me. The weight of a thousand chicken wings, large Pepsis, spiral-cut fried potatoes, and bearclaw pastries could not be displaced by fussy struggling. Guile was required. I went limp and tried to summon some.

"It's thirty-nine thousand dollars to repair. They need trained engineers, a crane, slate tiles from Scotland. Those sort of things can't be bought with Virtue Coupons."

I shook my head, which he permitted, and snatched a peek at Edward in the van. He appeared to be sleeping sitting up— not a relaxed sleep but the sleep of one who knows that doom will arrive very shortly, and right on time. Might as well be rested up for it.

"So Eff Sr. wrote a check. I asked, he wrote a check. I sent the check to Lauer. It was cashed. The engineer is driving up from Billings, the tiles are being loaded on an airplane. The donor won't even accept a modest bronze plaque. He understands history. Plaques don't last, he says. Correct ideas last."

In front of the main house, beyond my chin, Eff Sr. was standing with someone I'd not seen before. Both had binoculars hanging from their necks. Eff Sr. raised his to his eyes and indicated with an extended arm the direction in which the other was to look. The man obeyed, conspicuously submissive. He even let Eff Sr. touch his hip and slightly reorient his stance.

"This generous man who wants nothing but a hearing, a sincere, honest hearing, no plaque, no monument, is the man you're about to offend so grievously that even if Bluff and its people all caught fire—your friends, your teachers, Lauer, your sweet little five-year-old cousin with the limp—he wouldn't so much as spit to cool the flames. Don't make an enemy. Reconsider. Tell your writer friend he has obligations here."

I nodded, which he allowed, and then he went further by standing up off of my chest and slapping the dust from the knees of his dark slacks. I raised my sore back and sat up. Eff Sr.'s new underling had made a gun with his fingers and was shooting it, jerking up his hand to mime the recoil. Great beasts from the Ice Age were about to bleed, their necks too stout to turn and lick their wounds.

I sprang up and ran then. My partner's soggy bulk shuddered but didn't shift. I saw Eff Sr. elevate his binoculars to throat level as he and the other man watched me start the van, back up, go forward, and back up again, hemmed in between a machine shed and a fence. Edward woke up as I touched the van's back bumper to one of the fence posts, angling for more room. He raised his door handle, but not all the way. I finally got clear and straightened out the wheels. I'd dropped Edward's box of money in the fight and I thought about driving past it and reaching down, even if that meant running over my partner, but Edward, suddenly wise, said "Go. Just go."

Suddenly, out of nowhere, like life itself. It might sound like a lie in books, but it's the truth, and he knew this now, too. I'd sworn off proselytizing, but Edward had converted anyway, and Bluff, if Bluff still stood, would have to welcome him. I wished I could go away with him on the bus, but I had a funeral here. And a friend in danger. I watched him shrink and dwindle in my mirrors and wondered if he knew that I'd be back.

"I'm going Greyhound," Edward said. "I. Am. Going. Greyhound."

"I hear it's slow," I said, "but comfortable."

"For some of us," he said, "it's a rolling existential crucifixion."

"You're different now. You belong to a new 'us.' There's a bed and a sink in my parents' extra room. If it gets hot, there's a fan. It might need fixing. There's also a chair and a table where you can write. If you're bothered by mice, set a trap, or just try not to be."

"It sounds like heaven," he said.

I nodded. It was.

"I believe that I'm starting to get it," Edward said. "Think like a castaway. Adore the coconut. Forget the steak. Forget the chocolate ice cream. You live on a desert island. Adore the coconut."

Three or four hours in my kitchen drinking milk and he knew as much as I knew. On the ride to the station I had him roll down his window and stick his head outside, into the wind. Then I baptized him. All it takes is fresh air, a "Yes" or two, and less than a minute of your precious time.

# FIFTEEN

**The bird, a red-tailed hawk,** refused to fly, making me wonder if Lara had come back to us. My partner too, I saw, glanced down into the hole as though unsure the casket remained sealed. The regal bony mother, fully veiled, and her brawny sun-scarred new husband, in blue short sleeves, held their white feathers out in front of them the way that Christmas carolers hold candles. The Effingham men, in charcoal suits, stood between silky Hadley and dashing Lance, who'd attired himself in buckskin for some reason and wore a chunky cross of bleached gray wood inlaid with reddish agates and flecks of quartz. He patted Little Eff's back and rubbed his shoulders as the bearded young falconer whispered to his bird, then thrust his leather-clad wrist up toward the sun. Dozens of chins lifted, but not the priest's. He'd seemed out of sorts since Elder Stark's short talk, which hadn't sounded memorized like his had. When the hawk didn't fly again, the priest looked pleased, but then, when it finally launched itself, spectacularly, circling just a few yards above our heads before scooping down hard with its wings and streaking straight up until it was just a dark sliver in the glare, he busied himself picking lint from his black uniform.

Tilted heads swiveled, tracking the hawk's wide spirals. Elder Stark cleared his throat for attention and tossed his feather. I tossed mine and a flurry of them followed, many settling on or near the casket but quite a few of them catching a sideways breeze that fluttered them over the hole toward other mourners, who seemed confused about whether to retrieve them and try again to land them in the right spot. People here were too concerned with marksmanship. Feathers will drift. They aren't missiles. They aren't spears. Lance, whose feather had blown right back to him, picked it up off the ground and cocked his arm and threw it like a dart. It struck like a dart, in the center of the casket lid, and he smiled with his eyes as though he'd truly accomplished something.

Black Suburbans bore us to the Effinghams', where a new cook had covered several picnic tables with platters of thinly sliced rare bison meat (diseased, perhaps, but still fit for guests, apparently) and wedges of various cheeses whose blended stench killed my interest in all the other delicacies. My partner, of course, devoured everything, coating his plump fingers with crumbs and grease that he smeared on his sleeves before shaking hands with people. His funeral performance had won him many admirers—not only for his talk on Preexistence, which hinted that Lara's death fulfilled a plan she'd decided upon before embodiment, but also because they seemed to credit him personally for the astonishing antics of the hawk, which found another hawk behind a cloud somewhere and joined it for a synchronized ballet that climaxed with a high-speed double plunge.

I watched as Elder Stark consoled and hugged Lara's slim young cousin, Marguerite, whose leaf-and-vine patterned fluttery green dress was just the dress I would have worn myself that day if I'd been female and unmarried. He'd told me, when he found out about Betsy, that though his interest in securing a bride might not show in his actions or conversation, it emerged almost nightly in his dreams. Indeed, the Hobo had taken his right hand one day and guided it through a sketch of the girl's face, he said. I asked to view it, as a test. If a real girl appeared on his arm who matched the drawing, I'd concede that the homely tramp existed after all and wasn't just a device my partner used to make himself look prophetic after the fact. "I'm sorry," he said when I asked. "I had to burn it. I couldn't afford to have it stolen." I asked him who'd want to steal it and he said, "Entities."

I kept my distance from the other mourners, especially my partner and the Effinghams, who, in the wake of Edward's liberation, only tolerated my presence, I sensed, because other matters absorbed them: this afternoon's burial, tomorrow's slaughter, and Sunday's pack trip for the luminaries. My partner had been invited to go along to help feed and water the mules and llamas, and he told me the celebrated Ronald Howard would also participate in the expedition. "What about Cher?" I joked. She represented a type for me—I wasn't referring to the woman herself. But my partner was when he said: "She pled exhaustion. People had their hopes up. It's a shame."

The mourner I least wanted to spend time with had been slipping me periodic private glances, as though signaling me to wait in place until he satisfied other obligations. Since wiggling in beside him in the church pew, Lance had attached himself to Little Eff, continuously touching and stroking him. He behaved like a coach with a defeated athlete. Once in a while they'd slip off as a pair and Lance, drawn up square and in his fringed buckskin, his mighty crucifix knocking against his chest, would direct what appeared to be lofty words of solace and manly injunctions to be brave at Little Eff's shrunken, downturned face. The picture was one that early in my mission—before the stickiness with the Casper Wiccans, and maybe only for those first few hours when I-90 still felt like a road to princely feats—I'd imagined myself appearing in, my bearing and demeanor much like Lance's, sympathetic yet commanding. But genuinely so, I liked to think. Lance thought the same thing of himself, perhaps, and he probably still would after he finally killed someone.

Hadley neared, four or five steps behind her perfume. She had a pink drink with a cherry, which no one else had. She must have treated herself at the main house while changing out of her solemn slate-gray suit into the silvery T-shirt and denim skirt that announced the end of her long workday grieving for someone whom, she'd told me earlier, she'd met only once, under terribly awkward circumstances. "There's a reason that bedrooms have doors on them," she'd said. "I tried to explain it to her. Then she bit my tit."

When her body caught up with its perfume, Hadley gave me her drink to hold while she bent down and tightened one of the three black leather straps that fastened her left sandal to her left foot by wrapping around and around the ankle and calf, forming Xs where it crossed the other straps. The whole business looked cruelly complicated and painful, which might have been why it grabbed the eye and held it.

With her drink back, she said, "Where's your honey? You didn't bring her?"

"It was a funeral, not a birthday party. Anyway, we're apart now."

"Was it Aspen? He does that with new women. He pees on trees. He picked it up from his wolves, I think."

"Not Aspen."

"Errol briefed me about her. She used to dance, he told me. Contemporary American exotic."

"Only on computers."

"That's where it's at now. May I vouchsafe some good pragmatic advice?" The words this woman used. It was as though she was being paid to test them. "Pretty twentyish women need money, too. Sometimes they earn it in expensive ways. Then they get older and wiser. Or uglier. Put it out of your mind. Make room for other things. Have a peek at her medical records, if possible, and then, if there's nothing alarming, forget about it."

"None of that was my concern," I said. Just then, I couldn't remember my concern. I missed my Betsy. I missed her cleanliness. I missed the way she sterilized the tweezers by holding them over a lighted wooden match before she extracted pimples from my face. She made a procedure of every little task. After she bathed, she'd rinse her bar of soap and dry it with a washcloth, then rinse the washcloth. Why had I wanted to spare her? From what, exactly? She'd made her own life hard enough. Still, it seemed best to leave things where they stood. A new tire will go ten thousand miles without a leak, but patch it once and it starts to pick up nails.

Hadley tipped back her empty glass and let the cherry roll down onto her tongue. When she opened her mouth to speak, the cherry was gone, although I hadn't seen her chew it. "Who's John the Baptist? Or is it Davy Crockett?"

I offered a charitable summary of Lance. I left out his canvas-sack experiment. I left out plenty. The few things I left in, I trimmed and tidied the way my mother salvaged burned slices of toast.

"Poor Errol's ripe for the picking," Hadley said. "He blames himself for the psycho's overdose. By tomorrow, you watch, he'll be a Holy Roller and I'll be flying home commercial, economy class, eating bagel chips for lunch. Oh well, it happens. They all come back eventually. The King of Kings gets his turn, then I get mine. We've learned to share."

Hadley seemed to be waiting for someone to take her glass and looked deeply let down that it hadn't already happened. So I took it. She smiled. Her brow uncrinkled. Never having to hold an empty glass was part of the bargain she'd struck with life, I speculated; one that helped make the deal's other conditions more bearable.

"What's your buddy the scheming suck-up's name again? Eff Sr.'s new guru slash gastroenterologist?"

"Elder Stark?"

"Look at the dunce." She aimed her nose. "He's practically being visually cannibalized by a buxom olive-skinned size two who's never, that I can see, had any work done, except perhaps for a laser around her eyes and maybe a peel or two—just maintenance—but all he can do is stare daggers at Daniel Boone hypnotizing poor Errol with that big cross thing. I detect covetous territoriality. Territorial*ism*?"

I wasn't sure about the word, but Hadley appeared to be right about my partner. In Celestial Hall a dozen pillars were distributed around the seating area, blocking the view of the stage for many congregants and forcing them to lean way out of their chairs. So fixated did Elder Stark appear on our new bene-factor's son's looming Christianization that he was treating

Lara's cousin like one of those pillars. But unlike the pillars, the girl was mobile. Whenever he tried to peer past her, she shifted her stance so as to keep herself centered in his vision. If she knew what she was doing, she had no pride. If the dance was a reflex, instinctive, she'd fallen in love. Either way, she needed help, I felt.

"Excuse me," I said to Hadley.

"I'd rather not. I was thinking we could trade back rubs in the guesthouse. Yours seems stiff, and I know mine is. Too much churchy correctness makes me spasm."

My best reason for declining this proposition—if I really wished to, because it did present interesting opportunities, from taking revenge on Little Eff for Aspen to honing my crude romantic skills under the tutelage of a trained expert whose lathed and polished appearance I was used to now—vanished the very next moment when Elder Stark patted Lara's cousin on the cheek and hurried away to defend his vulnerable flock. I expected Lance to rebuff him, but instead he walked off toward the food, cleverly leaving Little Eff alone with someone too insulted and agitated to raise his spirits or regain his loyalty. He'd lose this particular contest, I predicted, and the prospect buoyed me. I wanted him back, and he needed to return to me. I knew him. No one else did. Maybe we could drive off toward Omaha, whose enchanting name excited in me a mysterious optimism, or maybe just straight north and home. We could throw our white shirts in the laundry, or in the garbage, and formally declare defeat to Lauer, whose own trips through Terrestria should have taught him that people here often felt that they'd been saved already—three or four times over, some of them, and by too many methods to keep track of—and the few who had no faith but wanted one were either so rich or confused or beaten down that enlightening them meant going crazy yourself.

Maybe Lara's cousin would come with us. He could impregnate her on the drive up and if Bluff disappointed her, she'd be stuck. By the time she gave birth, if she still wanted to leave, Elder Stark could adopt the baby and let her go.

"Okay, no back rubs. Oral copulation. That's all I can provide this time of month. If you're rugged enough to reciprocate, I'll let you. Whatever, though. We can eat Ding Dongs and play the Price Is Right. Which I bet you're really, really bad at. Which might precipitate riotous hilarity."

"Do you read the dictionary before bed?"

Hadley's face puckered up as though I'd pulled its drawstring. A scar I'd not noticed before near her left temple purpled slightly and became conspicuous.

"I try to make jokes and I'm not the type who should," I said.

"It's fine. It was funny. A wee bit obvious. 'Thesaurus' would have brought it up a notch."

"That's why I'm not the type. I'm obvious. If you're joking about a person, be original. Make that extra effort. They'll feel special."

"You asked me a question. About my verbiage."

"Mmm."

"Would you stop acting like you need to go somewhere long enough to listen to the answer? You do that a lot, you know. It's rude."

I looked over at Lara's cousin, so alone, and then at my partner, failing with Little Eff and probably feeling the deck begin to list as the great treasure ship scraped against a reef. There was always somewhere else to go and someone there in need of more assistance than the person standing in front of you. Universal helpfulness wasn't possible. Even the fireman rescuing a child was turning his back on some famine that was killing thousands.

"I'm here," I said. "You have my full attention."

Hadley paused to line up her thoughts. "My father, a disabled Bemidji iron miner, he followed me when I ran off to join the circus. He'd never been to New York. He packed a tent. No kidding, he thought you could camp in Central Park. He told me he wanted a farewell dinner, and make it a fancy place, maybe we'll spot DiMaggio. I picked '21.' I asked a cop. Dad loved it. Thirty dollars for a burger. He was a socialist—that just made his day. He said he couldn't wait to tell his union pals."

I turned then because I thought I heard a shot. "I'm listening. A thirty-dollar hamburger."

"I've made you all weird and self-conscious now," said Hadley. "Well anyway, we got drunk. We had a ball. We met a guy at the bar who said he knew a guy whose stepfather sold DiMaggio his Cadillacs. Afterward, on the street, Dad hailed a cab for me, and as I was climbing in, he started crying. I could see he wanted to tell me something. 'Read,' he finally said. 'Read everything. I've read one book in my life: a children's Bible. That's why I smashed my pelvis in an ore pit.' He reached in his raincoat and handed me a card then. 'These books will come once a month,' he said, 'forever. They're already paid for. I sent them three months' pension.' "

The next noise was definitely a gunshot. A practice round, or had the hunt begun? I searched the crowd for Eff Sr. but didn't spot him. It had to be a practice round. No one commenced to massacre their livestock an hour after a burial.

"The Library of the Ages, it was called. Flimsy, shoddy editions with fake gold leaf and leather so thin you could tear it with your pinkie nail. I called the company's office for a refund. I'm not even going to tell you how much Dad gave them. No luck, though. Soon, the first book came: the *Iliad*. And then the *Odyssey* and Plutarch's *Parallel Lives* and . . . I couldn't keep up. I sold the books to get a better head shot. I was in penury, flunking my auditions, hostessing at a men's club that stole the girls' tips. Dad telephoned me one day, we talked for a while, I lied about my work, and just before we hung up, he said: 'Your language, darling. It hasn't changed. Those books are too hard for young ladies, I should have known. I'll have them sent here to Bemidji.' And he did. When he died eight years later—a massive stroke, no pain, the way it should be—I flew to Minnesota to sell his house, and—"

Five booms in a row, an entire magazine. Little Eff and my partner had vanished also. I checked for Lance at the buffet, where people were still heaping paper plates with bison meat and spooning creamed horseradish on top, but it seemed that he'd joined the other target shooters. Capturing the Effinghams for AlpenCross would mean showing zest for all their games.

"—there they were stacked up in the garage, all seventy, still in their wrappers, immaculate. The hypocrite—he hadn't read them, either. Later on, after I shipped them to New York, I noticed a Hallmark card taped to Montaigne's *Essays*. 'My dear daughter,' it said . . . I should shut up. I'm boring you."

"I'm listening. I am. The shots," I said.

"Only talk to make the man feel good or to keep the conversation moving. I violated my first commandment."

The scalpels and chemicals and beams of light that had sculpted Hadley out of Gretel must have damaged the tear ducts in her right eye. It stayed dry while the other puddled up, the liquid collecting in a bulging dome that soaked the left side of her face when it erupted. I noticed again what I'd often noticed before: human teardrops aren't really drops at all. They're not that separate. We should call them "tearspills."

It was time to buy a second handkerchief. Hadley blotted her cheeks off, blew her nose, inspected the cloth, and folded it up tight. "Wash that in bleach unless you want an outbreak."

I'd thought things over as she cried and concluded that, if you're at liberty to do so, it's probably wisest to eat the meal in front of you. Who was to say you'd ever get a better meal, or another one at all.

"I want to play—what was it called?—the Price Is Right."

"I should get back and total up my invoice. They always stiff you once they've seen the light. Maybe I'll take a hot bath and read some Plato and see if the airline can whisk me out of here before the great white hunters start arriving. One or two of them know me, it might get messy."

She rose on her toes in her binding, strappy sandals and daintily kissed me between the eyebrows like a mother sending a child off to school. I'd misjudged her. Hadley was unselfish underneath, but she understood that her eagerness to please might leave her with nothing unless she reined it in and put it on a proper business footing.

"I'd like you to finish your story. This doesn't feel right."

"I so agree," she said, "but there you have it: the phenomenological crux of social mobility. We come in midway with people; we leave midway. We don't always get to hear the end of things."

She walked away with the assured light steps of someone who'd made a profession of departures. I waited until the wind had scattered her perfume before heading off to locate Elder Stark. All the smart people were leaving, I planned to tell him, and we should go, too, if we wished to be among them.

In a freshly cut alfalfa field about half a mile from the house I found the rifle range but not the riflemen. I poked a finger through a shredded target tacked to a stack of mildewed straw bales approximately as tall and wide across as a grazing buffalo.

Spent brass cartridges glinted in the stubble and I stuffed a couple in my pocket because the boy inside me still believed that all shiny objects were valuable.

The sportsmen had trampled a path between the bales and the spot they'd chosen as their firing line was no more than thirty yards away. Because buffalo didn't run from people (unless someone hollered or pitched a sizable rock at them, they barely hoisted their heads) I doubted that shots of even half that distance would be required in the safari. Unlike almost everyone else in Bluff, I knew some things about ballistics, since my father the deputy was the only resident other than the Varmint Warden—who dispatched rabid skunks and cat-killing coyotes with an open-sighted .223—who was permitted to carry firearms. When fired from close range, the smoky slow-speed ordnance issuing from Eff Sr.'s high-caliber blunderbusses would gouge broad channels through the hides and flesh, ruining a certain amount of meat but enabling efficient one-shot kills—assuming the hunter wasn't drunk or handling a rifle for the first time. I didn't plan to watch, though. Nor did I expect I'd be invited to.

My hope was that soon we'd be on the road to Omaha, but I knew it was a fantasy. My partner's emerging rivalry with Lance might keep him here for six months, a year. Even if guards escorted him from the ranch, he'd creep back through the National Forest at night, camp by the fence line nearest to the house, and monitor his quarry through binoculars, watching for indications of a fresh blockage in the old man's large intestines and scanning for any signs of cooling in Little Eff's ardor for AlpenCross. My partner's condition was as bad as Lara's, and hers had proven fatal. Unless it was in the talons of a hawk, he'd never leave the castle on his own.

I decided I'd have to take him away by force.

I found him at the table in our kitchen gobbling corn chips, swilling Dr Pepper, and reading a heavily underlined and starred copy of a book called *From Sea to Shining Sea*. A yellow notepad lay open at his elbow, but he closed it as soon as I came in. He also had his phone, which should have been locked inside the guardhouse. The phone was flipped open and its screen was lit, meaning he'd either just used it or was about to.

"The pack-trip guests start arriving at six a.m. I said we'd drive out to the airport and pick them up. They'll want help with their bags. We need to earn our keep here."

"They let you have your phone."

"I'm consulting with Lauer. He's been to see my mother. We're interested in what she thinks of this." He patted the cover of *From Sea to Shining Sea*. "As the new Executive Divine, Lauer's in charge of the Doctrinal Review. He's convinced her that new revelations are at hand. The truth is not a stone tablet. It shifts. It moves."

The blood surged through my head so rapidly and under such pressure that I heard the arteries squeak—an actual sound that struck me as a warning to lie down immediately or suffer a seizure. "What," I asked, "is an 'Executive Divine'?"

My partner folded his arms and scraped his chair back, perhaps to prepare himself for the assault he knew was inevitable if things went on this way. I'd already plotted the first two blows: a bony backhand clubbing of his right ear by my tensed right forearm followed by a tremendous head-on kick like the ones used by TV policeman to break down doors. I prayed for the strength to drag him to the van then, and the skill to resuscitate him afterward.

"The hierarchy," he said, "has been reorganized."

"That was sudden."

"In fact, it's not," he said. "Lauer's been planning it for a year or two. The goal is a more dynamic leadership, not so reactive, not so . . . calcified. The government of Great Britain would be the model here. There's a titular royal head, the king, the queen, but the locus of real-world, practical decision making—"

"These words of Lauer's, they sicken me," I said. "Especially when I hear them out of you. They coat my whole mouth with a rotten-banana taste."

He spread his knees, consolidating his defenses, and I responded by widening my own stance. Then a subtler strategy revealed itself. Soften, draw back. Perform a false retreat. Try not to wince at the gruesome terminology. Let him sing of the new dispensation unmolested. Then, when his breathing evened, smash his head in.

"So we'll still have a Seeress?"

"Of course we will. That's our tradition. We embrace tradition. We also embrace, as of now, the principle of 'Guided Institutional Evolution.' "

"Is that from that?" I nodded at the book that he'd been scribbling in.

"It's Lauer's phrase. This is just a volume on history that Eff Sr. said I should read to get my facts straight. About the wars and leaders and all that. The right names and dates and so on."

"You went to school," I said.

"We only got one side of things in school." He covered the book with one of his broad hands as though to remove it from the discussion. "Eff Sr. forgives you, by the way. He gave up on that Edward months ago. Truthfully, you did the man a favor there. I talked to him when we were shooting. He said the memoir was distracting him from more important problems, like his son. Little Eff is unsound. He's an unsound human being. He falls for things. He falls for anything. Then his father has to pick him up."

"Little Eff's with the Prince of Flocks now, isn't he?"

"This Lance—are you two friends? Lance said you were."

I shook my head as severely as people can shake them.

My partner scooped up corn chips from the bowl and crushed them past his lips, reducing them to a yellow mealy mash that I received several revolting glimpses of as he labored to make it swallowable by gulping up extra saliva from his throat. "He dresses funny," he said at last. "He also can't shoot worth a darn. He's laughable. The first time he aimed, he snugged the rifle stock—Eff Sr. and I just shook our heads, appalled—against the wrong shoulder, but also the wrong cheek! And then, once we'd straightened him out, he bumped the trigger before he had his barrel pointing level and blew a mirror off Eff Sr.'s truck!"

My partner's joy dislocated his features, stretching them and pushing them apart as his skull tried to burst through his face in sheer exuberance. He dipped his head to meet the straw sticking up from his Dr Pepper can and merrily, gurglingly sucked, crossing his eyes to watch the rising liquid. Here was my opportunity to avenge myself for the pummeling of the other day and then, once I'd whipped him, drag him to the van. I couldn't bear to touch him now, forever. That body, so glutted with grease and arrogance. That mind deceived by *From Sea to Shining Sea*.

Dropping my plan to take him by surprise meant I could speak again in my real voice. The words I chose weren't usual for me, but I knew they were mine because of where they came from. They howled up into the tunnel of my throat from some fundamental abdominal black pit that had been sealed off from me before but had been opened now, I understood, because there was real evil to be named.

"Vile decayed betrayer and despoiler. Defiled loathsome hog."

And then the pit closed over and I said this: "Lauer's worse, but he was born worse. Lauer was hatched in a brain aquarium. You're from Bluff, Elias. Remember Bluff? Elias and Mason. We used to be the same."

My partner laughed and I saw his horrid tongue, coated with golden curds of corn-chip paste. "No two are alike. Especially not us two."

"We're of the same body. Two different feet. Remember? I'm not going to forget that. Ever, Elias."

"Remember, forget, I don't care what you do."

Keeping an eye on me in case I lunged, he slipped his notepad inside the history book, tucked the bundle in one of his foul armpits, rose from his chair, gave another ugly laugh, and carried the bowl of corn-chip fragments over to the counter where the bag was. He shook out what was left inside the bag, which appeared to be less than he'd expected, judging by how vengefully he crumpled it. He crossed toward the stairs, picking chips out of the bowl and bowing his head to eat them from his hand because if he moved that arm the book might fall.

"Put the bowl in your other hand," I said.

"You see?" he said, turning as he made the switch. "Still brothers. We can't help it. Still a pair. Be as angry as you'd like tonight—in the morning you'll wake up and you'll remember that Could Have Been and Should Be aren't What Is. And then we'll drink our coffee. And we'll enjoy it."

I called him back when he was halfway up, this relentless young man who'd sold a whole religion to someone who needed his delusions solemnized, his twilight deliriums engraved and certified, and who longed to stamp his fine name on something more lasting than stock certificates and Asian factories.

"Have you ever used a gun before today?"

"Where would I have found a gun in Bluff? Maybe I aimed a stick once and said 'bang.' No. Of course not. They scare me witless."

"Did you manage to hit the target even once? People must have been laughing at you, too. You must have been as bad as Lance," I said.

"I had an important advantage," my partner said. "I am who I am. I knew better than to try."

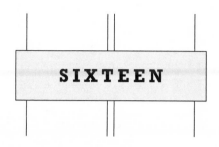

# SIXTEEN

**A Ford front-end loader,** the inside of its bucket rubbed
silvery smooth by the tons of soil and sand it had lifted and
dumped over its lifetime, was parked in the driveway in front of
the machinery shed. I carried my coffee to the guesthouse
porch, alone because my partner was at the airport hefting expensive luggage onto carts, and watched the old ranch hand
who operated the loader select a crescent wrench from a dented
toolbox and loosen a pair of black hydraulic hoses at their junc-
ture with the pump under the cab. I admired the way the old
hand submerged himself in the simple task before him, and it
struck me that what I'd been told last night was true: when the
sun reemerges to cast it slanting light on the factual and sufficent
All There Is and on the needful labors of the new day, the person who seeks to be happier than not must put aside his
resentments and regrets and quietly bear witness to these aston-

ishments. Look: the world is intact. It has no holes. The people have no holes. They work, they lift things. If there seem to be holes, the holes are in yourself.

I was here again, suddenly. This was where I stood, neither tilted back nor leaning forward, high on a wooded Terrestrian plateau that sloped up to meadowy foothills where bison grazed, inching along blade of grass by blade of grass, not backward, not forward, not up or down, just moving. And I, because I'd not slept well and wanted to sleep better, and because before going to bed I'd called a woman who'd chosen not to answer, as was her right—but mostly because the sun on my face was warm and my coffee was just the right temperature and sweetness—I resolved to live the way the bison did, bite by bite, while looking at the ground, always occupied, never out of place, indifferent to what was approaching from behind or getting into position up ahead.


The black Suburbans came and went all day, dropping the visitors and their heavy bags. I carried a few of these so I knew their weight, though I couldn't imagine what accounted for it. Summer clothing, even several days' worth, might add up to a pound or two, at most, yet some of the suitcases took two hands to lift. I didn't pry, though. I stayed quiet, invisible. Costumed according to various strange ideas about the situations that might arise this far west and this far from the city (I saw people dressed for saloon brawls, stagecoach rides, powwows, cattle drives, gunfights, poker games), the new arrivals spoke mostly to one another and mostly about matters I couldn't fathom. I heard talk about treasury coupons, the Harvard rowing team, a Chicago divorce lawyer nicknamed "the Incisor," new medications for swollen prostate glands, a store called Bergdorf's, and "the flat tax." I couldn't tell which of the guests were friends or strangers or relatives by marriage who hadn't met before but had communicated on the phone once. It was clear, though, that almost every one of them harbored some interest in almost every other one and assumed that the others were interested in them.

During one of the drop-offs and unloadings, my partner took me aside to let me know that the fellow whose duffel bag I'd just been handed was a high Terrestrian government minister in charge of "energy." He also owned, with a partner, the president's son-in-law, a fleet of tanker ships and a professional football team, "the Flood." The man, whom my partner called Secretary Barry, was here with his daughter, whom my partner pointed to as she was entering one of the large tepees that had been erected without my noticing on the main house's irrigated back lawn. My partner said the girl was "pleasant looking," but I couldn't confirm this from a distance. Without a smile, he said her name was Chipper. Not to smile at such a stupid name could only be a sign, I felt, of serious intentions toward its bearer. When she pushed back the flap on the tepee and stepped out, my partner waved at her, and then said, "See that?" I had no idea what he meant since I hadn't noticed her wave back.

I went to the guesthouse to wash up before supper, which I'd heard would be served near the tepees, off of chuck wagons. The house had been cleaned, I saw, and on the sofa I spotted a computer and a briefcase and an upside-down white cowboy hat still wrapped in plastic and stuffed with tissue paper. A tall white-haired man with much younger-looking skin appeared on the stairs. His shirt was gingham, girlish, his feet were bare, and he hadn't cinched his belt yet. "May I help you?" he asked.

"They must have moved us out."

"Perhaps you're residing in the village." All the guests called the tepees "the village" for some reason. It must have been mentioned on the invitations.

I thanked the man, who didn't thank me back, which hurt because I'd been so cooperative. I felt him watching me as I went out, and I made sure to shut the door firmly to reassure him that I was permanently, safely gone.

In the village a guest who'd put on denim overalls over the type of shirt that needs a tie directed me to an old-fashioned-looking map nailed to a tree trunk with square-headed nails. "Camp Shoshone" it said in rough black letters that reminded me of a poster in the café which read "Wanted: Dead or Alive— Motivated, Personable Baristas." Both the sign and the map were printed on stained brown paper edged in curly burn marks. One of the triangles representing the tepees was labeled "Lodge of the Two Elders." I memorized its position and, moments later, was reunited with my books and clothes inside a surprisingly spacious canvas cone outfitted with cots and rugs and lanterns.

Dinner, for once, was not buffalo but chicken. Young men I recognized from the downtown sidewalks, including the bob-sledder from the café whose family fortune was built on yellow markers and whom I'd suspected of having eyes for Betsy, were dressed as frontier cooks and armed with cleavers that, when swung down hard from shoulder level, split the roast chickens into equal halves that fell over onto their sides at the same time. The feat brought grins from the diners. Some clapped their hands. One man whooped. He'd been waiting all year to whoop like this, it seemed, and he did it again later on, when it was dark, and everyone was seated in a circle on pine-log benches, waiting for the speech.

I hadn't known a speech was scheduled. I'd been meditating on my cot, staring up through the tepee's little opening while my overfull belly burbled and leaked fumes. I'd kept up with my partner, right on through the pies, cramming down second double servings of everything to smother the hatred that flared up every time I heard that voice or saw that face. My morning serenity had simmered off, turned to steam by too much bulky luggage, too many middle-aged women in leather chaps, and too many loud conversations that grew subdued when I passed by too close or stared too long. Secretary Barry's rudeness finished things. He was the man in the guesthouse, it turned out. My partner met him in the chow line and called me over to be introduced. The man shook my hand but didn't meet my eyes—and not because he remembered me, I sensed, but because he deemed me unworthy of remembering.

When Elder Stark ducked his head inside the tepee and told me Eff Sr. was set to give a welcome speech, I rolled on my side and ignored him. He came and shook me. The speech was important. The speech could not be skipped. The names of the buffalo hunters would be drawn.

"I'm not going to watch the safari. I don't care," I said. "And who decided to call it a safari? Isn't everything Indian this weekend?"

"It's a mixture," my partner said. "The speech is starting."

"How many pages in *Luminaria* did you and Lauer give him for his writings?"

"This month? Four."

"Shoshone Indians don't have safaris. Apostles don't have Executives Divines. I don't approve of mixtures. I don't like them."

"They don't need you to like them. Get up off that bed. You'll brood yourself sick."

"I'm here because of you. *Only* because of you. I could have gone. I could have left you stranded in this place."

"And I acknowledge that, and I am thankful."

"Act it."

"I do. I love you. Be with me. I've done what I've done and I'm doing for the ongoing good of the Apostolic All. Believe it."

"What?"

"We're getting the better end of this." He winked at me.

"If that's how you really think, that makes it worse."

"It makes it what it is. The speech," he said.

I snarled at him to leave and said I'd be there, thinking the short walk over might vent some gas. I didn't care in front of whom.

With the collar turned up on his favorite sheepskin coat, the one with buttons of gnarled yellow bone, Eff Sr. stood up as straight as he was able, which was straighter than when we'd first met him, but not by much. My partner claimed he'd worked magic with the man, scouring and flushing his innards until they sparkled, and then pumping him full of Revealed Nutritional Science. But clots of tarry residue still circulated. Their particles clouded the corners of his eyes and darkened the backs of his spotted, freckled hands. The last time we'd stood near enough for me to scrutinize his nails, I'd observed the ridges, grooves, and furrows that meant the imbalance had spread to every cell, even the dry, brittle, dead ones farthest out.

He called for attention by swatting an aspen branch against one of the stones banked up to form the fire circle. He didn't seem to fear the column of sparks that every flicker of wind disturbed and scattered, sometimes landing black cinders on his gray head. And the smoke didn't trouble his lungs, that I could see. His breathing was quick and shallow, like a newborn's.

He dropped the stick and thrust his arms straight up the way that winning TV athletes do but also in the manner of a sketch near the end of Little Red Elk's *Thought Streams* depicting his vision of the Thunder Chief, a minor springtime deity who modern Apostles didn't give much thought to but who my great-grandmother sewed into a sock doll that, with dyed pipe cleaners for its upraised arms and flakes of obsidian for eyes, had vigilantly guarded me in my crib.

"Shoshone braves, Shoshone squaws!" Eff Sr.'s arms stretched as high as they could go, pulling his pale wrists out of his coat sleeves. "My gratitude be upon you, and my greeting!"

That's when the whooping man gave his second whoop. Some other guests whistled or howled like wild dogs, but the guests who appeared the least startled and most comfortable—perhaps because they'd attended previous gatherings—slapped their knees, their left knees, with their left hands. In unison, and for what felt like a full minute.

My partner, sitting with Chipper across the circle, knew just what to do, somehow. But Chipper didn't. She used the wrong hand until he pushed it down and grabbed her other hand with his. By the time she'd mastered the rhythm and the motion, though, Eff Sr. had dropped his arms and lowered his eyebrows and was rolling his shoulders and loosening his neck. He let out a long, showy sigh, and then said this:

"Now aren't we all glad to have *that* crap over with!"

I laughed with the others. The joke was a relief. It helped me feel much better about things.

The speech became practical and businesslike, setting out the schedule of events, the times and locations of the meals, and the weather forecast for the weekend. Rain was expected tomorrow, an inconvenience but also, Eff Sr. said—still grinning, thankfully—a sign that the "Directorate of Firmaments" looked favorably on the assembly because the storms would ease a six-year drought.

Eff Sr. called his son out of the crowd then and had him stand at his left shoulder. Little Eff looked embarrassed and abashed. In the V of his open collar I saw a chain similar to the one Lance hung his cross from. Hadley, it seemed, had been right: he'd met the Lord. The man who'd brought them together wasn't here, though; I heard he'd been banned for maiming Eff Sr.'s pickup.

"The details on the safari," said Eff Sr., "are all laid out in your orientation letters. This is a brand-new rite. It came to me. So: Are you ready for Freddy? Let's draw names. Errol, fetch the skin from Delbert there."

The new foreman stepped out of the shadows behind the benches and passed Little Eff a grocery-bag-size sack fashioned from a coffee-colored hide so crudely tanned that it still bore tufts of fur. The son held it open for the father; the names were already inside it, apparently. I expected more introductory fuss and bluster, but instead the old man plunged his hand into the sack, picked out a slip of paper, and said crisply: "Rear Admiral Retired Barnaby T. Amundsen!"

The crowd scanned itself until a hand went up. Prepared by the formidable name and title to behold an imposing master of the high seas, I found the sharp-eared, slit-eyed, short admiral, who was also bald and had a paunch, piercingly disappointing.

The second hunter was a husky woman who stood up, bowed, and waved, then made two fists. From about two feet apart, she rammed the fists together like butting rams, provoking a burst of knee claps and a third whoop. The next hunter was Secretary Barry. His prominence at the assembly felt engineered and made me think the drawing might not be honest. The strenuous way Eff Sr. stirred his hand around before he withdrew the fourth name from the sack seemed laughably, transparently fraudulent. I sighed and shook my head and turned my hands up, thinking these gestures might flush out other skeptics. There had to be a few, but they didn't show themselves. Too shy or too scared. It exasperated me. I was twisting around to leave the circle when a voice from across the circle said, "I'm honored, sir."

The hot little hiss of revulsion in my gut told me whose face I'd see when I looked back.

The fifth name didn't much matter after that.


The mother bison and their calves had been separated from the herd and driven by mounted ranch hands to a pasture on the ranch's southern border three miles away. Only bulls would be hunted. I counted twenty-one of them. According to Delbert's presentation at breakfast, the animals weighed a ton apiece, on average, and this was visible in the field by the depth to which their hooves had sunk in the soggy, churned-up turf. It had poured all night, and the trucks were mud-bound, too, burdened by the weight of all the spectators sitting in their cabs and on their hoods and standing in their beds. Waterproof field glasses had been distributed, but unless someone wanted to watch the bullets strike or note the precise locations of the entry wounds, they didn't seem necessary. The oblivious hump-shouldered targets were right there, so close to the trucks that when the wind picked up five minutes before the shooting was set to start a tiny tangled clump of coarse brain hair blew onto the front of my slicker. Standing next to me, Chipper got a little in her face.

Like me, she hadn't planned to watch the hunt and had come on behalf of Elder Stark. At least she said so. I doubted she really liked him; I think she was just intrigued by his attention, perhaps because her looks weren't pleasant at all but decidedly, painfully the opposite, beginning with her thinning, patchy hair that was already gray at twenty-six. They'd stayed up late together, huddled all alone on a log bench beside a still-glowing log end in the fire circle. To keep her there even after it started drizzling, he must have been acting very brave, however, because the pasty, fretful, sweating wretch who crawled back into the tepee after midnight would not have been appealing to any female, no matter how homely or starved for courtly words.

"When you've cocked it," he said, sitting hunched up on his cot, clawing his knees and curling his anxious toes, "when you've pulled back the part with the spring, behind the barrel . . . ?"

"It's called the hammer. That's the hammer."

He wiped a damp hand across a damper forehead. "Then do you have to go ahead and shoot? Can you wait? Will the thing, the hammer, stay in place?"

"It will if you don't touch it and don't flinch."

"Because when the hammer goes down it hits the . . ."

"Round. It pushes in the primer on the round. The primer ignites the powder. It turns to gas. The sudden, explosive pressure of the gas is what propels—"

"I know how bullets work."

"You have to give your turn to someone else. It's not a choice. It's what you have to do."

He covered his watering eyes with a damp hand and pressed his extended thumb against his temple. The hand started squeezing. Its knuckle points went white. He'd reached the edge of agony, it looked like, and was preparing to remove his face.

"They picked your name from a bag. They didn't ask you.

It's not your job or your duty. It was chance. Give your turn to someone who can shoot."

Still blind, and squeezing harder, he said, "I asked. I was there at lunch today when Eff Sr. decided to pick the secretary—there's an important business deal involved; permission to build a petroleum refinery—and I'd already talked to Chipper at the airport and thought about what a nice couple we might make if I could just show her, or prove to her, or demonstrate . . . I asked, understand? I asked a great big favor. He wanted to give my spot to Ambrose Dixon. Ambrose Dixon, the mayor of California."

I made an expression I knew he couldn't see but felt confident he'd sense. You are one of the world's immortal fools, my friend, and your foolishness will be carried by the Four Winds around the world and back to you. Perpetually. Forever.

"The mayor of *part* of California."

I stood with loyal Chipper and watched my partner step out of an idling Suburban. I craved some sign that my hours of late-night coaching and numerous drawings of rifles and their parts had not only calmed his flustered mind but stabilized his trembling hands. I felt responsible for his performance. It needn't be impressive, only harmless. He walked with the admiral past the men on horseback charged with keeping the herd in order and stepped up behind him onto the shooting platform: a truck trailer normally used for hauling machinery that had been parked in the meadow for two days now so that the bison—drawn there by a salt lick, a water tank, and quantities of hay—would, in Delbert's words, "feel cozy with it."

My partner's sturdy, wide stance encouraged me, and so did the studious angle of his head as Eff Sr. removed the Sharps rifle from its case, performed a diligent safety check (chamber empty, barrel unobstructed, trigger and hammer operating properly), and presented it to Secretary Barry, who kept its muzzle pointing correctly upward and shed an aura of competence and knowledge. In such a sure, commanding grasp, a gun posed no more danger than a toothbrush. I felt I'd been mistaken about the man, as we're often mistaken about those who chafe us. Viewed through the Seeress's "Lens of Perfection," the chilly curtness I'd condemned him for became a laudable measured prudence.

"Tell me when I can turn back around," said Chipper.

The shot came only seconds later—a brisk and echoless report that told me no second shot would be required. Gently, delicately, almost prayerfully, the bison kneeled down on its strangely spindly forelegs, then abruptly toppled sideways and lay still, showing the onlookers one curved black horn and a ragged flank of matted fur that was thick toward the neck but sparser toward the tail. I saw no hole, no gore. Because Delbert had warned against a head shot that might be deflected or blunted by the dense skull, I assumed the bullet had hit the heart or lungs. I told Chipper she could look again. The kill was as clean as anyone could have hoped.

Then something sad but fascinating happened. Instead of running off, the other bulls left their spread-out feeding spots and gathered near the dead one. The largest bull lumbered right up beside him, lowered its head, and shoveled at his belly as though he were trying to raise him to his feet. A second bull joined the effort, and then a third. Over them all a froth of buzzing insects darkened the air. The bull was down for good.

"That wasn't as bad as I thought," said Chipper.

"No."

"One way or another, they have to die."

The Ford front-end loader I'd seen yesterday moved in beside the carcass with its bucket down. The other bulls backed off a ways as the operator and a helper secured double chains around the beast's hind legs and anchored the chain to the center of the bucket. The operator leaped up into the cab, drew back a lever, and elevated the bucket until the bull hung a foot above the ground. The loader chugged off in reverse. The carcass twirled. The loader stopped maybe sixty yards away where a man with a knife stood ready to slit the belly. Chipper said she couldn't watch, but I did, and as the man stabbed the knife in, I saw her peek.

The colorful guts, enough to fill three wheelbarrows, sloshed onto the ground in one tremendous load. It was pyramid shaped, but then it spread and sprawled. I felt hungry insects whisking past my cheeks.

Back at the platform, my partner had the gun now. I'd thought he'd shoot last, I didn't know why. He held the rifle sideways. Wrong. All wrong. I think someone mentioned it to him—his head jerked up. The gun almost fell. His face looked terrible. Eff Sr. pointed a disapproving finger, Secretary Barry crossed his arms, and my partner, now pointing the barrel at his own feet, sagged at the knees, recovered, stiffened, and then began to shake so horribly I feared he'd vomit in the truck bed.

"Mason! Mason! Mason!" Louder each time.

"I think he really needs you," Chipper whispered.

There are times when the senses turn inward and one's actions unfold in a realm so far away from this one that afterward the mind cannot account for the passage of the body through space and time. I found myself on the platform where I'd been summoned, but whether I'd walked there or flew there I couldn't be sure. Who were all these somber, frowning men speaking to me so intently and deliberately? And what was this weight in my hands—smooth wood, cool metal—and this sweet, fragrant lubricant on my warm palms?

The fattest man, also the youngest, said, "It's yours," and stepped away to give me room for something. I heard him say to someone else, "He's good. He's much, much better than I am. He deserves this."

I'd seen how easy it could be. I'd seen how quickly it could all be over. And one way or another, they had to die. They carried this knowledge with them, it appeared, which was why they rarely hurried. I'd dug up two of their skulls once as a boy, scratching the tip of my spade against white bone in a crumbling soft brown stream bank. My father told me the college in Missoula had scientists who could estimate their age, but my mother, who was setting off for Riverbright to do some filing and typing for the hierarchy, suggested she take them with her, or just one of them, and ask the Seeress what she thought. She returned that evening with the answer: "Possibly much older than they appear." She'd also said illness had killed them, not violence.

"That's your animal," Eff Sr. said. He hovered behind my left shoulder, with leathery breath. "The boys cut it loose for you. Don't dawdle. Go."

"Just go," said my partner from my other side. "You're holding things up. Just pick your spot and shoot." Freed from all his burdens, freed from fear, suddenly he knew everything again.

It had to die sometime, and perhaps quite soon, but I would not walk away the man who'd killed it. This wasn't a refusal, but a vision; a vivid picture from the Thonic plane of a feeding male buffalo with a cracked right horn—the one in my sights, this specific creature—standing in another, lusher meadow in front of a different, steeper mountain. The time was the future, though maybe just later that day. The sun had slipped down to four or five o'clock and the mud had dried and cracked. The beast still lived. I hadn't interfered. And I couldn't, because what would be already was.

But I could kill something else. I thought of this. Nothing ruled it out. A person, maybe. Clobbered by ammunition of this high caliber, he wouldn't even suffer. And if I lived out the time allotted me in adherence to the Wisdom—enacting my story suddenly by suddenly, desisting from comparison, never pitting the rough against the smooth or the bright against the dull, discerning perfection, beholding the coconut—I might not have to suffer much myself.

"You're wrecking the safari. Damn you, Mason. Give it here! I'm feeling better. Let—"

If I'd cocked the hammer, as I must have or what took place next might never have occurred ("The habit of wishing backward from facts to likelihoods . . ."), I don't remember when I did so, or with what intention. Lately, I've thought I meant to fire wild, but not long ago I was equally convinced that the cocking, if it happened, was the first stage in a plan to force Eff Sr., my partner, and the other hunters to line up before me on the platform and bow one by one and plead their sorry cases, which I would inform them afterward I lacked the standing to adjudicate but did feel qualified to laugh at.

When the rifle discharged, the sulfurous hot fumes jetted straight up my nostrils and cleared my sinuses. I felt gravity claim the gun as I let go of it. I heard no screams, no panicked bustle, nothing; it seemed as though my ears were stuffed with wool. But other senses and faculties intensified. The mathematical wizard lurking in the brain who, in emergencies, calculates such things, such as the number of strides of a particular length that will let you reach the straying toddler before the oncoming mail van runs it over, computed trajectories and velocities and instantly steered my eyes to the black quarter horse rearing up under its rider, Delbert, who was sitting cockeyed in the saddle, madly jerking and swinging his spurred left boot. The horse returned to earth with planted feet and was still for a moment before it arched its back and, with one magnificent twisting buck, somersaulted Delbert into the air. The boot stayed in the stirrup.

A roaring shout from Eff Sr. unplugged my ears. His next shout, unleashed just inches from my shoulder, temporarily deafened me again. The snorting, jerking horse had bounded across the meadow and into the center of a triangle whose corners were made up of three bull bison. The jaws of their otherwise motionless raised heads went on grinding and pulverizing hay as they rather placidly observed the horse's distressed display. The crisis seemed over, though. Delbert had dragged himself over to a pickup and sat with his back against a tire. He rolled up his left pants leg. The sock was red.

The horse continued to kick and jump around, but the bulls looked untroubled. They held their ground and stared.

I turned and, for the first time since our tussle, laid eyes on Elder Stark. A bristling Eff Sr. thumped his heaving rib cage with a stiffly pointed index finger, backed him up a step toward the platform's edge. The admiral and Secretary Barry stood protectively at the old man's sides.

"You have defiled a historic western firearm, you miserable moronic lousy shit. You've crapped on the fucking ghost of Teddy Roosevelt. You had better pray that goddamn gun isn't fucking permanently . . ."

My tearful, nodding partner understood. He turned and

gazed down off the platform at the rifle. It lay in a puddle three or four feet off, its legendary barrel under water. Two deep intersecting scratches marred its stock. My partner crouched, swung one leg down off the platform, and hopped onto the ground to save the treasure.

Just then, the black quarter horse flailed in such a way that the boot—still wedged in the stirrup, by some miracle—flew loose and struck a bison on the neck. I was watching because I couldn't watch my partner. His humiliation was just too grievous. I'd hungered to see him laid low for quite some time by then, but around three that morning, in the tepee, toward the end of the grueling shooting lesson, while I was slowly bending his right-hand trigger finger to demonstrate the smooth motions of a good rifleman, pity seized me and all hard feelings melted. He'd despoiled himself, not the Truth, not Bluff, not me. None of those were his to ruin. Most pitiful of all, though, was his notion that he'd mesmerized Eff Sr. and looted his safe of some fraction of its gold without having given fair value in return. He'd traded away almost all he had to trade.

A boot in the neck to a creature of that magnitude—and to one whose reaction to his brother's slaughter had been to go on calmly chewing its cud after nudging the vast carcass with its nose and confirming that, yes, my companion's dead—shouldn't have been much of an annoyance. Then again, I'm not a buffalo. Perhaps the tiny, glancing blow brought back memories of larger insults that its species had absorbed over the centuries. Being stampeded over cliffs, for instance, or being cut down by the hundreds and the thousands by rifles aimed from the windows of tourist trains. I've done some reading since that day, and bison, I've learned, have certain grounds for anger.

The creature's advantage that wet chaotic morning was its ancient, inherited knack for maneuvering on saturated soil. My pill-addled, Egg McMuffin–swollen partner possessed no such agility. Hobbling him further was his visible terror—aggravated, undoubtedly, by the old man's unceasing croaky hollering—of fumbling the rifle a second time. The relic might have been a nursing infant, he clutched it that close once he'd wiped it clean of muck and proudly brandished it to show Eff Sr. how thoroughly he'd restored its fine appearance. I was shouting by then and trying to stretch a hand out, but the old man's invective smothered my words and Secretary Barry blocked my way.

My partner heard the pounding hooves and whirled, but his first and overwhelming thought, it seemed, was to shield not himself but Mr. Theodore Roosevelt, a dead potentate whose minister of taxation, I would learn, once sent an ugly missive to Mother Lucy demanding that she stop printing Virtue Coupons. Elder Stark wrapped his broad cushioned torso around the Sharps, slipped, stood up, skidded, recovered, and was gored. I saw the horns slice in and pull back out, and then I saw one of them—the one that stuck and allowed the furious bull to fling my partner right up onto the platform at our feet—impale his right shoulder and prick out through his back. And then he was tossed. And then he fell. And bounced.

But the gun never left his grasp. He hugged it tight. He hugged it tight and he never, ever let go.

# SEVENTEEN

**We made it back to Bluff,** with help. That's what I hope to write about someday, assuming anyone's still interested in what became of the Apostles: the way strange hands emerged to shepherd us home across the barbed-wire deserts of Wyoming. Our mission reversed itself along those highways, and the Terrestrians, whom I despised by then and blamed for the sad cargo strapped down in back, wrapped up in plastic inside a plywood box with a block of dry ice and a sachet of sage leaves, came forth in a bright new garb, as gentle seraphim.

There was the lady tow-truck driver from Riverton who worked on our van on the shoulder of the road, replacing a shredded fan belt at two a.m. by the shaky light of a sizzling orange flare. When she noticed that Betsy, who'd had no time to pack, was shivering in her thin T-shirt and nylon hiking shorts, she draped her black Windbreaker around her shoulders and wouldn't let us return it to her afterward, even though a patch sewn on the back identified it as a souvenir from the Las Vegas Hard Rock Cafe. She presented a bill for just twenty-seven dollars, giving me a discount for an auto club that I didn't belong to, but she tore it up when she saw me spread my wallet and bring out two limp, wrinkled twenties. "It's on Lou Anne," she said, adding that in a pocket of her jacket we'd find a king-size Pearson Salted Nut Roll that we were to split and eat immediately.

The next crisis came two hours later on the outskirts of Thermopolis. I'd stepped hard on the brakes to avoid a waddling marmot and one of the elastic cords that lashed the casket to a bunk frame snapped. To stop the box from skidding and bouncing around, Betsy sat on it with one leg on either side, but the wood was flimsy and cracked under her weight. I bellowed at her when I heard the sound, and I shouted again when she stood up off the box and I glanced in my rearview mirror just in time to see the box slide and bump the bathroom door.

We were both in tears when the quarreling subsided, though for different reasons, probably. Betsy asked me to drop her off in the next town. It seemed she'd forgotten that I'd saved her life. The evening before, as I was leaving Snowshoe, I'd driven to her mother's to say goodbye to her and been told that Lance had just then picked her up for a moonlight hike into the mountains. I sped to the trailhead, imagining the canvas bag lying among the boulders beneath the cliff. Banished from the Rocking F, the fellow was desperate now, I feared. I caught them as they were slinging on their packs. On Lance's belt was a scabbarded hunting knife and his face was broken out in purple blemishes that spoke of malnutrition and sleeplessness. I didn't argue with him, I just took her, sternly, in the manner she'd always favored, and only after we'd crossed into Wyoming did I explain the peril she'd been in. She shrugged and looked away. She knew, apparently. "Naked pictures go on and on," she said. "They're like the light from dying stars." She curled up on her seat and dozed, but restlessly, as though being pestered by biting flies. She'd told me the casket didn't bother her, though she didn't like the vapors from the dry ice, so I gathered that she was dreaming of her own murder. It was there if she wanted it, waiting, all prepared. What a peculiar feeling that must have been.

"There's a gas station, Mason. I mean it: let me go." Betsy sat on a bunk with one foot wedged under the box. "I'll call a friend to come get me."

"You can't go back there."

"I want my momma," she said. "I miss my momma."

I pulled over, too fatigued to bicker. Betsy sulked inside the little convenience store while I fueled up the van. At the adjacent pump a teenage boy was funneling motor oil into the crankcase of a jacked-up Ford pickup with spoked chrome wheels. "She's hot. She's a fox," he said, nodding toward the store. His hair had been knotted into greasy braids that lay parallel and distinct on his white scalp.

"She wants me to leave her here," I told him. Utter exhaustion bred utter candor. "We're transporting a body. It's gloomy. We've been fighting. At first she was fine, but now she's getting skittish." I clicked off the pump when the numbers on its display matched the amount of money I had left minus three or four dollars in dimes and quarters.

"Lay two of these guys on her," said the teenager. In his palm were three yellow pills with V-shaped cutouts. "Crush them up in some yogurt, if you have to. They don't have much of a taste. They're mostly sugar."

I did as he suggested, and it worked. Never dismiss unbidden late-night aid from people you might avoid if it were daytime. Someday, when I'm more settled, I'll fill a notebook with all the odd new latter-day commandments.

Dawn broke in the gas fields north of Worland, where cows and horses wandered among the rigs and the smell through the rolled-down windows of the van was just noxious enough that I couldn't stop inhaling it, helplessly savoring its chemical tang. The fumes made my brain shimmer with dreams and memories as tranquilized Betsy slumbered on the bunk, her right arm flopped out and resting on the box, which we'd resecured with twisted bedsheets. At one point, I heard a grumbly low voice that I associated with the Hobo. "He released me," it said. "I'm yours now. I'll stay close." A scene from our mission's second day took shape then: Elder Stark at a rest-stop picnic table, enjoying the last of the lunch his mother had packed for him: parsnip sticks, rosehip tea, and cold-smoked trout mixed up with barley and beet greens in a salad. It was the last wholesome food I'd seen him eat, his eyes so clear then, his nails so smooth and pink.

In Powell I left Betsy snoring in the van and roamed the aisles of a supermarket looking for a solid, sustaining snack to spend my last dollar and seventy-eight cents on. Lauer telephoned while I was shopping. He'd been calling every few hours for two days, first with instructions on caring for the body—no funeral-parlor preservatives, no tampering, just keep it cold and drive straight through to Bluff—and then with messages from Mrs. Stark, who'd broken down, he said, and resigned from office as the Seeress-in-Waiting. Her replacement hadn't been named but I suspected Lauer intended to seize the throne himself—that, or dissolve its duties and prerogatives into the post of Executive Divine.

"Status report. How far are you?" he said. "Mrs. Stark had a nightmare you'd crashed into a tree."

"That family overestimates its powers." When I got back I planned to wallop Lauer. Not with my fists—with an object. A length of pipe, perhaps. To bleed all that deadly gray language from his head.

"How are you and Sarah doing?" Never before had I asked the question plainly.

"In process. We're in process."

I hung up on him.

I left the store with a packet of smoked almonds that the phone call had distracted me from paying for. An elderly guard tapped my shoulder in the parking lot. I'd noticed this at Work-Mart, too, this practice of hiring the feeble and the old to wrangle with thieves over pilfered merchandise. The guard lacked a healthy larynx, apparently, and communicated by pressing a kind of buzzer against the skin of his throat. His tremulous syllables baffled me, and I didn't understand what he was getting at until he pulled the almonds from my shirt pocket. I apologized and gave him seven quarters.

"Truck from Powell food bank loading up in back," he said. I'd gotten used to his stilted electric voice by then. "Free day-old layer cake not picked up by customer. Mocha butter-cream icing. Shame to waste."

"I'm not from around here," I said. "I'm not from Powell."

"Any hungry person with a need. Also many fine items from our dairy case."

A procession of angels stretching to Montana, bearing us aloft on shining wings and feeding us on baked sweets and cold skim milk. When Betsy woke up near Billings and saw the cake sitting on the bunk across from hers, its sugar roses and frosting bride and groom still crisply outlined and intact, I think she changed her mind about our journey. We parked in a field along the Yellowstone River and prepared our feast. She unfolded two tracts on Perfection to use as plates and cut two generous slices of yellow cake, one with a flower, the other with a bow. We ate them with our fingers, off the casket lid, showering it in crumbs and hunks of icing that Betsy brushed into her hand when we were done and held out for me to lick.

This time the bird, a falcon, flew immediately. He'd done the job before. He knew the ceremony. So did the rest of us, everyone in Bluff. Only the ailing Seeress was absent. During the service I started counting heads to find out exactly how many of us remained, but I stopped at two hundred and twenty when I realized that the tally would come out much lower than I'd hoped. Once, these were all the people in the world for me, or at least all the people who mattered, who figured in, and they might as well have numbered in the millions, but now I could see that all of them together would fit in the lawn-care department of one WorkMart.

At the reception inside Celestial Hall I knelt before a seated Mrs. Stark and told her noble lies about our mission. I told her that her son had found love. A girl named Chipper. And it might have been true; she'd collapsed after the goring and followed my partner's body to the hospital in a second ambulance. I rode behind her in one of the Suburbans, squeezed in between her father and Eff Sr., who addressed me only once along the way, promising "timely, appropriate compensation to all affected parties." As they stripped off my partner's shirt in the emergency room and assailed him with their machines and instruments as though he were a broken television that could be shocked and soldered back to life, Secretary Barry grabbed a nurse and demanded the top doctor for his daughter, who'd revived and was sitting upright on her stretcher biting a thumbnail and swinging her dangling ankles. The nurse, my hero, wrested herself away from him and commanded a strapping young male orderly to usher him outside into the hallway. He reacted by going for his wallet and flourishing some plastic-coated credential, but there was death in the room and lots of blood, and the wondrous card had no potency for once.

Mrs. Stark interrupted my tales by looking past me and summoning Lauer with a bent, raised finger. Sarah strode over with him, arm in arm. She'd grown elegant during my absence, ambassadorial, her hair no longer in bangs but cleanly parted, her shoes an inch higher than any she'd owned before. It may have been the Saab. She drove one now—silver, with a black cloth top that would be unusable by late August, or even before then, if our frosts came early. I couldn't tell if she was happy.

"Mason," she said. She presented her left cheek and tapped it where she wanted me to kiss it. My lips came away feeling drier than they had.

"Where's your charming new lady friend?" she asked. "I chatted with her this morning at the co-op. She was trying to buy sandals with Virtue Coupons. Apparently they were yours. Hilarious."

"I gave them to her before I knew," I said. Before I knew Lauer had declared them valueless. And before I'd seen Celestial Hall's new entranceway—the Effingham Portal, a plaque informed me—all sided in redwood, with a redwood door. "Betsy's cooking supper at my parents' house. She felt it would show more respect if she bowed out of this. She's not an Apostle."

"Persuade her," Sarah said.

"I'd rather not."

Lauer, who'd been kneeling where I'd knelt, rose, and Mrs. Stark received another mourner. His name was Harmon Kluge, a talc miner. He'd arrived at the service in a car with Edward, who was standing beside the punch bowl across the hall admiring a little girl's embroidered dress. He'd welcomed me back in my parents' kitchen yesterday, already three or four pounds heavier, the backs of his hands and wrists scrubbed free of doodles. We'd talked for a while—about this Harmon, mostly; Edward was curious about the woman who'd crept out of town the night before their wedding after spreading a rumor that Harmon wore satin slips to bed—and when he left to trim the grass and shrubbery around my partner's burial plot, I knew he'd stay in Bluff for good. Most of all, he told me, he loved the views up here, because they only went in one direction. "We're part of no one else's panorama, but everyone else is part of ours. Ideal. It's what I've been looking for since age thirteen or so."

Lauer slanted his body to indicate to Sarah that he wished to speak to me in confidence. She waved like a princess, with the top half of one hand, and then vanished in the efficient manner of Hadley, withdrawing her essence first, and then her body. For a female Apostle, this was a new trick; usually it was the man who gave the woman room. But Bluff had changed. What was Lauer's term? "Evolved."

"I'm here to convey a message from the Seeress."

"She still lets you speak to her?"

Lauer snapped his fingers. "Enough. No more."

"That works with dogs, not people. Though Sarah might be the exception. You've trained her well."

The face of our new Executive Divine went rigid and royal but reddened at its edges. He dreamed of beheadings, this man, of bloody edicts. He longed for troops, for sashes, swords, and medals, for proclamations stamped with his wax seal and purple silk robes with lions on their breasts. We'd fled from him more than a century ago, across the prairies and on up into the woods, but we hadn't built fortifications, and we should have. They might have delayed him and forced him to lay siege while our queen devised other hazards to thwart the onslaught. But he was here now, and there was no defense. He'd marched through the garden that should have been a wall and planted his boots on our holy innermost center. The heat he gave off, the musk.

"She'd like to see you. Both of you," said Lauer. "You and the girl. Tonight. At moonrise."

"Where?"

"Riverbright. The Isis Room. Top floor."

"Why?"

"I don't know, but I trust you'll tell me afterward. Team-work. Brotherhood. Cooperation. Those are the keys. The lamps along our path. I've created a job in my office: Clerk Superior. Consider it, Mason. In Unity, Immensity."

"You made that one up."

"It's all made up," said Lauer. "You'll see that someday. And it will give you strength."


"Closer, darlings. Up here, beside the pillows. I like the warmth. I don't put out much heat now."

I stood behind Betsy. It wasn't just good manners. The woman on the bed was hard to look at. The shrinkage. The curling in. The crackliness. She'd been scoured away, just a thinness with a voice. Her eyes were the fattest things about her now, not sunken at all, but driven to the surface. They floated there, enormous, round, popped out. All of her other parts were curveless, flat.

"Your hand, honey. Let me hold it. There. Such pressure. So much wonderful leverage from such small bones. I miss that the most—that ability to squeeze things. It's a pleasure I wasn't aware of until it passed. It may be the greatest pleasure of all, in fact. Along with sucking, it's certainly the earliest. But sucking is really a form of squeezing, isn't it?"

Did this call for an answer? I gave one to be safe. "They're the same. You're absolutely right."

"Am I? Don't just kowtow. Think," she said.

I tried but I couldn't. I wished I'd never seen this. I envied Betsy for knowing nothing different.

"Sweetie, you're lovely. Do you know that?"

"Yes."

"Much lovelier than he is handsome."

Laughter.

"For a period," said the Seeress. "For now. Women slump, men stiffen. It all reverses. The squeeze and suck, the squeeze and suck of things."

The sound that's left behind when laughter stops and any further laughter seems impossible.

"If I could just bring more spit into my mouth I feel like you two young dears could hear me better. Words are wet things. Language is mostly moisture. I'm afraid I'll run out soon; I need to say this quickly. I'd ask for a glass of water, but it's useless. I can't seem to absorb it like I used to."

The Seeress reached for Betsy's other hand and it struck me that in the spaces between her words another conversation had taken place that included just the two of them and had already moved toward an agreement whose terms would never wholly be disclosed to me although they might determine my life to come. I was here as a witness, not a full participant. I was here to make the meeting legal, to attest to the fact that it had happened, not guide its outcome. When the women dropped their voices to a whisper, I stepped back from the bed and let them plot. Men can only stand guard over the mysteries. They don't belong to us. They never have.

The Seeress kissed Betsy's forehead and it was done. The kiss she gave me was a mere formality. It conveyed her affection but transferred no authority. That resided elsewhere now, passed safely along at the last possible moment through codes and signs I couldn't comprehend.

We didn't need fortifications after all. We had tunnels. We had tunnels out. One, the very deepest, was so narrow that only two people could pass through it, but two was enough, the Seeress assured us. Two was the All-in-One's own secret number.

"Take my big old Lincoln," she instructed us. "The keys are in the nightstand, in the drawer. There's an envelope under the driver's seat with money. It's finished here. It's complete. It's had its day. We've known it was coming since Mother Lucy. All of us. I'd tell you more, but I'm out of spit, my darlings. Now run along. Go. Go reinfold yourselves."

And so we set forth, that same night, into the world, and nothing was lost, because where would it have gone?

## About the Author

Walter Kirn is a novelist, journalist, and critic who lives in Livingston, Montana. He is the author of four previous works of fiction: *My Hard Bargain: Stories, She Needed Me, Thumbsucker,* and *Up in the Air.*